FIRST CAMPAIGN

LUKE SHORT

FIRST CAMPAIGN

Thorndike Press • Thorndike, Maine

Library of Congress Cataloging in Publication Data:

Short, Luke, 1908-1975.
  First campaign / Luke Short. -- Large print ed.
    p. cm.
  ISBN 1-56054-003-6 (alk. paper : lg. print)
  1. Large type books. I. Title.
[PS3513.L68158F57   1990]   90-34620
813'.54--dc20   CIP

Thorndike Press Large Print edition published in 1990 by
arrangement with H. N. Swanson Agency.

Cover design by James B. Murray.

The tree indicum is a trademark of Thorndike Press.

This book is printed on acid-free, high opacity paper.

FIRST CAMPAIGN

1

When Bowie Sanson heard the knock on the locked door of the reception room he heaved his two hundred pounds out of the chair behind his cluttered office desk with such abruptness that the lighted lamp on the desk corner teetered. The top volume of a carelessly stacked pile of law books slipped to the floor, but he paid it no attention as he moved into the reception room. He turned up the lamp on his secretary's desk and was heading for the door when the knock was repeated.

Unlocking the door he opened it, stepped aside and said with undisguised irony, "Evening, Counselor."

A man thirty years his senior slowly and unsteadily strolled past him and halted just inside the room. He did not speak or nod. He was in a state of quietly controlled drunkenness which appeared to excuse him from the amenities. Bowie closed the door and then regarded the older man with distaste.

"If it's money again, Abe, don't bother to sit down. The answer is no."

Abe Brandell regarded the tall, scrubbed-looking young man with the careful, almost sad curiosity of a man remembering something. His scrutiny seemed to say, "That's me, thirty years ago. Prosperous, arrogant, impatient of age, hot with ambition, sure of success." He tried to throttle a hiccup which he tailed off by clearing his throat.

"It's money, all right. But this time I don't think your answer will be no."

Bowie's full face, skilled in hiding his thoughts, did not bother to mask his impatience. He regarded the old man with the contempt that his dirtiness and shabbiness asked for. Abe Brandell's haggard face was softened by a week's growth of gray beard stubble, the whites of his eyes were red and rheumy, the blue somehow out of focus. His frock coat front wore stains on stains. He was collarless and even the dress collar button that held his shirt together was tarnished. His long white hair that touched his coat collar was unwashed and uncombed. He was, Bowie concluded, an unashamed derelict.

"You picked a hell of an hour and on the wrong night. I'm supposed to be up at the State House in committee meeting. The only reason I'm here is because when you underlined the word important in your letter you broke your pen point." He gestured toward the office. "Go in, Counselor, and tell me what's important."

The old man turned and led the way into the office. He saw the book on the floor and without bending over to look, he muttered, "Lytton on Torts," and made his way to the leather armchair facing the desk, which he carefully slacked into. Bowie, in his dark business suit that made his pale hair seem almost white, took the chair behind the desk. When he was seated, he said, "Well?"

Abe leaned forward. "Want to get your sorry candidate elected governor, Bowie?"

"Oh, no," Bowie said in disgust. "For a small sum, say a hundred dollars, you'll tell me how I can do it."

"For a large sum, I'll show you."

"How large?"

"Fifteen thousand."

The look of astonishment on Bowie's face dissolved as he laughed. Then his meaty face sobered. "Good night, Abe. Close the door on your way out."

"You don't even want to hear how?"

"Not for that kind of money. No."

The old man reached in his right pocket as he talked. "I brought three things with me tonight, Bowie. One is a gun." He drew out a small derringer and laid it in his lap, then reached for his left-hand coat pocket. "The second is a bottle, from which I will now take a drink."

Bringing out a pint bottle of amber whiskey from his pocket, he proceeded to uncork it and drink from it. Bowie regarded him wearily as he drank, coughed and corked the bottle which he also laid in his lap.

Then the old man reached into his inside coat pocket and drew out an envelope which he tossed on the desk. "That document will defeat Governor Halsey and elect your boy Asa Forbes."

Bowie didn't move immediately. He asked mildly, "What's the gun for, Counselor?"

"To shoot you with if you don't return the document."

Bowie smiled lazily and reached for the envelope. Holding it in both hands he read aloud the writing across its face. "To be opened upon the death of Governor Harold Halsey." His glance lifted to Abe. "A little premature, aren't you, Abe?"

"That's beside the point. Read it."

"This is privileged, isn't it?"

"Also beside the point."

Bowie murmured, almost musingly, "Who was it said, 'In God we trust, but lawyers never'?" Now he turned over the envelope and raised its flap. It had been sealed once, but that was long ago. From the envelope he drew out a single sheet of paper and spread it out on the desk top. Then, holding it flat with both palms, he leaned over and began to read. The expression on his broad intelligent face changed from curiosity to one of quiet elation as he read. Then he read it again before he gently folded the paper, replaced it in the envelope and moved it gently to the edge of the desk in front of Brandell.

"It's notarized, I see."

"I was a lawyer once. Remember?"

Bowie nodded and asked quietly, "When do you want your fifteen thousand, Counselor?"

2

I

GOVERNOR PROVEN LIBERTINE! SCANDAL ROCKS CAPITOL AS HALSEY BECOMES 'UNAVAILABLE'

Your editor read a document yesterday that proves beyond a shadow of doubt that Governor Harold (Hal) Halsey carried on a clandestine love affair for years with an attractive widow, that she bore him a son now living, and that before her death ten years ago she signed a document attesting to Halsey's paternity of her illegitimate child so that he could rightfully lay claim to a share of the Governor's considerable estate upon the death of the latter.

This news comes at a time when Halsey, former Territorial Governor and the State's first elected Governor, is battling for re-election against Asa M. Forbes, well-known rancher from Primrose County where both he and Halsey have extensive holdings.

If further proof of Halsey's scandalous conduct is needed, it was discovered that the Governor, perhaps from a guilty sense of obligation, has sheltered and employed his illegitimate son for years on his Hill Iron ranch near Primrose. It is necessary to name him, since the document did. He is Varney Wynn, son of Mrs. Elizabeth Wynn, and his birth date was noted as November 19, 1858.

Your editor could find nobody in the Halsey camp at the State House who cared to comment on the news, referring us to the Governor who is visiting his Primrose ranch where his guards bar access to all but family and political friends.

If the Halsey faction is silent at this disclosure, the Forbes faction is eloquent. Asked to comment on the shocking revelations, gubernatorial candidate Asa Forbes said magnanimously,

"We all make mistakes and Hal has tried to make up for his."

Asked if the disclosure might adversely affect Halsey's chances of winning the coming election Bowie Sanson, capital attorney and Forbes' campaign manager, said,

"The people of the State will not be

asked to vote on his (Halsey's) morals; they will be asked to vote on whether or not they wish to return to office a radical, unstable, power-hungry demagogue or choose a man with a legitimate family and legitimate ambitions for our State."

There was more, several columns on the front page of the *Capital Times,* but Governor Halsey tossed the paper among the telegrams and papers on the scarred top of the desk in his ranch office and looked across at his legitimate son. Cole Halsey was slacked easily on the cracked leather sofa across from the desk, his worn dust-colored Stetson beside him. He was taller than his father by some inches, leaner by many pounds, his thin face darker by shades, but in both their faces at the moment was the same troubled reserve. A flat shaft of morning sun from the window angled across Cole's denim pants and worn cowman's boots and halted abruptly at the base of the desk.

"Varney hasn't heard?" the governor asked.

Cole shook his head. His black hair, thick and Indian straight, was parted deep on the left side and was still damp from the morning's combing. His gray eyes, deeply recessed under thick brows, held an unaccustomed gentleness now.

14

"Well, what do you think of your old man now?" his father asked.

Cole's wide mouth tilted in the trace of a smile. "Just what I always did. Maybe more."

The governor gestured toward the paper. "This wasn't worth waking me up for?"

"Would it have changed anything? I figured you'd need some sleep to cushion it, Hal. Besides, what would you have to say to a reporter at two in the morning when he handed you that?"

The governor smiled wryly. His head was massive, both his white hair and his mustaches closely cropped. His thick neck and heavy shoulders under his calico shirt suggested that he had carried many a burden and that he was capable of bearing this one. He reached for a pencil that lay on the desk top, examined it as if it were a curiosity and without looking up, said, "Nothing. You were right. Let the old man get a night's rest and eat a big breakfast before he's tomahawked." He threw the pencil on the desk and looked up, his brown eyes livened now by curiosity. "You won't say how you feel about this news, Cole?"

Slowly, Cole rose, rammed both hands in his hip pockets, then turned his back on his father and stared out of the window. He could barely pick out the hazy fall color of the aspen

15

and oaks on the distant Raft Range against which the town of Primrose was nestled.

"After I chased off the reporter last night, I came in here and thought about it." He turned and looked at his father. "I don't feel any way about it, Hal. Only kind of surprised. No, not surprised either."

"Why not?"

Cole took a turn across the room, staring at the design of the boot and spur scarred carpet. He hauled up then and looked across at the governor. "Well, there's always been something special about Varney, hasn't there? You never treated him like an ordinary hand, so I didn't either. You said he was the son of a woman you'd always admired and that was good enough for me."

"Did you ever discuss him with your mother?"

"Never." He paused. "Did she know?"

"I told Priscilla. After you were born, Cole, there was no physical side to our marriage. There couldn't be. She understood. She told me she'd be damned if she'd ask me to be half a man the rest of my life and hers. All she asked was that I not tell her. When Varney was born, I thought she should know. She agreed that it was my obligation to help him and his mother. Priscilla was never jealous of Varney, Cole. You seemed to be all the son she ever wanted." He added drily, "Varney wasn't exactly planned, you know. By the way, where is he?"

"I sent him and Bert over to help Mrs. Schofield with some fence. She's getting too old for that work. Besides, I thought you'd like a little time before you talked with Varney."

"Thanks, but I've already got that speech memorized. I've had plenty of years to think about it."

Cole looked soberly at his father. "Have you got anything to say to me, Hal? If you want to — well, balance things a little more evenly between me and Varney, say so."

The governor stood up. "I like the way they're balanced now." He moved out into the room, restless, a stocky man in worn range clothes. Cole regarded him with quiet affection. He was an old lion, but still a lion, afraid of nothing, ashamed of nothing, not even of his admitted prejudices. It was typical of him that he had not even speculated on what damage to his chances for re-election the *Times* story would do.

"Hal, who dug up this story about Varney?"

His father looked sideways at him. "Why, Abe Brandell. He was Beth Wynn's lawyer, the best in the Territory until the booze got him. He's been trying to blackmail me with it for five years, but I wouldn't blackmail. Now he's got a buyer in Forbes, or rather that mining gang that's backing him."

"What happens now?"

A sudden smile creased the governor's face. "Why, if women had the vote I'd withdraw. I'll lose some votes from the preachers and the deacons, but I think I'll get them back when I show the source of Forbes' money. That crew would eat their young for a Confederate dollar and I'll prove it."

"I know one that better not," Cole said, and smiled faintly.

His father smiled too. "Burley Hammond. I know. Why don't you do something about Tish, Cole? You're reaching for thirty. I should be a grandfather five times by now."

Cole moved over and picked up his hat, saying, "Remember? I had to wait for her to grow up. By the time she did she was out of the notion."

"What you mean is, by the time she did old Burley was too rich for us."

"But it's not him I want to marry," Cole said wryly.

His father was laughing when the outside door to the office opened abruptly and Varney Wynn stepped inside. He was just in time to catch the tailing off of his father's laughter and now a flush of anger mounted into his thin, startlingly handsome face. He was of medium height, slim, dressed in working range clothes, and now he yanked off his work gloves with a swift impatience.

"That must have been a mighty short stretch of fence," Cole observed.

Varney's dark eyes were bright with anger as he said flatly, "Shut up, Boss! Shut up, half brother! Want to try calling me a bastard?"

Neither Cole nor his father spoke, only watched as Varney reached into his hip pocket and drew out a folded newspaper. He tossed it on the desk and saw the copy of the *Times* that still lay spread out.

"Mrs. Schofield gets the paper too," he observed. "Were you laughing over the story when I came in?"

Cole glanced at his father, then put on his hat and moved toward the door.

"You stay," Varney said thinly.

"No, don't stay," Hal said quietly. "Varney came to see me."

Cole skirted Varney, went out and closed the door behind him. For a moment, Varney and his father looked at each other, Varney with a quiet intensity. Then he said softly, "You don't look quite so tall this morning, Governor. Nor so white and shining."

"No, I don't suppose I do to you," Hal said

quietly. He came around the desk and sat down, while Varney moved over to the sofa but did not sit down immediately. He wrenched off his Stetson and tossed it on the sofa, then ran combing fingers through his blond hair. He was, Hal thought for the thousandth time, his mother's child — slim, delicately boned but sinewy, handsome, volatile, and basically shallow. Slowly, Varney sank onto the sofa where Cole had sat.

Then Varney said bluntly, "I don't know how to begin this. Why did I have to learn it the way I did?"

"You mean, why didn't I tell you? Well, there was always a good chance you'd never know. As you read in the paper, it was your mother's doing."

"Oh God, you're blaming her, now!" Varney said angrily.

"No, I'm trying to answer your question. This document the paper refers to was unnecessary. If it hadn't been executed, nobody would ever have known I'm your father. I would have provided for you, just as I always have."

"You call a ranch hand's wage providing for me?" Varney asked hotly.

The governor's voice was dispassionate as he said, "I call raising you from the age of twelve, schooling you, sending you to college and backing you on a small ranch and stocking it providing for you, yes. What do you call it?"

"I call it a cheap way of buying off your conscience!"

"Not cheap, exactly," Hal said dryly. "What more could I have done?"

"What you did for your other son!" Varney said hotly. "Who's boss of Mill Iron, him or me? Who gives orders and who has to take them? Who can live in the big house, him or me? Who goes to Kansas City with the shipment, him or me?"

The governor countered with questions too, but more quietly. "Who went to college and drank his way out of it, you or Cole? Who ran a nice little cattle spread right into bankruptcy, you or Cole? Who takes orders because he can't make *his* orders stick with anyone, you or Cole? Who hasn't any responsibility because he can't handle it, you or Cole?" Hal leaned back and shook his head. "No, Varney, I've given you every break except a legitimate name. And for that I'm sorrier than you'll ever know."

"What about the future? Now that I'm a proven bastard to everyone, I suppose you'll send me on my way!"

The governor said quietly, "I take care of my own."

"Just barely," Varney said bitterly. "Make me foreman and see what I do! You're afraid to!"

"You're exactly right. I'm afraid to. But when you can handle authority better than Cole or buy and sell land and cattle better than he can, I'll make you foreman. By that time I'm sure Cole will be the owner, employing you."

"Thanks, Father," Varney said sardonically. "You're too damn good to me."

"You know, you just might be right, there."

They regarded each other in silence, Varney with hostility in his dark eyes, his father with suffering patience in his.

"You hate me, don't you?" Varney said bitterly.

"Would you have said that before you knew you were my son?"

Varney thought for a moment, then shook his head. "I guess not. Still, being your son should change things for me."

"You're the only one who can change anything, Varney. I raised you just the way I raised Cole. Better, maybe, because things prospered for me. I wanted you to go to law school and be my partner in the firm." He shrugged. "I can't tell you how many times I've mentally repainted the name on my office door to read 'Halsey and Wynn, Attorneys at Law'. I thought of Cole as running the ranch operation and you taking over from me in the law."

"What you're telling me is that I turned out short weight. Is that it?" Varney's expression was sulky and resentful.

"Not exactly. What I'm saying is that the opportunity was always there and still is there. I've known lots of lawyers who began to read for the law when they were in their forties. You're only twenty-three."

"I'm not a book man," Varney said shortly. Then he grimaced. "I'm not a rancher either, the record says." Now he stood up and, regarding his father coolly, he asked, "Will I share in your estate, like the paper said?"

"Equally with Cole, but don't bury me yet."

The humor was lost on Varney. He asked now, "Who turned that document of my mother's in to the newspaper?"

The governor hesitated only momentarily. The boy had a right to know, he reflected. Then he said, "Abe Brandell," and told Varney what he had told Cole.

When he was finished, Varney said, "What are you going to do to him?"

"Why, nothing. He's punishing himself more than I ever could, even if I wanted to, and I don't."

"He betrayed my mother's trust," Varney pointed out coldly.

Halsey sighed. "That makes two of us."

Varney nodded smug agreement and started for the door, then halted, and turned to regard his father. "What do you want me to call you? Father? Pa, Governor, Dad, Pop, or what?"

"Cole's always called me Hal."

"I know, and I've never liked to hear him. Will Dad do?"

"I'll answer to anything you like."

Varney said dryly, "All right, Father mine. It'll be Dad."

He put on his hat and went out and now Halsey slacked back in his chair. It could have been worse, he thought. Oddly enough, Varney seemed to have little concern for what had been done to his mother and very much concern for himself, his ambitions and share of the estate. During the two-mile ride from the Schofield ranch apparently he had decided on two things — he would demand equality of position with Cole and he would make sure that he would inherit. In every way he was Beth's son — charming when he wanted to be, utterly selfish, quick tempered, and easily forgiven.

The governor saw clearly now that the three Halseys were entering a new relationship between them. With a kind of dismal certainty, he knew that the casual boss-ranch hand attitude between the half brothers had come to a sudden end. Cole could adjust to the new relationship with no hardship, but Varney would take some teaching. He would nourish his resentment of Cole's position while doing nothing to improve his own. If Varney had any sense he would work for someone else, but Halsey knew he wouldn't. Each judgment affecting the Mill Iron would come under his critical eye and he would voice an opinion he was not yet entitled to express. Long ago, Cole had been given complete control of Mill Iron, making the workaday decisions, hiring and firing, buying and selling, and shipping cattle and horses, obtaining and repaying loans, casually informing Hal of his actions. Really big decisions, such as the acquisition of land, were discussed between them, but Hal invariably left the final word to Cole, operating on the sensible theory that Cole was a more skilled rancher than he was. The yearly accounting was a boring formality which Cole insisted upon, the profits were plowed back into more land, breeding stock, wells, and fences. Now Varney, his father knew, would be pushed by his pride and vanity and greed into questioning Cole's decisions and it would be up to the Old Man to

25

play the role of arbiter. Well, that was no chore but he knew he would mostly side with Cole which would only stoke the fires of resentment in Varney. *Damn poor old Abe Brandell, anyway,* he thought.

Now his thoughts turned to the *Times* story and its repercussions. Bowie Sanson would make hay with this one and Red Macandy, the *Times* owner-editor, would abet him. Every newspaper in the state, whether for or against him, would carry the story because it was big news. Well, he would not deny the facts contained in the story nor would he elaborate on them. Now he pulled his watch from his pocket and noted the time, almost sadly. It was not only ten o'clock, but it was also time to face the music. The wolves at the capital would be waiting for him, so would his loyal but embarrassed staff. Irma Thruelson, his spinster secretary who adored him and was certain he could do no wrong, was in for a painful time of it — this Sunday her minister father would be forced to ascend his pulpit and denounce Governor Halsey as a grievous sinner who had broken God's second most important commandment and was therefore unfit to hold public office. *Maybe I am at that, but Forbes is less fit,* he thought wryly.

He rose and left the office through the door that led into the rest of the big house.

3

When Varney closed the office door behind him he halted on the single step, squinting into the sun that his hat brim did not screen. He had made a fool of himself before his newly found father, but he thought angrily, at the same time he had won an important point and obtained a promise. Nothing in his life was really changed by that not-so-brief conversation except that now he had a future where before he had only had hopes of one.

Stepping down now he turned right at the corner of the big white-painted three-story house and slowly headed through the tall cottonwood for the distant barn and corrals. He began to explore his feelings now. In a matter of an hour and a half the two people he had always tried unsuccessfully to please stood in an entirely different light. First and most important, the fear of them had been lifted. Where before his failures had scared him, each one adding to cumulative dread, now they didn't matter. The governor — no, his father — had openly acknowledged an obligation to him, a debt bonded by their blood. In the future his successes would count for him but his failures not against him.

With Cole, however, it was different. It seemed incredible that this tall, sober and quietly unrelenting man who seemed ten years older than his actual years could be his half brother. Their relations had always held a surface pleasantness. Cole, Varney knew, had always believed him unreliable, but at the same time he had been oddly forgiving, as if he had known of their blood relationship. Cole had treated him like a mischievous younger brother but not quite hiding a contempt for him that galled Varney. Had Cole, as well as his father, known all along that he was the old boy's son or had he tolerated him at his father's insistence?

There was a racket coming from the weathered shed that was the Mill Iron blacksmith shop and now Varney, curious, cut over in that direction. Hauling up before the open doors he saw Cole at the anvil hammering on the bit of a cold chisel that was fast growing cool. He watched while Cole gave it a last blow and tonged in onto the glowing coals of the forge. In the sudden silence following the hammering Cole heard Varney's boots scrape gravel and glanced up.

Varney put a shoulder against the door-frame and thumbed his hat back off his forehead. For the second time this morning he was at a loss as to how to start a necessary conversation.

"Reckon this is a day of surprises for me," he began, and added, "For you, too?" Some perverse urge prodded him further. "Or did you already know it?"

"I learned it the same way you did," Cole said evenly. He laid the hammer on the anvil, watching Varney with a look that was unreadable.

"I wonder how you feel about it — *really* feel about it," Varney said soberly.

"What's changed, except I have a half brother that I welcome?"

"Do you?" Varney asked maliciously. "Your inheritance cut in half?"

Cole rubbed a palm down the seam of his pants in a slow, thoughtful gesture and a faint, almost wry smile came to his dark face.

"Funny. I hadn't thought of it that way. Strange you should."

"How am I supposed to think about it?"

"Maybe that all of a sudden you've acquired a mighty fine man for a father."

"Give thanks for being a bastard, you mean?"

"I think I'd rather be his bastard than another man's proper son. You breed a fine mare and a good stallion knowing the blood lines will show in the foal. I don't think any words spoken before that breeding is going to make any difference in the colt."

Varney pushed away from the doorframe and said dryly, "That don't make much of a barroom argument."

"No, nor a church meeting one either," Cole agreed mildly.

Varney said abruptly then, "Just how do we stand now, Cole, you and me?" His tone, was suddenly and unaccountably challenging and Cole looked at him carefully before answering.

"Just the way we always have," he said slowly.

"I come when you whistle?" Varney asked softly. "You give orders and I carry them out? You boss Mill Iron and I work for you? I'm a thirty-a-month puncher while someday I'll own half the spread."

Slowly, Cole came over to him and halted. "What did Hal say?"

"That," Varney said bitterly.

"And he's owner."

Varney made an impatient, down-sweeping, loose-handed gesture. "Quit it, Cole!" he said angrily. "You know damn well what I mean! I'm the one that mends fences and cleans corrals and fixes windmills. I'm the chore boy that goes to town for supplies! I'm the — "

"Not any more, you don't. Your last two-day drunk in Primrose finished that," Cole said quietly.

Varney flushed. "Why the hell not get drunk? Around here, I'm in a class with a saloon swamper in town!"

"Your choice," Cole said quietly.

"No, yours and Dad's! You've always been against me and so has he! He's tolerated me just because I'm his. But who ramrods his spread? You, the silver-mounted saddle boy whose mother could show a marriage certificate! The old man's favorite, born in Holy — "

Cole brought his hand down from the doorframe in a sweeping open-handed clout that caught Varney on the cheek where it shelved into the jaw. It was not a hard blow, but it was swift and caught Varney unawares. He staggered off balance, then fell to the dirt floor on his side, landing with a grunt as the breath was driven from him.

Cole looked down at him and said mildly, "If you can't lick the teacher, you better study or quit school. Want to try, though?"

Varney raised himself to an elbow, then to his knees and came slowly erect. His lean and handsome face seemed on the verge of coming apart with an anger that was close to tears. For an uncertain moment, it seemed as if he would answer Cole's challenge and then the wildness in his eyes drained away.

"I belted you because Hal won't. We're through talking about him and you and me, Varney." He paused. "I sent you over to help Mrs. Schofield, go get along with it." He turned and started back toward the forge, but he had taken only a step when Varney said thinly, "I don't reckon I will."

Cole's next step was a change in direction. He walked around Varney, heading outside.

"Where you going?"

"After the paybook. You're through."

"Wait!" Varney called and now Cole halted and turned.

"Uncle!" Varney said, without smiling. He brushed past Cole, heading for the hitching post in front of the house where his horse was tied.

Ten minutes later, the governor crossed the veranda, went down the steps and through the wooden gate, then paused and looked back at the big house, surrounded by giant cottonwoods. Standing there in his black businessman's suit and black felt hat, he was an impressive-looking man, radiating authority and power and seemingly unaware of it. He was wondering now, as he had many times before, why he had built such a huge house when he and Priscilla knew they could have only the one child. He supposed that both of them, although they never said it, hoped to see the day when it was crowded with grandchildren. Heading for the bar and corrals, he passed under the massive cottonwoods sheltering the long adobe bunkhouse and cookshack. The leaves, yellow as lemons, were beginning to fall, spangling the dusty earth. A racket came from the blacksmith shed and he altered his course toward its open doors.

Cole was finishing the bit of a cold chisel at the anvil and when he saw his father, he gave the chisel a last blow, tossed it with the tongs into the tub of water where it sank hissing, put down his hammer on the anvil and came up to his father.

"I'm in my pretty clothes," Hal said. "Can you hitch up the buggy for me?"

"I'm ahead of you, Hal. The buckboard's waiting. I'm going into Primrose with you."

The governor looked over at the big log barn with its flanking corrals, to one of which a team and buckboard were tied. "Where's Varney?"

"Schofield's."

"You sent him back?"

Cole nodded. "Bert could do it alone, but it would take longer."

33

"Did he object?" Hal asked curiously.

Cole's dark face was expressionless. "At first."

"What changed his mind?"

Cole shifted his weight to his other foot, but he looked steadily at his father. "He made a few remarks about my being the favored son. I hit him. Not for myself, but for you." He reached out and took the black briefcase from his father's hand. "Ready?"

4

Primrose was, oddly enough, a combination of a pleasant, tree-shaded town and a rough and raw community, a mining town superimposed upon a ranchers' crossroads supply point. It lay in the fold of the last of the foothills before the land heaved up into the timber-clad shoulders of the Raft range. The rushing Raft River bisected the town and along its north bank a railroad crawled up from the prairie to end in the yards that were surrounded by mills and mines tunneled into the mountain. This north bank belonged to the mines and miners, their small log or frame homes were built close together, fronted or backed by small gardens. River Street, built so close to the Raft that some of the buildings were on stout piles, was a night street, a raw collection of dingy saloons, sporting houses, dance halls, boardinghouses, and eating places, with the railroad depot at its mountain end.

A bridge spanned the Raft at the lower end of River Street; crossing it, an observer was in another and different town, a substandard cow town. The streets were wider, lined by tie rails. Many of the buildings were stone or brick. The most impressive building, save for the new redstone courthouse, was the Primrose House on Grant Street, a big frame, two-story building with a deep veranda running its length that held three dozen barrel chairs made shiny with loafing use. On the beginning rise of the mountain were the fine big homes of the mine owners. These homes seemed to proclaim that the grime and smoke of the mines were just as intolerable as close association with the town's families; they were above or out of reach of both.

When Cole reined in the team at the depot on River Street, he could see the mixed train making up in the yards beyond. The platform held a couple of dozen travelers waiting for the train.

"Don't wait around here with me," Hal

said. "I see Jess and Mary Hanford to talk with."

He moved to climb down but Cole reached out and put a hand on his knee, and now the governor looked at him, a question in his eyes.

"This is just for information, Hal. Tell me what you're going to say when you get to Junction City and they're all waiting for you at the station?"

"How do you know they'll be waiting?"

Cole said dryly, "Burley Hammond has got every depot agent between here and the Junction in his pocket. Bill Carrell saw us drive up. I'll bet he's on the key now."

The governor was silent a moment. "Reckon you're right," he said at last. "Well, I won't deny the *Times* story. The rest of it is my business."

Cole looked at him carefully. "Brandell's blackmail try?"

"That's private."

"It shouldn't be, Hal." He fiddled with the reins, trying to frame this the way he wanted it. "You know, everybody likes a man who won't hold still for blackmail. It's sort of a one-man Declaration of Independence."

The governor thought it over and shook his head. "I know enough law to be certain I haven't got a case, Cole. I can't libel Abe when he tried to blackmail me and no witnesses to the fact."

"Don't name him," Cole countered. "Just tell them what you told me — the blackmailer finally found a buyer. Leave it there and let the voters figure it out. They will."

"Why, of course," the governor said promptly. He laughed. "Sometimes I have to trip over a thing before I see it." Now he climbed down and Cole handed him his briefcase. They shook hands briefly and Cole watched him ascend the platform. He stopped to talk with a couple Cole didn't know and progressed to another man. He was all right, Cole knew. Only death would change him from the friendly, magnetic, and honorable man he had always been.

Cole drove across the bridge and down Grant Street and reined his team in at the tie rail that stretched in front of the covered boardwalk of the Primrose Mercantile. It wasn't until he had stepped down and tied his team that he noticed he had pulled in beside a newly black painted, newly washed top buggy with red wheels; he recognized it immediately as belonging to Tish Hammond and for a moment he regarded it with puzzlement. The Hammonds, Tish with them, were supposed to be at their home in Junction City where

Burley could keep an eye on his men in the state legislature during the current session. Probably, it had been brought down from the big Hammond house on the hill by one of the stableboys who was proud of his new paint job.

Cole turned and headed upstreet toward the Primrose House in an easy, indolent walk. On his mind was the prospect of a drink at the Primrose House bar which was as close to a men's club as anything in town, and dinner afterward. He spoke to a passing couple, touching the brim of his hat, and then he saw Tish Hammond, a man with packages in his arms accompanying her, step down onto the boardwalk and turn toward him.

They saw each other at the same instant and both of them smiled, Cole without hesitation, Tish a little uncertainly. That would be because of the *Times* disclosure, Cole knew immediately as he took off his hat.

Tish Hammond was not a tall girl and her city dress of a light green that matched the color of her eyes, demurely hid a full figure and beautiful long legs that were revealed only when she wore a man's shirt and levis, a riding costume her father had long since forbidden. Her auburn hair was too luxuriant to be successfully penned under the small, silly feathered hat she was wearing. Her nose was small with a hint of flatness over generous lips that were commonly set in a placid reserve.

She came up to Cole, hugged his shoulders, rose on her toes and planted a brotherly kiss on his cheek. It was a warm-feeling kiss in the wrong place and it embarrassed him.

"Tish, what are you doing out here in the back brush?"

Before she answered him, Tish turned her head to address the man beside her. He was young, burly, dressed in a black suit and hat and had shifted his packages to his left hand, as if making sure his right hand had freedom to use the gun on his hip under his coat.

"It's all right, Hugh. You go on to the buggy and I'll be along."

The young man nodded, gave Cole a look of dark suspicion and passed him.

Now Tish looked fondly and carefully at him. "Cole, you simply never change, do you?"

Cole said soberly, "Well, this was a clean shirt this morning."

Tish laughed and Cole smiled too. Months back they had learned that this sort of inconsequential banter was safe ground, not holding any of the perils of conversations they both wished to avoid. In the two years since Tish had been with her family at their big house at the capital she had found an excitement in her life that Cole felt was alien to him and basically to her. Just before the beginning of that first year Cole had proposed they be married, since they had taken it for granted they would ever since they knew what marriage was. Tish, however, had begged for time. Her father, a rancher turned mining speculator, had suddenly seen one of his least favored properties turn into a bonanza gold mine that literally catapulted them into the class of the very rich. New homes, servants, carriages, social life, and travel here and in Europe were too tempting for Tish; she wanted to experience all this while she was young and free, she told him. There would be time enough and to spare for the more serious side of life. If Cole would free her for a time, she would come back, marry him and raise their children, knowing that the other and different things in life would never tease her because she had known them. But she knew them now and they still teased her; beneath her gloss Cole could find only a hint of the leggy, passionate, and directly simple girl he had proposed to.

And he knew at the moment they were both thinking this. He tilted his head toward the buggy. "Who's your scowling friend?"

Tish flushed in spite of her smile. "Dad's idea. He's — he's a kind of bodyguard, I'd guess you'd call him."

"In your home town?"

"Yes, here especially. Oh, it's this business with the miners, Cole. I don't know what it's all about, but Dad's getting letters threatening him and his family. Most of them come from Primrose, so Dad made me bring Hugh along." She added lamely, "He works for Dad and he's not a good friend especially." She hesitated, and then added with a faint anger, "He's not a friend at all."

Cole looked at her wonderingly. "You like having a bodyguard?"

"I hate it."

"Fire him." He added dryly: "Burley lets you do pretty much what you want, doesn't he?"

"But he won't go," Tish said bitterly. "He just laughs at me. So does Bowie when I ask him to tell Hugh to go."

"You just asked the wrong people," Cole said mildly.

Tish looked at him with an expression of irony. "Meaning I didn't ask you?"

"If you asked me, I don't remember it," Cole said dryly.

"Well, well," Tish said, her anger rising. "It's just like old times. Remember when I asked you to find out what was in the eagles' nest up at Officers' Gulch? You said you'd find out and you did. Of course, the eagle damn near cut you to pieces but you found out. There was nothing you wouldn't or couldn't do." She paused. "You're still that way, aren't you Cole?"

Cole didn't answer. He was surprised at her sudden and unaccountable turn of temper. Did she think his words had cast a slur on Bowie Sanson's ability to help her?

Tish said now, "All right. You fire him. I ask you to."

Cole regarded her with growing amusement. "I don't know why I don't walk away from you, Tish, like I used to when you were a kid."

"All right, walk away. But if you stay, remember what they say in poker — 'put your money where your mouth is'."

Cole looked at her carefully, seeing the naked temper in her eyes. "I think you mean that."

"I do! I talk with you two minutes. In the first minute you're superior to me. In the second you're superior to my father and Bowie! Well, are you?"

Cole gave her a lingering look, then turned and walked back toward the buggy. Hugh was leaning against the tie rail, watching them and, as Cole approached, he straightened up. The packages were deposited on the buggy seat, so his hands were empty. Coming up to him, Cole saw that he was a burly man, somehow out of place in the black business suit he was wearing. Probably recruited from behind the bar of a Junction City river-front saloon where the fighting was rough and for keeps.

Cole halted in front of him and said, "The train's still making up. Miss Hammond wants you on it."

"She going to put me on it?" Hugh asked with some amusement.

"I am."

"Try!"

Cole slowly extended an arm, as if to seize the lapels of Hugh's coat, predictably guessing that Hugh would grab it with his right hand and try to pull Cole toward him and wrestle him down. Hugh pounced on the arm and yanked and now Cole swiftly accommodated him. Instead of pulling back his captive arm, Cole drove against Hugh's body which was already braced to pull. Cole's weight drove Hugh off balance and he staggered back a step, beginning to fall before the tie rail across his back brought him up. Cole still drove and now, unable to make his feet find a purchase, Hugh was forced into bowing his back, Cole atop him, their bodies together. Cole's left hand reached down and snaked out Hugh's gun from its holster. Feeling it, Hugh released Cole's forearm and drove his hand for the holster and found it empty.

Now Cole, reversing the pressure, seized Hugh's shirt front and hauled him erect with a heave of his shoulder. As Hugh fought to straighten up he added to his own momentum, so that Cole's pull and his push carried Hugh forward. He lifted a foot to take a step and Cole tripped him.

Hugh fell to his hands and knees and now Cole raised Hugh's captive gun in a short arc and brought it down on Hugh's head. The burly man simply folded on his face.

Without looking around at the handful of bystanders who were watching, Cole punched the loads from Hugh's gun, threw them in the road and returned the gun to Hugh's holster. Afterward, he rolled Hugh on his back and dragged him feet first off the boardwalk and around to the rear of his own buckboard. It took him two tries to get Hugh's slack body onto the buckboard bed and when he succeeded he went back for Hugh's hat, returned to the buckboard and backed the team out, then swung around in the direction of the bridge. Not once did he bother to look and see if Tish had witnessed this.

The train was pulled up alongside the platform as Cole pulled past the depot and hauled up at the caboose where the brakeman was standing on the bottom step.

Cole gestured over his shoulder, saying, "One of Burley's boys. Help me get him on, will you?"

Since the Primrose & Midland Railroad was one of Burley's creations, the brakeman complied. They loaded Hugh into the caboose and later, as Cole swung the team around, the train pulled out down the valley. Crossing the bridge now, Cole reviewed what had happened and felt an overwhelming disgust with himself. He had been baited by Tish into acting like a show-off kid, but that was not the whole of it. Behind it lay something that was eating at them both. Tish had accused him of acting superior, and to himself he pled guilty to the charge. He did not like Tish's willful way of life or even her new philosophy of living all of it she could grab, nor did he like Burley Hammond's ostentation and he knew his feelings must show that dislike. He liked even less Burley's cynical assumption that when enough legislators had been bought and his own governor elected, he and his mine-owner cronies could run this state to their own liking. But least of all did he like what he heard of Tish's actions. He had heard enough capital gossip from Hal to know that Bowie Sanson was Tish's constant companion, that many people thought they were secretly engaged and some thought they were secretly married. Tish had never bothered to confirm or deny these rumors and Cole was not about to ask her to. Tish, he supposed, was like most women, dominating if they were allowed to be and changeable by the historical right of their sex.

What she thought of him now, Cole didn't know. Beneath her surface friendliness was a new will of iron. She had taunted him into challenging Hugh. Why? Did she hope Hugh would humiliate him or did she merely want to be rid of a bothersome bodyguard, thus proving to Burley that she would tolerate no interference in her way of life? *Or am I making this up?* he thought wryly. One thing was for sure, though. He was farther away from marrying her than he had ever been.

He threaded his team through the noon traffic, noting that Tish's buggy was gone from its place at the tie rail. At the Primrose House he pulled in at its tie rail and afterward headed for the saloon at its far end. He did not especially want a drink, but he wanted to be seen. In a sense, he wanted to show the family flag. For a moment, he wished he had brought Varney along, for Varney would have to face this some time and he wanted to be with him when he did.

He pushed through the batwing street doors,

swerved to get out of the way of the next customer, then halted to let his eyes get accustomed to the pleasant gloom of the place. The walnut bar was on his left and held a scattering of drinkers. Four empty card tables, leather-covered chairs framing them, filled the rest of the walnut-paneled room, two on each side of the big door that led into the carpeted lobby.

Cole moved up to the bar and got a good morning from Alec, the red-faced Cousin Jack who had been a timberman until a mine accident crippled him.

"How're things out your way, Cole?"

"Slow, Alec, but we'll bust out of that when roundup starts."

"I know. I won't see the lot of you till it's over. I won't sell two dozen drinks of whiskey, either." He reached down a bottle of Cole's brand from the back bar and put a glass beside it. Then Alec's glance shifted and Cole turned his head to see who had come up beside him.

It was Asa Forbes, Hal's opponent for governor. He was a tall man, just under Cole's height, dressed in worn range clothes. The hat covering his gray-shot hair was old and worn through at the creases, and it topped a pleasant hound's face that was bisected by full black mustaches that hid a too small mouth.

47

He was a weathered forty-five; his dark eyes, friendly but at the same time shrewd, were wide-spaced and now held a curious solemnity. He put out a hand which Cole took straightening up and saying, "How are you, Asa?"

"Cole, I just wanted to tell you. I had nothing to do with that *Times* story. I knew nothing about it, absolutely nothing. If I'd known of the document, I'd have forbidden Red Macandy to print it. I'm sorry down to the third level of hell that it ever got printed."

He was obviously speaking the truth, Cole saw, and he said mildly, "I believe you, Asa."

Forbes, still gripping his hand, turned and called, "Bowie, come here."

Bowie Sanson, with whom Forbes had been drinking, pushed away from the bar downroom, picked up his black hat from the bar top and walked toward them. He was a big man, both tall and solid under his pepper and salt suit. His pale hair was thick and curling, and there was a kind of fearless and amiable arrogance in his broad face that told the world he was used to winning. He halted beside Asa and nodded carelessly but in a friendly way to Cole.

Forbes now let go of Cole's hand in case Cole wanted to shake hands with Bowie. Cole didn't, and now Forbes said, "Bowie, tell

48

Cole here the truth. Did I know anything about that story Red Macandy wrote about Hal?"

"No, we sneaked that over on you, Asa. You didn't know about it."

"Why didn't he?" Cole asked softly.

"He would've kicked," Bowie said candidly.

"But you didn't?"

Bowie smiled crookedly. "No, and if you think I'm sorry it was printed, you're crazy. I'm out to beat Hal. This election is for more than marbles and I'll win it for Asa any way I can."

Cole asked mildly, "Did Abe come high?"

Bowie didn't make the mistake of looking at Forbes. He frowned slightly. "Abe who?"

"Brandell."

Bowie frowned. "Did Brandell come high?" he asked in a puzzled but pleasant voice, then shook his head slightly. "You've leapfrogged me there. I was talking about the election."

"So am I. I wondered if Abe finally struck pay dirt with Mrs. Wynn's deposition."

Bowie deliberately shifted his glance, a questioning one, to Forbes as if to ask Forbes if he knew what this was all about. Then he shifted his glance of feigned puzzlement back to Cole. "What's Abe Brandell got to do with the deposition? Did he ever see it?"

49

"He drew it up," Cole said quietly. "In a way, I'm glad he made some money out of it. I admire a crook that really works at his business. Abe's been trying to blackmail Hal with it for the last five years, but Hal wouldn't blackmail."

Bowie was silent a long moment, but Cole could see the muscles along his heavy jaw slowly cord and he knew he was telling Bowie something he hadn't known until now that angered him. He only said carelessly, "Then I think Hal was foolish not to buy it up, because it's too late now."

"It's too late, all right, but I wonder who for — you, Asa, or Hal?"

Forbes looked at him in puzzlement. "What's that supposed to mean, Cole?"

"Bowie knows. Tell him, Bowie."

"Come on, Asa. You've got a drink down there," Bowie said crisply. He took Forbes by the arm and Forbes, puzzled still, lifted his hand in a careless parting gesture before the two of them went back to the far end of the bar. Cole was suddenly aware that Alec, arms folded across his chest, was leaning against the back bar, the expression on his ruddy face unreadable. As Cole poured his drink, he said, "Hear that, Alec?"

"If I wasn't supposed to, that's what the tables are for."

Cole grinned and so did Alec. Cole tossed off his drink then put a coin on the bar. Alec took it and picked up the bottle and glass. "'cess to your old man, Cole. Tell him I said so."

"You're for sin?" Cole asked dryly.

Alec carefully put down the glass and bottle and lifted his left leg. With his fist he rapped sharply on his shin, producing the muffled sound of wood being knocked on. "I'm for mine laws that don't leave a man with this, like the governor is. As for what's born on the wrong side of the blanket, 'tis no affair of mine."

Cole smiled and nodded and gave Alec a lazy salute as he moved through the door onto the sidewalk. Turning toward the buckboard he felt a sudden hunger whetted by the whiskey. As he was passing along the veranda, he heard a voice call, "Cole."

Halting, he turned and saw Tish just rising from one of the barrel chairs. She crossed the veranda and Cole moved toward her and folded his arms on the railing which was just under shoulder height.

Tish halted and looked down at him. "You are an idiot, bless you. I lost my temper and I'm sorry."

"Well, you're rid of your friend. That's what you wanted, isn't it?"

"Yes, but I'll probably get another. You — shouldn't have listened to me."

"Next time I won't."

"Let's don't quarrel, Cole. What I really wanted to tell you when we met was that I'm sorry about that newspaper story. I'm especially sorry for Hal. For Varney, too, except I don't know him well." She hesitated. "How did Hal take it?"

"Like anybody facing his own mistakes."

"What a foul thing to do," Tish said vehemently.

"Have you told Bowie Sanson that?"

"I have, but why do you ask? You don't think he had anything to do with it, do you?"

Cole scrubbed his jaw with his left hand and then pushed away from the railing. "He only bought Mrs. Wynn's deposition from Abe Brandell. That means he had everything to do with it." He turned away and started downstreet.

"Wait, Cole," Tish called.

Cole didn't stop, and Tish didn't call again. When he climbed onto the buckboard seat, he couldn't see her anywhere on the veranda.

5

The Primrose & Midland tracks clung to the bank of the Raft for some miles, joined the line from the south, then swung north to service Burley Hammond's coal town before it turned east to the prairie towns that were mostly livestock shipping points. At each of its nine station stops the agent, having listened to his key, had spread the word that the governor was on his way back to the capital. Hal's friends, along with the just plain curious, were gathered on the platform of each depot. Hal, wanting more than ever to show he was the same man he had always been, got down at each stop and, holding his hat in his left hand, shook hands with all who wanted to speak with him. His friends were encouraging, although not one of them said exactly why, and it made Hal feel good.

It was on the sunny, windswept platform at Westhaven that the only unpleasantness occurred. A middle-aged woman in a black dress with a ravaged and bitter face accosted him and said, "You are nothing but a sinful monster, Governor." Hal bowed courteously and said, "Very true, madam, but a contrite one."

At the Junction City station, he was met by young Joe Eames, his bright and tough young secretary who worked for him days and divided his nights between studying for the law and studying saloons. He was a lanky young man with a deceptively mournful face whose cap of thick, curly hair was the only hat he had ever known. He stood a little aloof from the crowd that was waiting, but when the governor stepped down he came forward and took his briefcase.

"It's not a lynch mob, sir. They just want to see if you've grown horns and a tail."

"All I've grown is older," the governor said wryly. He looked over the gawking crowd with a calmness that was so deliberate, it was almost defiant and then he put on his hat.

A heavy, grumpy-looking man in a rumpled suit came forward, a half-smoked cigar jutting from the corner of his mouth. "Can you spare us a minute, Governor?"

"Who's us, Red?"

"Three-four editors and me."

"Not here, Red. Come up to the State House and I'll talk with you."

"While I spit on you, Macandy," Joe said.

"That's enough, Joe. Let's go," the governor said.

The governor's carriage was waiting at the far end of the platform and the crowd silently parted for them as they headed toward it.

The drive was a short one down the wide main street of Junction City. This was already a substantial town with brick and stone buildings almost outnumbering the frame ones. The slow-moving wagon and buggy traffic made Albert, the colored stableman, swear inaudibly. Since the governor's carriage and driver were easily recognized, they drew attention. Sidewalk strollers paused and pointed and occasionally waved and were answered by a wave from Hal.

The State House, whose top floor was still being worked on was at the crown of the river bluff, a stone building of quiet dignity, set in well-kept grounds. The carriage swung around the circular drive and halted at the bottom of the broad steps that lifted to the first floor. Hal could remember when the territorial capitol building was an unused store building down in the town. At the top of the steps, Hal paused long enough to look down and see a rented hack drive into the circle. That would be Red Macandy and the others.

Inside the marble-floored corridor, they turned left, heading for the corner governor's suite. Joe said then, "The reception room is jammed, Governor. There's half a dozen preachers there, along with a lot of your friends. Why don't you sneak in your office door while I calm the animals?"

"All right, but I want to see the editors first."

The governor moved on to his private door and stepped into his carpeted office, hung up his hat, then looked about him. His big square desk was placed crosswise at the far corner of the big room, a standard with the American and state flags behind it, a padded-leather swivel chair with arms facing it. Glass-fronted bookcases solidly filled lined the left wall and there were several leather-covered armchairs around a big conference table. Between the windows in the right wall was a horsehair sofa.

He moved around to his chair and was looking at the sheaf of letters awaiting his signature when Joe came in from the reception room. Wordlessly, Joe moved up four chairs in a semicircle facing the desk and then said, "Ready?"

The governor nodded and Joe moved over to the door and opened it, saying, "Come in, gentlemen. And you too, Red."

Red Macandy led the group. He was a dumpy, mussed man with cigar ashes graying the front of his unpressed dark suit. A saddle of thin red hair bridged his near bald, pasty white skull. A slack-bodied, sour-visaged man, he was utterly without principle, a lackey of the man with the fattest pocketbook. He was also the owner-editor of the bright and venomous *Times*. The three men with him, one young, two middle-aged, exchanged a cordial handshake with the governor before they all took their chairs facing the desk. The governor seated himself and waited while Joe crossed behind his chair.

Then the governor looked around the room and saw they were waiting. Joe Eames slacked into the chair to one side of the big desk, laid his hands across his thin belly and now he said, "Well, the governor's waiting. Why doesn't somebody begin?"

Seth Bainridge, the owner-editor of the Conifer *Democrat* and a loyal Halsey supporter, said quickly, "Hal, do you affirm or deny the facts contained in the *Times* story?"

"I affirm them," the governor said quietly.

"You do have an illegitimate son called Varney Wynn and he does work on your Mill Iron outfit?" Seth persisted.

"I confirm that, too."

Red Macandy came close to smiling around his cigar. "I thought you'd deny it, Governor, and make us prove it."

Joe Eames said dryly, "You'll claim he denied it anyway, Red. You're wasting the governor's time."

"Why would I claim he denied it?" Mac-andy asked in an injured tone.

"Because on any given day you'd rather print a lie than the truth," Joe said. "You accidentally got ahold of something true and printed it, and now you're afraid it's spoiled your record."

"All right, Joe," Hal said quietly. He looked at Red Macandy and saw that he was unruffled and even enjoying this. Now Morgan of the West Haven *Herald*, which opposed him, asked spitefully, "Care to describe the late Mrs. Wynn, Governor?"

"Not to any of you," Hal said calmly.

"Had you known about Mrs. Wynn's deposition before you read it in the *Times*, Governor?" This was from young Burke, the son of the editor of the *Argus Basin Free Press*. It must have been one of his first assignments, for his voice was shaky and he was obviously impressed that he was talking to the governor himself.

"Why yes, I knew. I've known it for five years."

Red Macandy leaned forward, suddenly interested. "How did you know?"

"Because the man who had it has been trying to blackmail me with it since June of 'Seventy."

Macandy said sharply, "You expect us to believe that, Governor?"

"It's a matter of total indifference to me whether you believe it or not, Red. Why don't you ask that blackmailer if you want the truth. He's got his money, so he'll talk."

"If I knew where to find him, I would," Red said. "Who is he?"

Hal said quietly, "You're forgetting something, Red."

"I never forget anything, but what did I forget?"

"That I'm a lawyer. If I gave you his name, it would be actionable. Obviously there were no witnesses to his blackmail attempts."

"Try again, Red," Joe jibed.

The governor said mildly to Joe, "Red is baiting us, Joe. He knows the man's name."

"I'm not a mind-reader, Governor," Red said sardonically. "I know everybody in this state, so you'll have to be more specific."

The governor said quietly, "Why not ask Asa Forbes?"

Bainridge and Burke laughed while Morgan and Macandy exchanged glances. Macandy said then in a surly voice, "What would Asa know about it?"

"I doubt if the blackmailer made a gift to you of Mrs. Wynn's deposition, Red. He's hungry for money and since the deposition is in the hands of Forbes' gang, it's reasonable to believe they paid something for it."

"You're saying Forbes bought it?" Red challenged.

The governor shook his head. "You won't get me to say that, Red. What I'm saying is that the deposition was for sale and that the blackmailer finally found a buyer. I'm also saying the buyer is a Forbes backer, else why is it being used to try and defeat me?" He smiled and said, "Is that mealy-mouthed enough?"

Red leaned forward and pitched his long dead cigar into the spittoon. "I wondered if that's what you were tasting, Governor," Red said dryly.

Bill Morgan said sardonically, "Now that the contents of the deposition are known, I suppose you'll make some gesture toward your illegitimate son?"

"A gesture like what?" the governor asked curiously.

"Like setting him up in business or bossing one of your ranches." He added with open malice, "That would be a great vote getter, and you're not one to miss that chance are you?"

"I made my gesture twenty-three years ago, Bill. I specified in my will that my property was to be equally divided between my two sons. It's still in my will."

Burke and Bainridge were both scribbling on copy paper; Red looked at them with disdain and Joe caught his look.

"You're not taking notes, Red. How can you misquote a man if you don't write down what he said?"

"He hasn't said anything yet that's quotable," Red growled. He looked insolently at Hal. "Say something I can use, Governor."

"Like what Forbes' backers want from him?"

"That'll do for a start."

"Why, they want him to come out against the appointment of a Mining Safety Commission. They want him to say it's interference by the state government in private business. They want him to say he's against crippling taxes on the mining companies, the greatest source of wealth and jobs in the state. They want him to say that high taxes will kill the goose that's laying the golden eggs."

Joe Eames spoke before Red could answer. "They also want him to say that a man who has a bastard son is unfit for office, but he won't. You will, though, won't you, Red?"

"I'm interviewing the governor, not his squirt secretary," Macandy said testily. To the governor he said, "You keep referring to Forbes' backers. Who do you think they are?

What are their names?"

"Why, they're the same men who pay you, Red. Surely you know your bosses," the governor said.

Red Macandy stood up. "I'm wasting my tine here."

"When you could be in a nice warm saloon, cheating at cards," Joe Eames said coldly.

Hal rose and the rest of them came to their feet. "One more question, Governor. Are you going to keep to your speaking schedule as announced?"

"Definitely. I intend to speak in every town in the state before election."

They thanked him and shook hands, all except Red Macandy who simply walked to the door and went out.

When Joe closed the door behind them, he came over to the desk behind which the governor had seated himself again. "You've been holding out on me, Governor. I didn't know about the blackmail part."

"How would I have told you without telling the reason for it?"

"Right. But that was sweet, real sweet. It makes you a stubborn cuss with guts, just in case anybody doubts it. And it makes that deposition a pretty shabby piece of business." He shook his head in wonderment. "God, but isn't the truth a beautiful thing?"

He turned. "Ready for the wolves?"

At Hal's nod, he walked over to the reception-room door, paused, and with his hand on the knob, turned and said quietly, "You know, after searching my soul for weeks, I've decided I'm going to vote for you."

6

Varney stepped into the Mill Iron office and halted just outside the circle of light cast by the desk lamp. Cole was seated in the chair behind it, reading a letter. On the desk top were scattered a dozen folded newspapers.

Cole looked over his shoulder and Varney said tonelessly, "Bert said you wanted to see me."

Cole rose and extended the letter. "From Hal. Sit down and read it."

Varney took the letter and slacked into the chair Cole had vacated, while Cole circled the desk and opened the first of the newspapers, flattening it on the desk under the lamplight. His fleeting glance at Varney told him there was no pleasure, no sense of anticipation in Varney; his still, expressionless face held only the same faint sulk that it had contained all week.

Varney carefully removed his hat and laid it on the floor, then turned his attention to the letter, which read:

Dear boys:

The enclosed newspapers may interest you. Save them as a record of my own private Gethsemane. On the whole, I came off better than I deserved. If I can read between the lines of most of the editorial comment, it's not they like me or condone what I did, but they are angry that Forbes' gang would use this weapon.

Varney, I'm troubled that we parted on the note we did. Understandably you were angry and I may have appeared unfeeling to you. I am anything but that. I know what you will be facing now, but I urge you to face it without temper or bitterness. Spend your bitterness on me, not the man who calls you a name.

If I have read my history rightly, there has never been any moral disgrace attached to being born illegitimate. The disgrace was directed at those who caused the birth, simply because they had created a threat to the sanctity of property by lawful inheritance. What I'm saying poorly is that economics was the basis for the moral judgment, not religion and certainly not nature. I'm not excusing myself or making light of your burden when I say that the economics of your illegitimacy is already settled fairly between the three of us. Cold comfort, but comfort nevertheless.

Cole, I know you'll be repping for us at roundup starting this week and then go on to Kansas City with our beef. I don't often make a suggestion to you, but this time I wish you would ship everything you can without jeopardizing our future. This election has cost money and will cost more. I can't hope to match Forbes' dollar or spend it for what he does, but I must both entertain and travel. But more importantly, I must help the people who are helping me. A little help on a pressing mortgage to a good man is not only good politics and good business but it is also necessary. Forbes is putting pressure on the banks to put pressure on politically doubtful borrowers, and I have to step in the breach. I have been offered financial help, but I prefer not to be beholden.

I had a rough week, but things are better now. The preachers, as expected, were the worst, but I think there's enough of the Old Nick in most men that they don't like being told who to like or dislike.

Varney, once you've shipped come on up and see me. Cole, take care in the big city. Their whiskey will taste better than ours, but it's still whiskey.

> Affectionately,
> Hal or Dad

Varney read it again. Cole pawed through the papers, reading only those sections that his father had marked. When he saw Varney toss the letter on the desk, he said, "Listen to this, Varney. From the *Argus Basin Free Press*. Quote. When you look at Hal Halsey and then at the fat cats backing Forbes, you wonder if a few illegitimate children wouldn't be good for them. At least it would make them human, something they aren't and Halsey is. Unquote." He looked at Varney, who did not smile.

"There's nothing like a bastard son to hold up the campaign platform, is there? It's almost as if he planned it that way, or wanted it that way. He even writes like he's proud of it," Varney said sourly.

Cole looked searchingly at him, a surge of temper rising and dying in him. "That's right,"

Cole said quietly. "He bribed Abe Brandell to give your mother's deposition to Red Macandy."

"But he's close to bragging about being my father!"

"He's doing what any man with courage would do. He hasn't denied it." Cole paused. "Come to think of it, he could claim that the deposition was hers but that the facts are wrong. He could say that she kept the company of other men and that she named him as your father only because he was Territorial Governor and prominent. Other men would do it. Some have, but the point is he didn't." He paused long enough to circle the desk and halt beside Varney, who followed him with his glance. "I've got one more observation to make, Varney. You must like getting knocked down and losing teeth."

"All right. You're boss and you could do it and the governor wouldn't give a damn either."

"No, I'll sit this one out, but the next time I won't. And next time after that I won't, until I knock some sense into you or shut you up." His voice still held iron in it as he said, "Now get away from me before I change my mind this time."

Varney said, "Then let's talk about something else."

Cole turned away from him and crossed over to the sofa and slacked onto it. He could feel his stomach knotted with anger and he was shaking a little. He closed his eyes and relaxed and when he opened them he saw Varney watching him. Varney had leaned both arms on the desk and his hands were clasped before him. In the shaded lamplight that cut across his lower face he had the bedeviled look of a man nerving himself into speech. Cole let him wait.

Finally, Varney said, "Cole, I'm not going on roundup. I've made up my mind and you can't make me change it."

"Why won't you?"

Varney shook his head in wonderment and asked softly, "You have to ask me that? Don't you know?"

"Tell me."

"I — I can't face those men, not with them knowing what they do about me, laughing behind my back, prodding me into cussing them so they can fight me. I can't do it."

"It's the best time *to* do it, Varney. Most of the older men you know will be there. So will the fellows you grew up with. The odd rider that's new won't know or care. You get it all over with at once. They'll be more careful than you'll be about what they say."

"No," Varney said stubbornly.

Cole sat up. "Dammit, they're *with* you, Varney, if you give them a chance to be. The first man that brings it up, they'll be on him to a man."

"Why would they be?" Varney challenged. "I haven't done much to be respected for."

"They'll do it because you're Hal's boy." He came slowly to his feet. "Don't say it, Varney, or this'll be the next time I was just talking about."

Varney stubbornly held his glance. "No, I can't do it, Cole. Maybe later, but this is too soon."

"Start running and you'll never quit."

Varney smiled crookedly. "It's easy for you to preach. Suppose you were the bastard instead of me. What would you do?"

"I'd go to roundup and I wouldn't pack a gun. I'd look every man in the eye. If anybody named me, I'd fight him until I was knocked cold or he was."

Varney smiled with self-pity and leaned back in his chair. "But you're not the bastard and I am, and your medicine isn't for me. No, tell them I got thrown from a horse and hurt. Or tell them I've gone to Junction City. Hell, tell them anything."

"I'll tell them the truth, Varney — that you didn't want to come. They can make anything out of that they want, but I don't even have to guess what they'll think."

"Hell with what they think," Varney said angrily. "It's my life."

"Then make it as miserable as you want."

Now Varney reached down for his hat, then eased out of the chair. "I thought you'd make me go. Anyway, thanks for the favor."

Cole shook his head. "It's no favor, Varney, and I want no thanks. You've made some mistakes in your life, but none like this. If you can't make yourself do it, I'm not the one to make you."

"Let's leave it right there," Varney said quietly. He turned and went out, and Cole fought the impulse to open the door and call him back. Instead, he tramped over to the desk and slowly sat down in the swivel chair, his face brooding and dark with an obscure dislike of himself.

He had failed utterly to reach Varney and Varney's decision to avoid the roundup could shape the rest of his life. It was the act of a young man not yet a man, and Cole had a growing and dismal conviction he never would be one. Granted that Varney's heedless life had been given a savage wrench, but he would not face the change that must be made. He either had to face it or inevitably turn into a recluse, afraid and ashamed to meet the world. There was an alterative, Cole knew.

Varney could leave the country and take up a new name and a new life, but he wouldn't, Cole judged. He would be protected here, assured of a living, knowing that the crew he worked with would fight his fights out of respect and affection for Hal. Maybe it was time to give him more responsibility, but he had already shirked the little that he once had. When Cole thought of the slow, reliable, and sturdy qualities of Fred Enders, his *segundo*, he could not imagine Varney replacing him. Varney had not even the makings of a top hand, all of which the other nine riders for Mill Iron most certainly were. No, responsibility wasn't the answer. There really was no answer, he thought gloomily.

Cole rose and stretched. Tomorrow they would breakfast before dawn. The chuck wagon and horse herd would head for Calico Flats, the crew headed by himself following, stopping at the Flats only long enough to check in with Tom Mather, the roundup boss. They had already been assigned the country they were to sweep, so they would head immediately for the high country in the Rafts.

Cole blew the lamp out, then stumbled his way to the door that led into the house. Maybe, just maybe, he thought, Varney would change his mind after a night's sleep, but Cole doubted it. Varney had already started run-

71

ning, *the thing he does best,* Cole thought.

From the house porch, Varney watched the crew with Cole at the head, take off. They were a little late, because Cole had taken time to cut out Varney's string from the remuda. He should have done it for himself, he thought, but it was too late now. That was just one more thing Cole would hold against him.

When the crew mounted, Varney stepped back into the house and watched them through the curtained window as they rode past the house in the direction of Calico Flats. They were talkative and happy, Varney saw; even solemn Fred Enders riding alongside Cole on his big chestnut, had a smile on his face. For a moment Varney felt a keen disappointment. This was the good time of year for every owner and puncher, the time when they worked like hell, slept little, ate seldom and saw how their stock had prospered. It held the same satisfaction for them that the sight of the autumn harvest held for a farmer.

When they were gone by Varney shifted his glance to the distant corrals where young Bert Prince, left behind to do the few required ranch chores was watching, a picture of dejection. Varney knew he should and could have offered to do Bert's chores, thus freeing him to join the roundup crew, but he hadn't. It would have stamped him as the willing menial in the eyes of the crew who were contemptuous enough of him as it was.

Then Varney turned and for the first time really looked about him at the big living room with its huge fireplace, Indian rugs and deep leather easy chairs and sofa. He was familiar with the office, but he had never been through the house. Now, room by room, he made his tour. Cole's room next to the office held little more than a narrow bed and a chest of drawers whose top was littered with shotgun shells, worn gloves, and a bottle of whiskey. Varney took the bottle, drank from it, then carried it with him as he resumed his tour.

The governor's bedroom upstairs was a big, sunny corner room that contained a fine old littered desk, a fourposter bed, a sofa, and some easy chairs. The floor was covered with a big Oriental rug. The room across the hall was just as spacious and had been the room where Priscilla Halsey spent years of miserable invalidism. It was utterly feminine, with fragile chairs, a chaise longue and a big bed with a frilly canopy; the curtains were bright and lacy. *I saw her maybe three times*, Varney reflected, recalling only a slight woman with a pain-ravaged face. He took another drink, a long one, before he moved down the hall to the other bedrooms.

They were guest rooms and all looked un-lived in. *One of these is mine, Cole said this morning,* Varney thought, and now he smiled faintly. As a point of pride he would never move in here. The fact that he wouldn't would embarrass and anger Cole, but Varney would be adamant. When he was given proper responsibility that fitted his new position then he would become a member of the family and move in, but not before.

For each room Varney took another ritual drink. When he reached the kitchen he had emptied the bottle and he took a long drink of water. He was pleasantly on fire inside and he had come to the surprising conclusion that he was about to have a good time instead of licking his wounds.

There came a knock on the living-room door and Varney, scowling, moved in to a front window. He could see a saddle horse at the tie rail, but it was unfamiliar to him. Now he moved unsteadily toward the door and opened it.

Tish Hammond stood on the porch. She was dressed in a divided skirt, a man's shirt and a buckskin jacket; her hat hung down on her shoulders by its chin strap, and her long auburn hair was gathered at the nape of her neck by a green ribbon.

Tish said, almost uncertainly, "You're Varney, aren't you? It's been so long since I've seen you, I'm not sure."

"Varney Wynn," Varney said firmly. "You were almost going to say Varney Halsey weren't you?"

Tish flushed. "Not really, but it would have been a natural mistake."

"Oh no. *I'm* the natural mistake," Varney said. He laughed at her embarrassment and she could smell the liquor on his breath.

"I'm really looking for Cole," Tish said, half angrily.

"Well, if you're up to a twenty-mile ride, I can tell you where to find him. He'll be at old Marty Frost's cabin at the head of Cooper Branch." Varney smiled at her expression of puzzlement. "Roundup's on, Miss Hammond. You're the only one in three counties that doesn't know it."

Now Tish blushed furiously and gave him a look almost of hatred. "I — I did know it. I just forgot it started today."

Varney nodded, his face reflecting amusement. "Go on and ask," he said then.

"Ask what?"

"Why I'm not on roundup. By now you're wondering."

"Yes, you're right," Tish said sharply. "Is

75

it because you'd rather stay here and drink?"

"You guessed it," Varney said cheerfully. "Will you join me? Or don't you drink with bastards?"

"I've drunk with plenty of bastards, but not in the morning," Tish said flatly. Then she added, "That was a poor joke and I wish I hadn't said it. But you're so sorry for yourself, you invited it."

"I'm not sorry for myself. I'm sorry for all the people that think they have to be nice to me. They don't have to dirty themselves if they don't want to."

Tish looked at him curiously. "Just for the record, how many people have called you a bastard yet? Besides yourself, I mean."

"Well, the *Times*, for one."

"In the course of printing a dirty but legitimate news story. Who else?"

Varney shrugged and said sullenly, "That's coming."

"You sound pretty sure of that." She paused, and then asked quietly, "Do you know anyone born illegitimate?"

Varney scowled and didn't answer immediately. Then he said, "No, but there must be lots of them."

"Exactly. But I don't know of one either. When it's discussed, and that's not very often, it's the mother who's blamed, not the child. I never heard anyone called a bastard except in fun or in anger. Never when it was meant literally."

"Then why is it a fighting word?" Varney asked sullenly.

"I wouldn't think it would be to an illegitimate child. It would be the simple truth, so why take offense? Anger in the son won't get the mother married."

"That's easy for you to say. You aren't — "

Tish cut him off. "No, it's not been easy to say any of this. I just don't like to see a man slink and hide when he has every right to walk with pride. As much right as any other human being."

"That's something Cole might have said," Varney said, with open sarcasm.

Tish studied him with a thoughtful curiosity in her face. "Does that make it wrong? If Cole said it, it would be wrong. Is that what you're trying to say?"

Varney hiccupped and it seemed to make him angry. He made a down-sweeping gesture with his hand. "Damn it, you talk too much!"

"I guess I do," Tish said. She turned and walked to the edge of the porch, then said over her shoulder, "Good-bye, Varney."

She was not answered. As she mounted her bay mare, she glanced over at the house. Varney stood at the edge of the porch, hands on hips, watching her. He even refrained from a good-bye gesture.

Pulling her horse around, Tish headed back for Primrose. This whole visit home was wrong so far. Yesterday her father had returned from Junction City with a new bodyguard for her. He had been furious with her, almost as furious as she had been with him. They had argued far into the night and she had gone to bed with his parental edict ringing in her ears: she would have a bodyguard whether she wanted one or not. Before daybreak she had wakened and dressed, sneaked a cold breakfast in the dark kitchen and had then gone out to the stable and saddled her mare. Her father, house guest Bowie, the bodyguard, the maid, the cook and the stablehands all slept as she rode out into the gray dawn.

Before defying her father's orders, she had done some planning. If she succeeded in sneaking out alone, she would head for the Mill Iron. If her bodyguard caught up with her, she would ask Cole to throw him off his ranch. This, in a way, would be a test of Cole too. She had told him there on the hotel veranda that he shouldn't have listened to her when she dared him to rid her of Hugh. What had he answered? "Next time I won't." Well,

78

this might be the next time, she had thought, and wondered what Cole would do.

Her successful escape, though, was the only thing that had gone right. She had forgotten roundup, probably because Burley and Bowie were both townsmen, interested in politics and mining rather than cattle. Too, she had lost touch with old ranching friends. So she had missed Cole and instead found Varney. She had been disconcerted by his appearance and was momentarily at a loss for something to say. Well, Varney himself had provided her with a subject to discuss and, as usual, she had talked too much and too strongly.

Varney, his words and his actions added to his appearance, appalled her. Years ago, she had known him as a leggy kid Hal had picked up, but during Varney's college and ranching years she had never seen him. Lately, she herself had not even been close to the Mill Iron. After her refusal to marry Cole, they had gone their separate ways, seeing each other occasionally in town but keeping things as impersonal as possible.

Now the whole situation at the Mill Iron troubled and bewildered her. Hal was fighting for his political life and had no time for the social amenities, at least not with Burley Hammond or his family. Cole was friendly but withdrawn and she had an indefinable feeling that he was privately contemptuous of her life and her friends. Now Varney, scandal clinging to him in spite of his innocence, was thrust upon both the Halseys. If Varney had been like Cole, the new relationship would have been easy, but from what she already knew of Varney and had seen of him this morning, it would be anything but easy.

Ahead of her, a mile or so from Primrose, she spotted a pair of riders approaching. As they came closer, she saw it was Bowie and her new bodyguard, Abel Lynch. Abel was a gangling, middle-aged, and taciturn man who was their gardener in town, a saloon brawler and surly tyrant. Her father kept him at her mother's insistence because plants and trees grew for him as they did for no one else.

Both of them reined in and waited for her. Bowie, she saw, was dressed in range clothes and looked strange without a business suit. When she pulled up before them Bowie only shook his head reprovingly. "Why don't you give up, Tish? You're a nuisance."

"Oh, I haven't even started."

Abel said, "Your Pa says I'm to sleep in the hall across from your door from now on." He was wearing bib overalls under a soiled duck coat.

"Then do it, Abel, if you want a jug of hot

80

water poured over you every night."

Bowie laughed. "He's thinking about a pad-lock on your door."

Tish shrugged. "Let's go." Then she looked at Abel. "Ride about twenty yards behind us, Abel."

"What for?"

"I don't especially like your company and I want to talk with Bowie." She added venomously, "You think my father will trust Bowie not to shoot me?"

Abel flushed but said nothing. Tish and Bowie moved off and presently Abel started after them.

"Where'd you head for, Tish?"

Tish smiled faintly, but did not look at him "Mill Iron. Where were you looking for me?"

"Same place. Your father had an idea you'd go there to get Cole to beat up Abel. He's pretty good at that, I understand."

"I wish you were as good," Tish said tartly.

Bowie laughed again. "Did he turn you down this time?"

"He wasn't there. I'd forgotten about roundup starting. Varney Wynn was there but I don't think he's the man to do it."

Bowie asked curiously, "What's he like?"

Tish hesitated a moment and then said, "I don't know. He was drunk both on booze and self-pity." When Bowie asked, "How's that?"

she told him of her conversation with Varney and Bowie listened without much interest.

He was nodding as Tish finished. "Your father said he'd already caused Hal a pack of grief."

Tish looked at him now. "Was Dad mad this morning?"

"Never seen him madder." Bowie's broad face held amusement as he told her now. "You know, you can't win this one, Tish."

"I could if you'd help me."

"By doing what?"

"Just what Cole did with Hugh."

Bowie moved his head so impatiently that his jowls quivered. "Can't you get it through your pretty head that your father isn't punishing you, that he's protecting you?"

"But from what?" Tish exclaimed. "Is there a miner in Primrose who'd knock me down and kick me?"

"Plenty of them," Bowie said flatly. "Look, some of these miners are no better than animals. They're foreigners, used to beating their women. Even the sporting girls are afraid of them. When they fight, they use knives and they know how to carve a man without killing him." He glanced over at her. "It would take one of them less than ten seconds to disfigure you for life."

"But Bowie, what I can't understand is why

they'd want to! Is it to get even with Dad? What's he done to them? If it's something wrong, why doesn't he stop doing it?"

"He's done nothing wrong," Bowie said grimly. "He hires miners to dig ore. They go underground of their own free will. If they don't like it, let them find other work. Your father pays them enough to live on and raise their families and get drunk on."

"Do they want higher wages?"

Bowie snorted. "Did you ever see a workingman who didn't? Of course they do. But your father's first obligation is to provide for your mother and yourself, then for the people who loaned him their money, then for the others who are skilled enough to run his mines. The miners come last and that's as it should be. They've got nothing but muscle to sell and muscle is the world's cheapest commodity. Besides, they're making dollars now where they were making pennies in the old country."

"Did they knife the owner's daughters in the old country?" Tish asked with some asperity.

"If they even looked at the owner's daughter they'd have been thrown in prison," Bowie said shortly.

"But they do get hurt in the mines, Bowie. I've seen men who were crippled in them."

"Of course they do," Bowie answered impatiently. "Mining's dangerous work. So is being a law officer. So is being a trail hand. But I'll say again, Tish, that nobody's making them go down a mine. If they think it's too dangerous, let them find other work."

"Maybe there isn't any other work."

Bowie's glance held a mild dismay. "So there isn't other work. Well, why do we work? Isn't it so we can eat and stay alive?" He snorted. "I could take a rifle and go up in the Rafts and live off the country for years. So could they if they don't like their work." He regarded her closely and said, "You couldn't be blaming your father for anything, could you, Tish?"

Her glance at him held surprise. "No, Bowie. I'm just trying to understand what makes it necessary for me to have a bodyguard."

"Have I explained?"

Tish sighed. "I guess you have. I'll — I'll put up with it here, but I won't like it."

"You're not here enough to make it a nuisance. And when we're married, we'll live in Junction City. I'll be your bodyguard and a damned good one."

"*If* we're married, not when."

Bowie smiled faintly. "We'll be married, honey. All it takes is a single word, and that word is 'yes'."

Tish did not reply. In this bright morning with the tang of fall in the air, with the close Rafts ablaze with color and the good smell of warming sage in the air, she was suddenly sad. Why had Cole been in such a rush and why was Bowie? She'd keep, and what she needed was time. Bowie was good to her because he was in love with her and no man could be more physically attractive, but did she love him any more than she loved Cole? And was it love at all and why wasn't it? Did she lack that quality of self-deception that made other girls fall wildly in love? For it was self-deception, she was sure, else why did some girls' eyes light up and glow at the sight of some laughable lout? Did she demand too much, or was love only a willingness to accept an imperfect someone you could live with? *Big and profound questions, Letitia,* she thought wryly.

In Primrose they took a quiet, tree-shaded street that ended at the beginning of the gate-guarded hill with Burley Hammond's big brick house planted in the tall pines atop it. Abel trailed them.

They turned over their horses to the stable-boy and Tish led the way to the side door that let into the library. At their entrance into the paneled room, Burley Hammond ceased his floor pacing and turned to face them, a bull of a man in a dark suit. His heavy face under his bald head was divided by full brown mustaches and now it held an anger that was close to explosive.

Tish said quickly, "All right, Dad, it's over. I won't do it again and I'll be Abel's good little girl. But only here. Not in Junction City."

"Did I ever say it had to be Junction City?" Burley demanded flatly. His voice was rough, in strange contrast to his correct suit, white shirt and flowing tie. He looked as if he were about to open a Board of Directors meeting of one of his mines. His hands were big, now gone soft, their size the only indication that he had once worked with them.

"No, you didn't," Tish conceded mildly. Now that she had given in she was no longer interested in discussing it.

Now she indicated the heap of newspapers atop the massive desk by one of the windows of the too-dark room. "What are all those?"

"Newspapers," Burley said, and now he gave Bowie a quick and almost angry glance before he looked back at Tish. "Get out of those men's clothes, girl. You're too old to dress like a child."

"Maybe I'm dressing like one because I'm being treated like one," Tish said. Without speaking further to them, she crossed the carpet to the far door and stepped into the living room, closing the door behind her.

Burley now made a gesture toward the newspapers. "The office sent these on the morning train. Almost every paper in the state."

Bowie tossed his hat in the big chair facing the desk and as he moved over to the newspapers, he asked, "What's the reaction around the state?"

"Not, by God, the one you anticipated, Bowie!" Hammond said angrily.

Bowie halted, glanced briefly and curiously at him, then picked up the top newspaper, which happened to be the *Capital Times*.

"Don't bother with that. You already know what Red would say. It's the others."

"What's the gist of them?"

Burley grimaced in answer. "Did you know that Abe Brandell has been trying to blackmail Hal with that deposition for five years?"

Bowie said easily, "Not until Cole told me the other day."

"Why didn't you tell me?"

"What could you have done?" Bowie countered.

Burley glared at him, then shrugged. "Nothing, I guess."

"Did Hal say it was Abe who blackmailed him?"

Burley shook his head in negation. "He's

too smart for that, but everybody will know it." He rammed both hands into his hip pockets, a countryman's gesture that his millions could never erase. He began to pace the big room.

"What do the newspapers say?"

Burley didn't even look at him. "That we bought the deposition."

"Do they name us?"

"Only by calling us 'the Forbes' Gang' or 'the Fat Cats' or 'the Mining Midases'." Now Burley looked at him with a scowl. "The whole damned thing has been turned against us, Bowie. Hal was interviewed. He didn't deny his bastard and even Macandy's original story said he'd been providing for the boy. The blackmail part was the clincher. People hate blackmail and they admire a man who won't pay it under any circumstances. The best Red could come up with was that anybody could claim they'd refused to be blackmailed because the blackmailer would never identify himself to confirm it."

"That's not bad, Burley."

"*I* think it's bad, but it's all we've got. Hal killed that by saying that obviously the blackmailer had found a buyer. That's what all the papers say, too." He pulled his hands from his pockets, then fisted his right hand and pounded the palm of his left. "Damn the day the telegraph was invented! The story's all over the state. One jackal editor telegraphs the story and every other editor picks it up."

"Where's Asa?"

"Somewhere on roundup. I sent a man for him but he'll have to find him. I don't know when he'll be here."

Bowie moved over to the big chair, lifted his hat off the seat and tossed it on the floor, then sat down. "I think you're overestimating the damage."

Burley crossed over to the desk and slapped the heap of papers with his open hand. "Read these!"

"I will, but you've forgotten one thing, Burley. The women."

"I've never yet seen a man take his wife to the polls so she could watch him vote," Burley said sourly.

"But she influences his vote."

"The hell she does," Burley contradicted. "His vote is the *only* thing she doesn't influence. And the easiest thing in the world for him to lie about is how he voted, because nobody can prove he's lying."

Bowie flushed, recognizing the truth in what Burley said. "But claiming a bastard is death to a politician. It's even deadlier than denying you have one."

"Has Hal's claiming his changed your opinion of him?" Burley demanded.

"Frankly, no."

"It's changed mine. I admire him for it," Burley said flatly, then added with a touch of malice, "You're soft in the head if you don't think every man in the state feels like I do."

Now Burley sat down and regarded Bowie with a scorn he didn't bother to hide. "All right, Master Mind, what do we do? You sold us on buying the deposition and look what it's got us. What do we do now?"

Bowie crossed his legs and slacked lower in his chair. "I've been thinking about that for the past few days, although I didn't anticipate this newspaper reaction." He held up a finger. "One. You raise the wages of your miners, all of you."

"That'll cost us tens of thousands," Burley said sourly.

"Well, it's better than hundreds of thousands if Hal wins. It's an obvious move that Hal will pounce on. Let him. A full lunch bucket and more booze money will talk louder than Hal can." He held up another finger. "Organize the churches and the preachers. Get a half-dozen jack-leg revivalists to tour the state promising hellfire and brimstone for anybody voting sin into office. And believe me, Burley, this is sin with a capital S. Everyone with a daughter knows it. Make them hate Hal as they love their daughters."

"You can't hate Hal. That's the hell of it," Burley said gloomily.

Bowie ignored that. "In all our speeches and in all our papers we should hammer home the word 'trust' — or rather the lack of it. Hal can't be trusted if he'll betray a woman."

"A lot of men will hate you for that," Burley said dryly. "They've betrayed women, but they all figure they can be trusted." He rose. "You through?" When Bowie nodded, Burley said, "Well, go think some more. All you've said is piddlin'. It won't get Forbes in."

Bowie rose, gathered up the newspapers, said, "I'll take these up to my room," and went out of the library.

Upstairs in the room that Tish always prepared for him on his visits to Primrose, he hauled a big easy chair to the window, pried off his boots, then slacked into the chair. All the papers were weeklies except the *Times*, which was a daily. Halsey had given his interview the first of the week in order to give the country editors time to ponder his words, Bowie judged. He began to read each paper carefully, but he paid especial attention to the editorials.

After an hour he discarded the last paper, rose and stretched. It was worse than Burley made out. Except for five newspapers whose owners Burley had bought or threatened, they were all sympathetic in varying degrees to Halsey. The old fox had been smart enough to voice his contrition, so every editor only gently scolded him for his sins. But the blackmail revelation had taken the sting out of their pious censure. How could you hate a man who had not only refused to pay blackmail but had never denied his son and had provided for him? All the editorials seemed to say, Yes, their warrior was tarnished, but look who was responsible. Examine their dirty method of discrediting Halsey, but more particularly, examine their motives.

"A guilty man but a brave one who will not quit the good fight. Praise God," one editorial had said, and Bowie thought that summed it up. *Damn and triple damn Abe Brandell,* Bowie thought too. Well, Halsey must have another weakness. He'd been womanless since the death of his wife and of Mrs. Wynn. Anything there? Bowie doubted it, for Halsey was too much in the public eye to risk an affair. Could he be discredited through his son Cole? No, Cole was liked if a little bit feared, by everyone who knew him. The fear came from the knowledge that Cole was a proud man who would fight like a lion for the people he liked and the things he believed.

Now Bowie took a slow turn around the

room. *Through Varney?* he wondered. Re-calling what Tish had said of her visit with Varney this morning, Bowie thought he wasn't worth bothering with. The boy was a nothing, a drunk. Still, he was ashamed of the fact he'd been identified publicly as a bastard. Who would he hate for that?

Suddenly, Bowie halted. What was running through his mind made him hold his breath for moments before exhaling. No, it was too dangerous. But *was* it? *Was* it? Involuntarily, he glanced up at the door, as if he had spoken aloud and might have been heard.

Crossing over to the chair he sat down and looked out the window. The whole of Prim-rose lay before him; he saw it and yet didn't see it, for he was calculating the risk. If he dared to go through with it, two men could do it. And the two would have done nothing very wrong and need never know why they'd been asked to do it. Burley would never know either. The risk wasn't great and the re-ward was already pledged: for electing Forbes, he would get not just the present frac-tion of Burley's immense legal business, but all of it. He would sit on the boards of a half-dozen corporations, sharing generously in their earnings.

Yes, he thought, *I'll risk it.*

At noonday dinner Burley was sullen, still

smarting from his morning session with the newspaper accounts of Hal's interview, and he excused himself immediately after eating. Tish had been hungry and then was immediately sleepy. She went upstairs to nap, leaving Bowie to finish his coffee alone. He rehearsed his scheme and could see no flaw in it. He would wrap up the Primrose end of it this afternoon. Tomorrow he would take the morning train to Junction City where he would take care of the rest of it. It didn't matter that Burley and very likely Tish would return with him. In fact, it would be better if Burley was in the capital when the news broke.

Bowie changed from his boots to street shoes, then left the house and walked down the winding drive and through the gates into town. He made two stops, one for a drink at the Primrose House bar, the second to cash a check at the Stockmans Bank before he crossed the bridge and turned down River Street. Except for drays and an occasional four team, high-sided ore wagon from the outlying mines, there was little traffic here. River Street waited for this Saturday night to come alive.

At the Miners Rest Saloon, a big barn of a building with high and dirty windows painted half their height, Bowie shouldered his way through the half doors and went up to the long bar that bore the scars of many a brawl. There was no mirror behind the bar and the liquor was kept under the bar itself. Only boxes of cigars and plug tobacco plus a couple of sawed-off pool cues graced the back bar. The bar was stripped for action that came almost nightly.

Bowie signaled the bartender away from a couple of men drinking beer. As he approached, Bowie noted a five-handed poker game going on at a rear table under a high wall window. The rest of the room with its tables and sturdy chairs and overhead, unlit kerosene lamps was murky. The whole room smelled of spilled beer and spent cigar smoke.

"Dave in?" Bowie asked.

The beefy bartender gestured with his thumb to a door in the side wall. "Just come in. Go on in."

Bowie skirted the free-lunch counter whose contents were covered by a couple of dirty towels, halted before the closed door, rapped once and then entered a small office whose four walls were covered with a superb collection of whiskey posters. A very fat man seated at a roll-top desk turned and when he saw Bowie he smiled and rose, shoved his chair back and extended a meaty hand. "Back in town again, Bowie? I figured you'd be stumping out in the state."

"I start next week. Asa had to get his cattle shipped first, Dave."

Dave Hardy was one of Bowie's heelers and, in spite of the hatred of the miners for the owners, he would deliver, Bowie knew. His broad and ruddy face was at the same time genial and cruel. Now he gestured to a chair in front of an old and sagging sofa and Bowie sat down. Dave seated himself in his extra-wide chair and they talked politics for a few minutes.

Bowie said after that, "Dave, I need some help. Can you get me a couple of fellows who can really hold their liquor without getting into fights?"

"That's some order," Dave said dryly. "That's why most of them drink." He laughed, his belly jiggling in rhythm under his white shirt. "Let's see." He thought a moment, then said, "There's a couple out there in the game that might do."

"I don't want riffraff," Bowie said, then added, "Well, sort of riffraff, maybe. But good drinkers first of all."

"Take a look at 'em," Dave said. "They ain't ever really sober except when they work and that ain't often. They'll easy handle a quart a day without fightin'." He went to the door, opened it and called, "Albie, you and Henry come here."

He turned from the door, leaving it open.

"They owe you money?" Bowie asked.

"Both. Not much, though."

"Don't name me, Dave," Bowie said, and Dave nodded his understanding.

The two men entered the room and halted, only glancing at Bowie before regarding Dave. They were both miners, but at the moment clean ones. "These two fellas are Albie Wright — he's the tall one — that bandy-legged rooster is Henry Bohannon."

Bowie nodded, as did the two men. The young one, a pimply man with an undershot jaw, would be about the right age and the slight, older man had the ravaged face and burned-out eyes of a lifelong drinker. Both wore old duck jackets and the usual miner's round hats.

Dave said, "Want me around?" and when Bowie nodded, Dave closed the door.

Bowie said quietly, "How would you two like a job drinking whiskey for a week?"

"Free whiskey?" Bohannon asked in a hoarse voice.

Bowie nodded. "The drinks are on Dave. I'll pay him and I'll pay each of you a double eagle besides."

"For doin't what?" Albie asked.

"Getting a man drunk and keeping him drunk for a week."

The two looked at each other, then Albie said, "We like the idea."

Bowie nodded and gestured toward the worn sofa against the wall. "If you two would like a paid up drunk sit down and listen."

Bohannon moved immediately to the sofa but Albie looked at Bowie with a careful skepticism before he shifted his glance to Dave. "This on the level, Dave?"

"If you don't think so, walk out," Dave said coldly. Albie hesitated, as if the thought might not be a bad idea, then he changed his mind and joined Henry on the sofa.

"Can either of you read?" Bowie asked. Both men shook their heads in negation and Bowie sighed. "Then maybe you've heard the talk going around about Governor Halsey having a bastard son. They just discovered it and it was in the papers. Name's Varney Wynn."

"I heard it," Albie said. "I know him."

"How well do you know him?"

"I have a drink with him maybe once every couple months. Don't know him good, no."

"That's fine," Bowie said, and turned his attention to Henry. "You know him, Henry?"

The older man shook his head and Bowie said, "No matter." He leaned forward now, arms folded across his knees. "I want you two to get a bottle of whiskey apiece from Dave.

Then go to the livery and hire a couple of saddle horses. You know where Halsey's Mill Iron ranch is?"

Albie nodded yes, Henry nodded no.

"All right. Varney's there alone. He's drinking a little and feeling sorry for himself. I want you to make him drink a lot and for a long time."

"Why would he want to drink with us?" Albie asked. "We ain't special friends."

"But you will be," Bowie said mildly.

"What'll make us?"

"Why, you're both bastards too."

Albie looked puzzled and wholly angry. He looked up at Dave, who said, "He wasn't calling you bastards. What he means is you'll tell Varney Wynn you are."

"You'll sympathize with him," Bowie cut in. "Tell him you two can't read, but you were told about the papers calling him a bastard. You got to arguing with a bunch of fellows about it and you and Henry were the only ones who felt sorry for Varney. Afterward you two had a drink together and each of you told the other that his mother had never been married." He looked away from Albie to Bohannon. "Henry, have you got that?"

"I got it," Henry said and added, "With me, it's true."

They all watched him in silence and he looked defiantly at them from eyes so red-rimmed they were almost bleeding.

"Then you know firsthand that being a bastard doesn't amount to a damn," Bowie said. "Varney doesn't know that. Sympathize with him, tell him how you lived with it."

"I lived with it with a bottle," Henry said quietly.

"Then tell him that." Now Bowie looked back at Albie. "That takes care of your welcome from Varney. When you first meet him, tell him you both came out to comfort him. The rest should be easy."

"I reckon," Albie said slowly. "What do you get out of this though?"

"Nothing you need to know about," Bowie said curtly. "And I'm not anywhere near finished, Albie." He stared at the young man until Albie's gaze dropped away. "Now listen carefully. Tomorrow I want Varney in town here. I want people to see him drunk, but I don't want him to get in trouble. The next day is the most important." He looked back at Albie. "The day after tomorrow — that's a Monday — I want you two and Varney Wynn on the train to Junction City. You understand that?" He looked up at Hardy. "Dave, I'm relying on you to see this is done."

Albie nodded, but it was Henry who spoke.

"What do we do there?"

"Keep Varney drinking in the waterfront saloons. I want him seen and I want him identified. Let him sleep that night and bring him back to Primrose on the morning train. Then let him do what he wants to, only keep him out of trouble." He paused and leaned back in his chair. "Now tell it back to me, Albie, starting from here."

Albie did and with no prompting from Henry. When he was finished Bowie rose and reached in his pocket. He drew out two double eagles and gave one to Albie and the other to Henry. "You'll each get another when the job's done. Now, on your way. Don't forget to pick up a couple of bottles on your way out."

The two men left and after Dave closed the door behind them he went back to the chair at his desk and eased his vast bulk into it. He looked speculatively at Bowie before he said, "I see what you're trying to do, Bowie. You don't think this would win sympathy for Halsey?"

"I do not," Bowie said firmly. "If Varney turned out a fine boy, friendly with people and proud of his old man and not ashamed, I think it would win votes for Hal. People would say, 'Well, he made a mistake but what grand results.' But if Varney shows up a surly, slobbering drunk, people will say, 'There's bad blood there, and even his father can't control him'."

"Yeah, maybe you're right," Dave conceded.

"There's no maybe about it," Bowie said quietly.

7

The roundup this year started out with flawless weather. There was some snow in the high country of the Rafts but not enough to trap any cattle who had moved lower of their own accord. Cole and Mill Iron had been assigned Cooper Creek and its tributaries, which was their normal summer range anyway. Starting just below timberline, they swept all the canyons and open parks, pushing everything ahead of them toward the distant flats that seemed a vast brown table stretching east to infinity.

The first couple of days were rough on the horses but easy on the crew. The canyons were fairly tight and thick with brush and the cattle hung in the small pockets of grass close to the stream because that's where the feed and water were. The canyon walls hemmed them in and there was no direction to go but down, while the fleeter game that was flushed headed for the ridges.

It should have been a pleasant time for Cole; the weather was crisp enough so that when he rode in shadow he was glad for his worn sheepskin. The cattle looked fat and were a little reluctant to leave the known for the unknown. The shrill whistles and shouts of Toby Hanson, a new hired hand who was his partner at the beginning, were cheerful sounds as they mingled with the bawling of the sparse cattle ahead. But all that day and that evening when the two of them made camp in the canyon, Cole was strangely depressed. He had chosen Toby to side him because he was new and Cole wanted to know him, but the gawky and eager young man striving to please the boss could sense his mood and their camp that first night was almost a silent one.

When Toby had checked their horses on picket and they had both sought their blankets, Cole lay awake, alternately watching the dying fire and the stars, listening to the night sounds of a distant coyote and of the horses stirring. He hadn't been much company today, he conceded to himself. But how could he explain this premonition of coming trouble that had been with him ever since he rode out of Mill Iron. Varney, of course, was the cause, but there were other things as well. Hal was getting his lumps right now, with nobody to help him. Why, he wondered, hadn't he had sense enough to send Varney to Hal after Varney refused to join the roundup? He and Hal could have faced this business together and Varney might have had some of Hal's courage rub off on him. He himself had handled Varney badly, with plenty of understanding but with little patience and some anger. And how was he going to handle him in the future, this half brother for whom he could find no affection in his heart? As a troublesome ranch hand, no relation, he had only been a nuisance, but now as a blood member of the family he deserved loyalty and help. But how could Varney get it when he wouldn't accept it?

Staring up at the almost dark night sky, Cole saw a cruising night owl on utterly soundless wings fly down canyon above him. The sight seemed to fit in with his mood. The owl was trouble for something this night, something that would never see him or hear him until it was too late.

Cole shifted his back to the fire and closed his eyes. Tomorrow some time they would pick up Joe Easley and Harry Shore with their gather from another canyon. Maybe people was what he needed to shake him out of his depression.

That didn't work either, Cole found. The others joined them the next noon and now the country spread out a little from the canyon walls. That night they reached the wagon which had come up as far as it could negotiate. Two more of the crew, including Fred Enders, were there, Cole saw. They pushed their gather into the sizable herd which was now grazing across a big meadow hemmed in by the pines that seemed black in the failing light. Some of the cattle, early arrivals, had grazed and watered and were bedding down.

Cole and Toby turned their horses into the rope corral and lugged their saddles and blanket rolls over to the wagon. The fire held a welcome warmth in the chill of the evening and Cole could sense that this crew was a happy one as he approached. They taunted him about being slow and he threatened their jobs if they continued to run all the tallow off the beef. It was easy and friendly and he began to relax. A second fire, for warmth, had been built away from the cook's fire; a couple of hands were dragging in dry wood and the cook, "Annie" Anderson was bawling for someone to light a lantern so he could get on with supper. Nobody was paying him any attention.

It was then that a rider came out of the timber and rode up to the fire. Talk trailed off and Fred Enders came slowly to his feet from his place beside Cole. He was a stocky man twice Cole's age and his square, weathered face proclaimed a kind but stern task-master.

The rider reined in, looked around at the crew and asked, "This the Ladder wagon?" Ladder was Asa Forbes' brand. Fred cleared his throat, the signal that he would do the talking. "Who you lookin' for?" he asked mildly.

The rider, as was apparent to all, was no cowman, for he wore a corduroy mackinaw and the round hat with uncreased crown that was miner's dress. He was middle-aged and looked as if he would be reliable in his line of work.

"Why, Asa Forbes. He owns Ladder, don't he? They said he'd be up here on roundup."

Fred came slowly toward him saying, "He is. You come from town?"

The man nodded. "I work for Burley Hammond."

"You run across anybody today?" Fred asked, with seeming irrelevance.

"Nobody. Why?"

"Too bad," Fred said. "You just rode through the country Ladder's sweeping. If you'd met anybody they could've put you straight."

Cole started to push himself to his feet, then sank back. He saw his men look at each other, then at him, then back at the rider.

"You mean I've overshot Forbes' wagon?"

"By many a mile," Fred said in a kindly tone. "Light and eat. We can rustle up some blankets for you."

The rider was the picture of despair; he didn't have to *say* that he was weary and lost in strange country because everyone watching him saw it.

"Well, I thank you," he said and then asked, "It ain't likely I could find him tonight?"

"I'd hate to try it myself and I know this country," Fred said and he turned to the crew. "Toby, take his horse and feed him."

The rider sighed and his expression of gratitude seemed to say that Fred's words had got him off the hook and that he had done all a man could be expected to do.

He swung out of the saddle as Toby approached. Another hand in a friendly gesture came over too.

Fred turned and tramped back to Cole and sat down.

Cole said quietly, "You know damn well the Ladder wagon is south of us."

"He don't, though," Fred said quietly.

"Why'd you do it?"

"Well, Hammond must want Forbes bad if he can't wait till we hit the Flats." Fred smiled. "There ain't many ways any of us can help your pa, Cole. If we can rawhide Forbes a little, it might help."

Cole laughed so loud some of the crew glanced at him. Suddenly, for the first time since he'd left Mill Iron, he felt good.

His feeling lasted through the next day. Hammond's man had left at daylight, riding in the wrong direction, so innocent of the cattleman's world that he did not know that the brand on every horse and cow in sight was that of Governor Halsey's Mill Iron. This day Mill Iron's full crew was working together. Cole sent a couple of hands direct to Calico Flats with the cattle already gathered while the remainder of the crew swept their assigned portion of lower slopes, pushing all cattle of whatever brand ahead of them to the holding grounds a half-day's drive from the Calico Flats' big tangle of stockpens. On the Flats there, each outfit would be cutting out the shippers and strays before loading the shippers onto the trains which would be backed up and waiting. On a high point, Cole paused to look out over the Flats which were already in darkness. Pinpoints of campfires were barely visible there, cookfires of the wagons whose outfits had been assigned the prairie divisions of the roundup and had made their gather.

When Cole joined the others pushing the cattle past the wagon to the meadow where they would be held for the night, the light was fading. He noticed a saddle horse tied to the front wheel of the chuck wagon, but paid it no attention. When the cattle were turned loose to mill around the creek for water, Cole headed for the horse herd and turned his horse in. The crew already had the big fire started and as Cole approached the wagon he saw a slight figure leave the fire and head for him. It was Bert Prince and for a moment Cole felt a touch of anger that Bert would leave Mill Iron unattended. Then he remembered Varney was there and had probably sent Bert to join the crew at roundup.

Cole dumped his saddle by the wagon as Bert hauled up beside him. "Well, Bert, you made roundup after all. Everything all right?"

"Everything's quiet, Cole, and I'll make it back by early light."

Cole looked closely at him in the light of the distant fire. His unformed thin face held a worry that sobered Cole immediately. "Anything wrong, Bert?"

"That's what I don't know Cole. That's why I come, even if I had to leave the place."

"What's happened?" Cole asked quietly.

"It's Varney. He's gone. Him and these two fellows left three days ago, the day you left," Bert said hurriedly. "I know I shouldn't of left but — "

"All right, Bert. Take it easy. Start from when we rode out."

Bert nodded. "After you left, about an hour after, Miss Hammond rode in and went up to the house. She talked there on the porch with Varney, then rode back toward Primrose. In the middle of the afternoon a couple of men rode up and Varney took 'em into the house."

"You didn't know them?"

"No. Anyway they stayed and stayed and — and it got kind of noisy up there."

"Were they drinking?"

Bert nodded soberly. "Reason I know is they never went to bed. Next morning early, Varney came down and told me to get him his horse. He couldn't have managed it himself, and neither could the other two. Then they all rode off. Varney never said where he was going."

"Primrose, you think?"

"That way. Varney never took his blankets and them two didn't have blanket rolls. Late that afternoon Mrs. Schofield dropped off the mail. She said she had to pick up some freight at the depot and on her way she seen Varney

110

out in front of one of them River Street saloons. He was drunk and fightin'." He
paused. "That's all. He ain't showed up, but
nobody's rode out to say he was in trouble. I
just got to worryin', Cole, and it just kept
eatin' at me. It ain't any of my business, but
them damn fools he was with don't care
about nothin'."

"Why do you say that?"

"Well, after they'd gone I went up to the
house. The front door was open and when I
went to shut it I smelled smoke. I went in and
followed my nose to the office. Somebody'd
throwed a cigar in the governor's wastebasket
and it was burnin'. I got it out all right, and
cleaned up the rest of the place, but them two
was pigs. Maybe Varney was too drunk to notice." He hesitated. "I'll get back now, Cole.
My mind's easier long as you know."

Cole sighed. "Thanks, Bert. You did the
right thing. Eat and then get back."

"No, Annie'll give me some biscuits and I'll
take off. I shouldn't of come, but I done it
anyway."

"I'd have fired you if you hadn't," Cole
said.

Bert smiled, almost shyly, and turned
toward the cook's fire. Cole stood there,
watching him get his biscuits from Annie,
stuff them in his jumper pocket and disappear

around the wagon in the direction of his horse. He sighed, then. He didn't know what trouble Varney was in or even if he was in any — yet. But if he kept drinking, trouble would find him. He reflected a moment. He could make it to Primrose tonight, but when he got in not even the saloons would be awake to direct him to Varney. No, he'd take off early in the morning, leaving Fred to rep for Mill Iron at the roundup. A cold wrath came to him then. Varney was ashamed to face the men at roundup, but give him a bottle and he would face the whole town, the whole world.

8

Sunday, Bowie, along with a still disgusted and unforgiving Burley Hammond, took the train into Junction City, two impressively dressed professional men. Both wanted to be at work early Monday morning and the single daily train leaving at noon would get them there at three, wasting most of a day. Burley was angry that Asa Forbes hadn't showed up in Primrose before they left, but could do nothing about it except curse. At Junction City, Burley's carriage was waiting and Bowie asked that he be dropped off at his office.

In his deserted office, Bowie got down to work immediately. His scheme, of course, would elect Asa Forbes easily if it worked and it would, but he must go through the pretense of carrying out the plan he'd outlined to Burley. He found Governor Halsey's speaking schedule which had already been published, then settled down to write letters. First he wrote to four ministers, asking them to schedule revival meetings on the nights before Governor Halsey would speak in their towns. He enclosed a check to each. He wrote a dozen letters to party chairmen, asking them to try and arrange for a hostile crowd at Halsey's speeches. Lastly, he made a note to visit Forbes' campaign headquarters in the Prairie Hotel first thing in the morning to arrange for the volunteer workers to have handbills printed for the revival meetings. Since he lived in a corner suite of living room and bedroom at the Prairie House, he could get this done first thing in the morning. After supper tonight he would work on the text of the handbills which must not name Governor Halsey but which must point to him.

Next day Bowie saw his campaign people and gave them the text of the handbill, then spent the rest of the day seeing clients, except for one hour in the afternoon. He spent this hour in the depot, waiting for the train to arrive from Primrose. When it arrived he was watching through one of the station windows that looked out on the platform. When all the passengers had descended from the coach, Bowie felt a panic mixed with rage. Albie, Henry, and Varney were not on the train. And then, as he was cursing them silently, they descended the steps under the glowering gaze of a conductor. All three were drunk, Varney the drunkest. He stumbled on the last step and would have sprawled on his face if Albie hadn't caught him. They both went down, but got up immediately, brushed themselves off and headed down the platform where the station hacks were ranked. Bowie saw them climb into one and drive off, and afterward he strolled back to the office. So far, so good.

That evening he had supper with a client and excused himself afterward, pleading press of work. Returning to his office he lighted the lamps and actually did work at his desk. A person watching him would have thought he had nothing on his mind as he sat behind his desk reading, making notes on a tablet and marking citations with slips of paper as bookmarks. He glanced occasionally at his watch and when it was eleven o'clock he rose, put on his overcoat and hat and left his office after blowing out the lamps.

The streets were almost deserted at this hour as Bowie headed across the town. He passed the Prairie Hotel and went on down-street heading for the Grandview Hotel. It was a big frame building of three stories, the capital's second best. As in most capital cities, the politicians and legislators had marked a hotel for their own. It was seldom the best hotel where both the prices and the formality were forbidding; it was usually, as with the Grandview, second-rate, a little seedy, comfortable, and informal. Its big lobby was the equivalent of a caucus room, smelling of cuspidors and old leather.

Bowie passed the lobby doors and turned left at the corner. He followed a rotting boardwalk to the alley and then turned into it. There was a covered stairway entrance here which served as a fire escape and as an entrance to the building for people who did not want to be seen and identified by the clerk. These included politicians on secret deals and girls on equally secret deals. Long ago the tolerant management had let it be known that the doors opening onto the stairs would never be locked.

Bowie climbed the first flight of stairs using the handrails. A glass door at the landing held a dim light from a corridor lamp. He halted, getting his breath, then continued up the stairs to the second floor where again the landing was dimly lighted. Here he opened the door and went down the ill-lighted corridor.

When he came to room 43, he knocked sharply on the door and waited. He was about to knock again when he heard a stirring behind the door and his hand dropped. The door opened and Abe Brandell stood there in his shirtsleeves.

"Evening, Counselor," Bowie said dryly. "I figured you'd be up."

"Can't sleep much any more," the old man said thickly. He was pleasantly drunk; beyond him Bowie could see the bottle of whiskey standing beside the glass water pitcher.

"Come in, Bowie."

"No, I'll wait here. Get your coat on, Abe. We're having a meeting."

"Who?"

"You, Burley, Asa, and me. Better wear an overcoat. It's chilly."

"What do you want with me, Bowie? I've given you everything I can."

"No. This regards a long ago court appearance of yours. With Halsey." He paused. "There's money in it Abe, so hurry, will you?"

Frowning, Abe turned and headed for the coat over the straight chair. Bowie stepped in, so he would not be visible to anyone using the corridor.

When Abe had his coat on, he went over to the curtained-off closet and took out a black overcoat so old it was green in spots. Shrugging into it he picked up his hat from the dresser and motioned for Bowie to lead off.

"Take a drink, Abe," Bowie said contemptuously. "If you don't, I'll just have to wait down the hall while you come back here for something you pretend you forgot."

"All right," Abe said mildly. He went over to the bottle, poured some whiskey into the glass, drank it, poured water into the glass and drank that. Bowie watched him and then stepped out into the hall. It was empty, he saw.

Abe came out and closed the door behind him, then turned toward the interior stairs.

"Not that way, Abe. We can't be seen together and we shouldn't be seen here even separately. We'll split up on the street. Let's take the fire escape."

"It's so damn dark."

"Hold on to my arm, then."

Bowie turned and walked toward the fire-escape door. He opened it, stepped out and waited on the landing, watching Abe's shuffling progress. When Abe stepped out onto the landing, Bowie carefully closed the door.

"Let me get on your other side," Bowie

said, and he stepped behind Abe. Then he halted, braced his foot against the back wall for purchase and drove both hands into the middle of the old man's back.

Brandell had not even touched the handrail yet and he went sailing out into space. Bowie's shove was so violent that the old man's head hit the slanting roof over the stairs with a crash before he dropped heavily on his side and went cartwheeling down the stairs, his body thumping and turning and crashing.

He cleared the second landing, never touching it and Bowie, racing down behind him, saw the body slowly lose momentum, skid, turn over and over down the steps and finally come to rest close to the entrance.

Bowie raced down the stairs, a match already in his hand. When he came to Abe's grotesquely sprawled body, head foremost and on his belly, Bowie wiped the match alight. Abe's Roman nose was flattened and bleeding, and the only reason Bowie could see his face was because Abe's head was turned far around as if in death he had performed the impossible task of looking at his own back. Bowie blew out the match, reached the street and turned into the alley.

Once through it he headed for his hotel. If he had any feeling at all it was not one of regret or remorse. He had simply beat John

Barleycorn to Abe Brandell by a few months. Abe's death in a bed of cirrhotic liver would have been meaningless, but his death on the Grandview backstairs was anything but that.

9

Tuesday, Cole arrived in Primrose just after midday in a cold and driving rain which, in their last camp this morning, had been snow. He was cold and his mood was grim as he stepped down from his saddle in the center drive of the feed stable. He turned his chestnut over to the hostler with instructions to rub him down and grain him, and then he stood in the big doorway out of the rain and regarded the street which was fast becoming a mire. Roundup, he knew, would be miserable, what with the men and their mounts wet and muddy night and day and the cattle sullen, their brands difficult to read. If this held on it meant shipping wet cattle, which would double the normal losses.

Now to find Varney. He stepped out into the rain which had wet him in spite of his buttoned slicker collar and headed downstreet on the slippery boardwalk. At the corner he crossed the muddy street to the Primrose House and tramped through the lobby into the bar. There were two card games going on and Cole waved to the players at both tables. The very fact that nobody asked him why he wasn't at roundup told the story that Varney was on the loose. Nobody was at the bar as he bellied up to it. Alec took down Cole's brand of whiskey and a glass from the back bar and came over and put both before him.

"Haven't seen him since day before yesterday, Cole," Alec said in answer to the unasked question.

Cole nodded and poured his drink and tossed it down. Then he asked, "What kind of shape's he in?"

Alec looked uncomfortable, but he held his glance steady. "Well, I had to ask him to leave, Cole."

Cole nodded understandingly. "Think he's home?"

"I know he isn't, because the sheriff saw him at noon. Try River Street."

"Yes, that would be it," Cole said tiredly. "Thanks, Alec." He paid up and went out the street door, but instead of turning toward River Street he retraced his steps to the feed stable and livery. He asked for a top buggy with rain apron and a livery horse and waited in the doorway while the buggy was hitched.

Afterward he drove down Grant Street, crossed the now muddy Raft and turned up River Street. He stopped at the first saloon, a squalid box that held only the bartender who had a newspaper spread out on the bar before him.

"Seen Varney Wynn?" Cole asked.

"No, he drinks at Dave Hardy's place."

Cole thanked him and went out and drove the block to the Miners Rest where he put the buggy into the tie rail.

Entering the saloon whose overhead lamps were lighted against the gloom of the day, Cole saw Varney immediately. There was only a scattering of customers at the bar but they all seemed clustered together, listening to Varney talk.

Cole tramped down the bar toward Varney who had stepped away from the others so he would have room to tell a story that required gestures. Cole halted at the edge of the bar and regarded Varney, who did not see him. Indeed, Varney was seeing very little. The sight of him brought a feeling of sick shame to Cole. Varney had not shaved in days and his beard-stubble seemed to deepen the hollows of his ravaged face. He was dirty too and sometime during these last few days had exchanged his usual Stetson for a black miner's felt hat. He was weaving on his feet and his talk was incomprehensible. The men around him were laughing, not at his story but at his drunken inability to tell it. There was a scabbed-over cut on his right cheekbone and his eyes were barely open. When he ceased his gesturing, Cole saw that his hands were shaking almost uncontrollably. He was, Cole saw, steeped in alcohol, sick with it, all his senses succumbing to it, yet his heart was fighting to carry its impossible burden.

Cole walked up to him and put a hand on his arm. "Come on, Varney. Let's go home."

Varney turned in the direction of his voice and fought to get his eyes in focus. When he did, an expression came into his face that struck Cole like a blow in the stomach; Varney's face tautened into naked and blazing hatred.

"Come to get your basherd bruvver?" Varney shouted. "Go 'way! Go home! Go to hell!"

"Come on, Varney. The fun's over."

"Whyncha leave him be?" a voice asked.

Cole half-turned to see a tall, rawboned young man, his face ugly with drunken anger. But what Cole saw above the pimply face decided him. The man was wearing Varney's Stetson and had to be one of the men Bert said had come to Mill Iron to see Varney. Cole hit him hard, hurting his fist against the shelving jawbone, and the man went down.

Instantly, bewilderingly, the room exploded. Someone jumped on his back just as another man hit him in the face, touching enough of his nose to flood his eyes with water. The man on his back had an arm across his throat, effectively choking him. Desperately Cole turned so his back was to the bar and backpedaled two strong steps until he crashed the man on his back against the bar. The man's grip broke and Cole's head came down to meet another fist.

Close to a dozen men were fighting, not only him but each other. There seemed to be no sides taken, or if there were he didn't know who was on his side. There was no room to really fight; he wrestled a man out of his way, hearing wild curses around him and it was only when a pool cue was brought down on his forearm, almost breaking it, that he was aware the bartender had joined the fight.

Putting his head down and covering his face with his good arm, he bulled his way toward Varney, receiving a kick in the leg and a blow on his back before he broke from the melee. Varney had found a chair from the gambling tables and he was staggering toward the fight, the chair held high over his head. Cole moved into him from the side, hitting him, and Varney simply melted to the floor.

Cole swept up his hat from the floor where

it had fallen when he was jumped. The fight was moving down the room, over and around the body of the man whom he had hit first.

Quickly now, Cole heaved Varney to his feet, then ducked swiftly as Varney fell forward. Cole's shoulder moved into the jack-knifing body and then Cole straightened up. Varney was over his left shoulder, and Cole wrapped both arms around him and headed for the door. The battle, which the bartender was inevitably winning, was raging on as he stepped out into the rain.

At the buggy he dumped the unconscious Varney on the buggy seat, sat him upright, jammed his hat tight on his head, and spread the splash curtain over his lap. Across the bridge, Cole took the first street on his left and headed out of town. The town had seen enough of Varney the last few days without adding a final parade down Grant Street, he thought grimly.

On the drive to the Mill Iron, Varney roused. He looked around, glanced bleakly at Cole, then shut his eyes. Cole said nothing to him since there was nothing to say. Varney was still drunk and sick and talk would be useless.

At Mill Iron, Bert helped unload Varney from the buggy. Varney between them, an arm over each of their shoulders and his boots leaving twin furrows in the mud, Cole and Bert went into the house and Cole's bedroom. Bert left to put up the horses and Cole undressed Varney. He was barely conscious, just able to move his body as Cole stripped him and rolled him into bed. He was snoring by the time Cole had rounded up an extra blanket.

Cole built a fire in the big kitchen stove, grunting from the aches and pains of the brawl. Just as he lit the fire Bert came into the kitchen, after knocking.

"Anything I can do, Cole?"

"Yes. Rustle up some grub from the cookshack and bring it here." Cole smiled wearily. "You're probably tired of talking to yourself, so eat with me."

When Bert was gone Cole slacked into one of the chairs surrounding the big kitchen table and folded his arms on the table. This, he reflected, was a day he wasn't apt to forget. It had a lunatic quality about it, from Varney's appalling drunkenness to the senseless brawl that everybody seemed to welcome.

Now, for the first time, he had a chance to assess Varney's drunk. The look Varney had given him when he had first recognized him in the saloon still wounded him. It was a look that said Cole was his mortal enemy, not the look of a man who wanted help or could accept it. There was no reason to think that when Varney sobered up he would feel any differently. He would hide it but it would always be there. He resolved then not to tell Hal about Varney's drunk or about Varney's feelings toward him. Hal would learn of the drunk himself and Varney inevitably would express to his father his true feelings for Cole. For a brief moment Cole felt a pity for his father and was immediately ashamed of this. There must be some way he and Hal could work this out with Varney. The story of Varney's spree would get around, of course, and Cole knew that Forbes' gang would make the most of it. Hal would accept that but Cole knew Varney's action would hurt and bewilder him.

Then Bert came in with grub from the cookshack, saying, "This ain't ever going to let up, Cole. If them corrals weren't anchored to posts, they'd of floated away."

"Nice roundup weather," Cole said dryly.

They fixed a supper of sorts and ate it at the kitchen table with the lamp lighted against the early dark. Bert was careful to avoid talk of Varney, but eventually Cole forced him to. Cole asked for the description of the two men who had come here the day after he left for the roundup. As Bert described them, Cole knew the man he had first hit in the brawl, the man who was wearing Varney's hat, was one of them. The second he was almost sure was the small man who had jumped on his back, trying to choke him. Cole didn't even bother to ask Bert why they had come. Bert didn't know and neither did he, but when things were normal once more he would learn just why two saloon riffraff had triggered Varney's drunk.

They cleaned up the kitchen and Bert, after saying good night, went back to the bunk house in the still-driving rain. Cole went into the office and sat down at the desk. Four days' mail had accumulated and going through it he saw there was no word from his father. Hal, of course, would know Cole was on roundup and out of reach of mail. Cole leaned back in his chair, now his long face sober in speculation. Could he go back to roundup, leaving Varney alone again? Could he trust him not to do the same thing again? Then too after roundup Cole would have to ride with the shippers to Kansas City. Altogether he'd be gone over a week, leaving Varney to his mischief. Then it occurred to him that he didn't have to leave Varney. He would take Varney with him.

That decision made, Cole read the sparse mail and glanced at the back copies of the *Capital Times*. Red Macandy was doing his best to keep the story of Hal's bastard son alive. His columns were full of letters from readers excoriating the governor. As for the straight news of Hal, there was none. He had been on a speaking tour in the northern part of the state these last few days and Macandy, of course, would not bother to report the speeches.

Cole had set aside the next to the last copy of the *Times* and was reaching for the last one when he heard the sound of a horse passing by in the night. Rising, he left the office, stuck his head in Varney's room, saw he was sleeping, closed the door and went through the lamplit living room toward the front door, picking up the lamp on his way. When he opened the door he saw a slight and slickered figure approaching the steps to the porch. When it came into the circle of light cast by the lamp, Cole was startled as he recognized Tish Hammond. She came up the steps, her outsized slicker dripping and her Stetson channeling water from its brim.

"What in the hell are you doing out tonight, Tish?" Cole asked roughly.

"Being sworn at it sounds like," Tish said as she crossed the porch. She halted then, then turned and called, "Go down to the bunk house and get warm, Abel."

Cole stepped aside and Tish entered the room where she opened her slicker, took off her hat and swung it to shake the rain from it.

"I don't know why I bothered with a buggy. We got just as wet as if we'd ridden." Cole, still holding the door open, looked out into the night. He saw that Bert had come up to identify the caller and now Cole called, "Put 'em under cover, Bert." Then Cole closed the door and moved over to the table where he put down the lamp. By that time Tish had shrugged out of her wet slicker and dropped it on the floor. This was the first time in more than a year that Cole had seen her in the range clothes her father had made her give up. Somehow they made her much different from the ladylike Tish who wore the town dresses a rich man's daughter was expected to wear. Cole noted without much curiosity that a flat oilcloth-wrapped package jutted from the hip pocket of her levis. He could not guess why Tish had come to Mill Iron at all, let alone on such a night as this, but he knew she would tell him in reasonably good time.

"Let's get some coffee down," he said, starting for the kitchen.

Tish followed him into the big kitchen and watched him stir up the fire and pull the big coffeepot to the front of the iron range.

"How's Varney?" Tish asked.

Cole turned and regarded her curiously. "All right. Did you come out here to ask that?"

"Partly," Tish said. "Mostly this though." Moving over to the table she pulled out the oilcloth-wrapped package and put it on the table.

Cole came over to the table and was about to reach for the package, when Tish put her hand on it.

"Not yet, Cole. Where did you find Varney?"

"The Miners Rest on River Street, so drunk he couldn't stand up. I brought him home, and put him to bed."

"Did he talk? Did he say anything?"

"Like what?"

"Maybe you'd better look inside now," Tish said. Lifting her hand from the package, she unwrapped it. Then Cole saw it contained a folded newspaper. She extended it to him and said, "It's on page one."

Cole unfolded the newspaper and saw it was this morning's edition of the *Capital Times*. The center of the front page was a box outlined in black to attract attention. He read the text. It was headlined FOUL PLAY? and the text read:

As we go to press, word has reached us that Attorney Abe Brandell was found dead this morning at the foot of the outside covered fire escape of the Grandview Hotel. He

130

was dead of a broken neck. The Sheriff's office believes he either fell or was pushed to his death.

That was all.

Cole's glance lifted from the paper to Tish. "I can't say I'm sorry about Abe, but what's it supposed to mean to me?"

Tish pulled a chair out from the oilcloth-covered table and sat down. "Cole, Varney was in Junction City when that happened."

Cole scowled. "How do you know that?"

"Louise Selby came back from Junction City on today's train. I saw her in the Primrose House late this afternoon. She told me that Varney and two other disgusting drunk men were in her car." She paused. "Don't you see —"

"I see that Varney was in Junction City when Brandell died, that's all."

Tish nodded. "Did he do it? Could he do it, Cole?"

Cole slacked into a chair, folding his arms on the table. He was looking at her but he did not answer immediately. Then he said, "I know what you're thinking, Tish, and thanks for thinking of me. We know that Abe Brandell gave Mrs. Wynn's deposition to Red Macandy to print, but does everybody else know that?"

"The deposition made a bastard out of Varney, didn't it?" Tish asked quietly.

Cole nodded and was silent, his forehead creased in a scowl.

"Don't you see, Cole. Who'd have a reason to kill that old man except Varney? Varney got drunk because he couldn't face being called a bastard in public, didn't he?"

"You must know so, Tish. Bert tells me you talked with him the morning I left for roundup."

"He was bitter, Cole, and oh, so sorry for himself."

"Did he mention Abe?"

"No, but he must hate him. He knew about Abe surely."

"He knew," Cole said grimly. "Hal told him everything just as he told me."

"Did he kill him, Cole?" Tish asked again. "Is he like that?"

"No," Cole said. "He's weak and he can be vicious but he's also a coward."

"Even a coward can push an old man down a flight of stairs. That doesn't take bravery."

Cole said quietly, "Do you want him to be guilty of it, Tish?"

Tish answered furiously, but in an equally quiet tone, "I'll never forgive you for asking that, Cole."

"I asked it for one reason, Tish. If Varney

didn't kill Brandell, then somebody wanted to make it seem as if Varney did; and who would stand to gain if Varney really was guilty? Have you thought it out that far?"

"No, I hadn't, but I know the answer. My father would be one of the gainers, wouldn't he?"

Cole only nodded.

"Then I do forgive you for asking the question," Tish said. She stared at Cole but Cole could tell by the faraway look in her eyes she was not thinking of him but of something else. "No, Cole," she said finally. "I won't accept that. I can't. My father would never be a party to that, never."

The crackling of the fire in the stove reminded Cole of the coffee heating; he rose, moved over to the stove, took two heavy mugs out of the warming oven and poured their coffee. When he set Tish's cup down in front of her, she looked up and he could see tears in her eyes. Now Cole sat down and, staring at the coffee in front of him, he said, "Maybe Abe Brandell did fall."

"Won't you wake Varney, Cole?" Tish asked impatiently. "Can't you ask him?" She added suddenly, "Ask him now."

Cole rose and said, "Maybe with some coffee Varney will talk."

Tish rose. "Can I come, Cole?"

"Close enough to hear him but stay out of the room. He won't talk with you around if he'll talk at all."

Cole led the way through the living room and headed down the corridor, a feeling of dread within him. If he had really been the man he imagined himself to be, he would have made Varney go on roundup. He should have fought him if he refused to go instead of giving in to Varney's feelings. Now the situation was intolerable, both for him and for Tish.

Cole entered the room, leaving the door open while Tish waited in the hall. He put the cup of coffee on the chest of drawers, then moved over to the bed and began to shake Varney's shoulder. He was rough and abrupt, hoping he could startle Varney out of his drunken sleep. Varney's slack body gave with every push. Now Cole stopped and applied the wet cloth to Varney's face and still there was no reaction from Varney. He breathed slowly and deeply and Cole knew that at last the days of drinking, the lack of food and probably lack of sleep had finally caught up with him.

"Varney, wake up," he said loudly, then put two fingers in his mouth and whistled shrilly. Still Varney slept. Cole pinched his arm savagely, but if Varney felt the pain, his gaunt face did not show it. It was almost as if nature had taken over to heal him and would let nothing interfere with her process. It was just as well that he couldn't wake Varney, Cole thought. The odds were that Varney would remember little or nothing of what he had done and where he had been these last few days. Even if he could have remembered, he was not likely to tell Cole; Hal maybe, but somehow Cole even doubted that.

Cole pulled up the blankets to cover Varney, then picked up the coffee and left the room, closing the door behind him. Without a word Tish led the way back into the kitchen. Tish sat down while Cole took both their cups of coffee back to the stove and refilled the cups. Again he gave Tish her coffee and sat down.

"I don't think he'll even remember much when he wakes up. I'll have to wait till morning."

Tish nodded somberly and sipped at her coffee. Cole was thinking that even if Varney could remember the events of the past few days, he would probably lie about them. It had been plain ever since the morning he had walked into the office with Mrs. Schofield's copy of the *Capital Times* and confronted them with it that he considered his father and his half brother as enemies. Everything he had done and said since then, especially to their father, confirmed this. There was not a trace of blood loyalty in him, only hatred for the man who had conceived him and for the half brother he believed was favored. Cole knew what he must do if Varney couldn't remember or would lie about what he did remember. He would have to hunt down Varney's two companions and some way learn from them what went on in Junction City, checking their stories against whatever story Varney might tell. Then he must take what he had found to Hal as quickly as possible.

Tish's voice interrupted his thoughts. "Cole, can I stay here tonight?"

Cole tilted his head in the direction of the bunk house. "Who did you call Abel? Is he your new bodyguard?"

"Yes. He's our gardener in town."

"If you stay, your father will hear about it from him, then what?"

"I'll handle him, so don't worry."

"Will you handle Bowie too?" Cole's tone of voice was dry but it held no malice.

Color came into Tish's face but she held his glance. "Bowie too."

"Why do you want to stay the night, Tish? To talk with Varney tomomow?"

Tish nodded. "I think he'll tell me more than he will you, Cole. You're not so blind you don't know he hates you, are you?"

"I know that better than you, Tish."

"He hasn't any reason to hate me. Maybe he'll talk to me where he won't talk to you."

Cole pushed his chair back, walked around Tish's and went into the living room. He returned with Tish's slicker and hat and held them out to her.

"Please, Cole."

Cole shook his head in negation. "It's my trouble, Tish, not yours. Now put these on and go home. I'm grateful you came but go home now."

Tish rose and accepted the raincoat and hat.

Cole walked to the kitchen's outside door, opened it and whistled shrilly into the steady rain. Both of them heard Bert's distant voice call, "Coming."

Cole turned and saw that Tish had shrugged into her slicker. She was watching him with sober worry in her face. "Will you tell me what you learn from him?" Tish asked.

Cole nodded. "Can you be at the depot before the train leaves tomorrow?"

"Are you going to see Hal?"

"I've got to," Cole said grimly.

"With Varney?"

"No, tomorrow morning I'm going to hunt

up those other two that were drinking with Varney. If you can be at the depot I'll tell you what I've found out from Varney and from them."

"I'll be there," Tish said. Then she added softly, "Poor Hal. Poor you."

"No. Poor Varney," Cole said.

They heard the buggy approach and now Tish tucked her auburn hair up atop her head and put on her hat. Cole opened the kitchen door and as Tish stepped out into the rain Cole bade her a subdued good night.

Tish halted and looked back at him.

"It won't be, but let's observe the conventions. Good night, Cole."

10

Red Macandy, never a patient man, was seated at his desk in the office of the *Capital Times* this morning. Earlier he had written up the Brandell story that even now was being set up by his printer behind the railing that separated his single desk office from the printing shop. The desk was a square one with two knee slots, one for his side and one for Billy Foster's side. Billy, half reporter, half advertising solicitor, was out now and Red was awaiting him impatiently. He had already, while waiting, smoked and chewed down two cigars and wanted a third, but his stomach was sourly protesting.

The Brandell story hadn't been much but he had made the most of it. Sheriff Morehead, a stanch Halsey man, had refused to speculate on whether Brandell had fallen or been pushed down the Grandview stairs. Red had made it seem in his story that the sheriff's office might still be in doubt as to the circumstances leading to Brandell's death, but he did not dare to put quotes in Morehead's mouth. The sheriff, no man to trifle with at best, hated him, Red knew, but then almost everybody did. There was a story here and a big one, Red felt, but the pieces weren't all in place. There was a better than even chance that the old drunk, Abe Brandell, had really tripped on the dark stairway and fallen. But could he have rolled down almost two whole flights if he had only tripped? Chances were he had hold of the handrail as any sane man would have held it. Even drunk, Abe wouldn't walk down those stairs without using the rail. And why was he using those stairs anyway, when he could have used the interior stairs? True, the covered stairs were closer to his room, but why would he risk them at night? He had chosen them over the interior stairs. It must have been because he didn't want to be seen. Was someone with him? Maybe a woman? Red doubted that, for the old boy, a womanizer in his time, had of late years lost interest in the opposite sex mainly because his chief love was booze. Had a man been with him? And if so, who? Here, back again full circle, maybe nobody was with him.

In his story Red had been afraid to print these speculations, even under the guise of rumor. He had also been leery of giving any political color to the story. Since he had printed the interview with Halsey it was pretty common knowledge that it was Abe Brandell who had attempted to blackmail Halsey and had provided Forbes' crowd with Mrs. Wynn's deposition. Would Halsey have pushed the old drunk down those stairs in revenge for Abe's having disclosed Hal had a bastard son? Even to Red, the thought was preposterous, although he would have loved to have it turn out to be so. Would Forbes, angry at the sympathy Halsey had won all over the state by confirming the fact that he had a bastard son, push the old man? That was equally preposterous.

The big, many-paned front window of the *Times* office was painted white halfway up to insure some degree of privacy in the office and Red long since had learned to identify passers-by by their hats. Now he saw Billy Foster's rakish brown felt travel across the window before he heard the door open.

Billy was a tall young man who was as much of a fop in his dress as his meager salary would allow. He was, Red thought, aggressively buoyant and optimistic — traits that were desirable in a seller of advertising space but were deplorable in a man writing news stories. Billy sailed his hat toward the coat rack, missed and didn't bother to pick it up. He had curly blond hair that the girls liked and that he liked too. Long ago Red had assessed him as a vain ass but useful.

Now Red rose. "Took your damn time. What's the talk on the streets today about Brandell?"

"Just that anybody who drank as much as he did had to fall down sometime. He just chose the wrong place."

"Ah," Red said in disgust. He moved over to the coat rack, shrugged into his rumpled suit jacket and covered his near bald head with a disreputable-looking black felt hat. As Red headed for the door, Billy said, "Remember that brawl down at Kelly's Saloon that I wrote up yesterday?"

"What about it?" Red asked indifferently.

"One of the Primrose drunks was Varney Wynn. That ought to call for a follow-up, hadn't it?"

Red halted, his hand almost on the doorknob, and looked at Billy. "Say that again," he said slowly, letting his hand drop.

"I asked if it ought to call for a follow-up."

"No, what you said before. Did you say Varney Wynn?"

Billy nodded.

Red looked at him with a fathomless contempt. He turned and came back to the desk and said with loathing, "If I were to call you a god-damned idiot, it would be gross flattery."

"What did I say wrong?" Billy protested.

"What you just said will elect Forbes governor, you stupid fool." Now Red leaned both hands on the desk and spoke to Billy with a quiet vehemence. "You go back to Kelly's, you get his story of everything Varney Wynn did. Who did Varney talk to? How long was he there? What was he talking about? What started the fight? Where did he eat? Did he sleep? Was he ever alone? Don't bother to come back until you can account for every minute of Varney Wynn's time. If Kelly can't tell you, find out who can." He straightened up. "Now get out of here, jackass."

A chastened Billy Foster fled the office and now Red, hat still on his head, began to circle the desk slowly. What he had was almost too good to be true and he wondered how best to use it. His first move should be to see Sheriff Morehead and make a deal with him. By the time Morehead got his two deputies working, Billy would have a head start.

Red halted now and double-checked something on a slip of paper on his desk top. Yes, Governor Halsey had spoken at West Haven last night and he was due back in Junction City this afternoon. They had had a hell of a storm down south yesterday but a telegram this morning had said Halsey, in spite of the rain, had drawn a good crowd. Well, that was the last partisan crowd he would draw, Red thought jubilantly. He would draw crowds from now on, sure enough, but they would be the same sort of curious crowd who in the Middle Ages used to throng the castle court-yards to watch a beheading.

Now to business, Red thought. He felt so good that he recklessly lit another cigar and then stepped out into the street. Turning left he reached Main Street, then took the board-walk left again to the County Courthouse which was a frame box of a building converted from one of the early warehouses. It was a clear day and cold and Red could see in the distance the capitol atop the river bluff. Before the interior of its third floor was finished and long before its dome was in place, there would be a new governor in that first-floor corner suite, he thought with satisfaction. The retainer that he himself received monthly from Bowie Sanson would undoubtedly be increased after tomorrow's story broke.

He wove his way through the morning boardwalk traffic, nodding occasionally to acquaintances. Usually he would have been halted by one or two people who wanted more detailed information on some story the *Times* had printed the day before, but this morning he was not stopped. At the courthouse Red turned in through the double doors closed against the October chill. He was in a long corridor that ran the length of the building. Signs of the various county offices projected out above the doors on either side proclaiming the identity of the official within. The sheriff's office was in the rear-left corner and consisted of two rooms. The first held two desks, one for each deputy, and a number of chairs lining its tan colored walls from which the paint was already flaking. The door between the two desks let into the sheriff's smaller office at the end of which was a railed stairway leading down into the basement jail.

The deputies' room was empty of both petitioners and deputies when Red entered. He saw the door into the sheriff's office was open and he moved up to it and knocked firmly on the frame. A big man dressed in working range clothes was seated at a large roll-top desk, writing. At Red's knock and his greeting, "Morning, Sheriff," the man straightened and turned his gray thatched head. Sheriff Sam Morehead had a lean, deceptively sleepy-looking face, bisected by full black mustaches that if they were worn by any other man but Morehead, Red would have known were dyed. Beneath these was a straight mouth and a jutting chin with such a deep cleft it might have been made with an ax. Still looking at Red, the sheriff laid down his pencil; he could not quite keep from his pale blue eyes his dislike of Red Macandy which was shared by almost everybody.

"Morning, Red," he said civilly enough and watched Red close the door to the other room. Cigar pasted in the corner of his mouth, Red crossed the room and without being invited took the chair against the wall next to the sheriff's desk. His slack body of seemingly boneless fat suggested the only exercise he ever took was striking a series of matches to light his damp cigar.

Now he took the cigar from his mouth and said, "You still think Brandell tripped and fell down those stairs, Sheriff?"

"I haven't heard anything that would change my mind," the sheriff said coldly.

"Well, you're about to," Red said matter-of-factly. "Before you do though, I want to make a deal with you."

Instantly Sheriff Morehead said, "No. I won't make a deal with you, Red. What I'll do if I think you're withholding facts I should have, is throw you in jail."

"I didn't mean a deal in that sense," Red said. "I won't withhold any facts from you if you won't withhold any from me. People will talk to you and your deputies because you've got a badge. I haven't."

The sheriff thought a moment and then said, "I don't think I will, Red. I don't trust you."

Red smiled sourly and replaced the wet cigar between his yellow teeth. "I kind of think you will, Sheriff. If you don't cooperate with me, if you withhold any facts from me, the *Times* will blow you out of the sheriff's office. I guarantee it."

Sheriff Morehead smiled thinly. "If I ever had a mind to help you, I haven't now. You see, I don't scare."

Red already knew he didn't and decided on another tack.

"All right, Sheriff, I'll let you be the judge. If the information I give you is useful, will you give me full access to the further information you develop?"

"I think I'm required by law to do that, Red," the sheriff said. "Yes, of course, I will."

Red moved his cigar to the opposite corner of his mouth and watching the sheriff closely, he said, "All right. Varney Wynn was in town here on a drinking spree Monday night — the night Abe Brandell was killed."

For a long moment the sheriff said nothing. Then he asked quietly, "Can you prove that, Red?"

"Prove it?" Red said roughly. "Hell, I'm not on trial. What have you got two deputies for if you can't get proof?"

A flush of anger came into the sheriff's face but he said mildly, "I guess they could find out if Varney Wynn was in town drinking, but what's that supposed to mean to me?"

Red took the cigar from his mouth and pointed it, butt first, at the sheriff. "Because he's a murder suspect, that's what." Red snorted and then he said with savage sarcasm, "You've got a murder on your hands, Sheriff, and you call it an accident. I've named you the murder suspect and you ask why you should be interested in him. Good God, you *do* hate your job, don't you?"

"But you like yours, which is printing any

slime about Governor Halsey that comes into your mind."

"If you change that to read any slime about Governor Halsey that comes into public view, I'll plead guilty," Red countered. "Did I make up that Wynn deposition?"

"No, but you printed it."

"And am I making this up that Varney Wynn was in town the night Brandell died? No, but I'll print that too."

Red stood up. He saw that the sheriff was troubled and that his dislike for him, Red, was coloring his judgment. He knew the sheriff couldn't be cowed by anything he said, but he thought he could be chastened.

"All right, Sheriff, I'll tell you exactly what the *Times* will print tomorrow. It will say that in spite of the strange circumstances surrounding Brandell's death, the sheriff still maintains it was an accident. I'll list those circumstances. What was Brandell doing going down a back stairway at night? If he fell, how come he fell as far as he did? Why did he fall when there was a handrail he could grab?"

"You said that before," the sheriff said coldly.

"Ah, but never in print, Sheriff. But there'll be more in tomorrow's story. All facts. I'll say that the presence of Varney Wynn in Junction City on the night of Brandell's death has been confirmed. Right there I'll repeat

148

that Varney Wynn is Halsey's bastard son. I'll link this fact with the rumor — rumor, mind you — that Abe Brandell was the blackmailer the governor referred to in his interview. The best comes last, Sheriff. You know what it'll be?"

Morehead nodded. "Yes. That the whereabouts of Varney Wynn on the night of Brandell's death is being investigated by the sheriff's office."

Red smiled. "Aha! That saves me writing an editorial, Sheriff."

The sheriff stood up now. "All right, you've got what you want, Red. I'll let you know what this office finds out."

"That's better." Red was almost crowing.

The sheriff said with barely controlled anger, "The day I leave office, Red, I've got a date with you."

"Can I print that, Sheriff?"

"No, don't print it. Just remember it."

"You've paid me a tribute, Sheriff. Your threat must mean that I'm doing my job. Thank you."

He left without saying good-bye and once on the street he turned into the traffic on the boardwalk, the closest thing to a smile he could muster on his face. Inwardly he was crowing. These last minutes almost but not quite made up for the insults and the open contempt he had taken without protest from Sheriff Morehead. In tomorrow's story he would be charitable regarding the sheriff's delay in conceding that Brandell's death might be murder. He would be fair, so fair in fact that any reader, even the most stupid, would think that Sheriff Morehead had been trying to cover up Varney Wynn's murder of Brandell. He would, of course, identify Sheriff Morehead as an avowed and loyal supporter of Governor Halsey. It would make, Red thought, a classic newspaper story. Small-time, but flawless.

Bowie Sanson's office was on the second floor of one of the brick buildings on Main Street. Now Red headed for it. Climbing the stairs he wondered if Bowie might not have already heard of Varney Wynn's visit to the capital. In Bowie's reception room he asked the young man behind the desk who was reading law under Bowie if Bowie was in and was told to go inside.

Bowie was coatless and Red noted that the buttons on his vest were straining against his massive chest. Bowie closed the volume he was reading after marking his place. "You look fired up, Red. Sit down. What is it?"

Red took a seat and recounted the day's events, including the details of his victory over Sheriff Morehead.

When Red was finished, Bowie was smiling with pleasure. "That's perfect, Red. That story will jar the whole state." He shook his head and said softly, "Varney Wynn in town that night. It seems incredible." He looked carefully at Red now. "You think Varney did it? You think Varney pushed Brandell, Red?"

Red snorted. "Hell, I don't know, but what difference does it make if he did or didn't? Even if Morehead can't find anything on him the suspicion is still there on Varney. It's on Morehead and his damn coroner's jury too. If Varney did it and he's arrested and stands trial, we win anyway. Forbes can't lose, the way it stands right now."

"You're sure of your facts, Red?"

Red laughed. "The sheriff is going to make sure for me. He can't lie and say Wynn wasn't in town because I'll have witnesses to prove he was. If he tells the truth that's even better because it's official."

Bowie leaned forward and folded his arms on the desk. He said soberly, "You know we've got to move carefully on this, Red, or it will turn around and bite us."

Red smiled crookedly. "I make up lies only when I have to, Bowie, and this time I don't have to. It can't be denied that now the sheriff has a suspicion of murder. It can't be denied that Varney Wynn had a reason for killing

Abe Brandell because Abe made him a bastard. And it can't be denied that Varney was seen in town the night of the murder."

"Just leave it there, Red," Bowie said. "No editorials and no speculations. No sympathy to Halsey for his wayward son. None of that stuff. Just write it straight."

"I know, I know," Red said. Then he cleared his throat. "Do you think this is worth more money for me, Bowie?"

Bowie nodded. "Let's raise that two hundred a month to three hundred, Red." Then he laughed and said, "For lord's sake, buy yourself another suit of clothes with the raise."

Red rose. "No. If I cleaned up people might stop hating me."

"No. They hate you for yourself, not your clothes, Red," Bowie said dryly.

11

That same morning Red Macandy had his confrontation with Sheriff Morehead the day was crisp and clear, but at Primrose to the south the weather was gray and still drizzling. The heart of the storm had moved east across the plains but when Cole awakened that morning before dawn he knew the tail end of it was still with them.

He dressed by lamplight in the room across from his own room where Varney was sleeping. He looked in on Varney, saw he was still sleeping, went into the kitchen, built a fire and put on coffee. He ground enough coffee beans to half fill the big granite pot and while he waited for the coffee to boil he thought of what lay immediately ahead. Varney, with more than twelve hours' sleep behind him, should be able to answer questions once he had a couple of cups of scalding coffee down him. How would he answer them? With contrition or defiance? Cole couldn't guess. He must remember that he couldn't bait or goad Varney and there must be no censure in his questions. Looking out the window while he waited, he saw a lamp in the bunk house in the light of the first hint of dawn. It was a gray day for gray trouble, he thought.

When the coffee was done he poured it out, almost syrup-thick, into two cups and tramped back to Varney's room. The night lamp was still burning and he put down the coffee, turned up the lamp, moved over to the bed and shook Varney. Varney came awake slowly and groaningly hoisted himself to his elbow. He did not look at Cole who went over to the dresser, took both cups of coffee and returned.

Cole extended a cup saying, "Watch it. It's hot."

With a shaking hand, Varney accepted the coffee, then sat up in bed. It was an illusion, Cole knew, but the sinewy muscles of Varney's arms and shoulders seemed to have grown closer to the bone, as if this last week of dissipation had burned up some of the flesh under his skin.

Cole returned to the chest of drawers and leaned against it, coffee cup in hand. Varney drank cautiously at first and then when he found he could handle the heat, he gulped the coffee down. Wordlessly, Cole brought the second cup over, took the empty and went back to the kitchen for more. When he returned with a fresh cup, the second cup was empty. He put the fresh cup in Varney's hands and asked, "Think you can eat?"

"Let's see if I can keep this down first," Varney mumbled. While Cole had been in the kitchen Varney had pushed the pillow up against the headboard and was leaning against it. He looked weak and drained and still half sick, Cole thought, and now Cole sought a way to begin this. Finally, for lack of anything else to say, he said, "I got worried about you when Bert told me you'd gone."

Now Varney looked full at him and with his free hand he brushed back the pale hair off his forehead. He said tonelessly, "All right. Start the sermon."

"There's not going to be any sermon," Cole said easily. "I just want to know a couple of things before you go off to sleep again."

"What things?" Varney asked suspiciously.

"How much do you remember?"

Varney frowned and shook his head. "Not much, big half brother," he said with a quiet defiance. "What am I supposed to remember? Did I burn down a church?"

"I don't know what you did," Cole said patiently. "That's why I'm asking."

"Well, I got stinking drunk and stayed stinking drunk."

"That you did," Cole conceded. "And I don't care why. Try and remember, Varney. Where were you? What did you do?"

"Why do you want to know?" Varney asked curiously.

"If you broke anything, I want to pay for it. I just want to pick up the pieces, that's all."

"I'll pick up my own pieces," Varney said sullenly. He looked at the cup to drink again and his shaking hand clicked it against his teeth. He saw that Cole noted it and waited for a jibe that didn't come.

"You hit the River Street saloons, didn't you, Varney?"

"Three or four."

"Where did you pick up the cut on your cheek?"

Varney started to raise his hand and let it drop. "In a fight," he said resentfully.

"I know that, but where?"

Varney's tone changed to real anger now. "Hell, how do I know? I was in a couple or three fights."

"But where?" Cole asked patiently. "Here? West Haven? Primrose House? Haley's Crossing? Where?"

Varney was watching him closely. "Why do you say West Haven?"

"You were seen getting off the train yesterday. Where had you been? Junction City? To see Hal?"

"Did he telegraph you?" Varney asked.

"No. No," Cole said. "Nobody's telegraphed me. I've been at roundup. I just want to know where you've been while I was gone."

Varney was quiet for several moments, his gaunt face sobering by the second; then he shook his head. "I don't know, Cole. Damn it, I was drunk. I've got pictures in my mind of places, saloons, and people, but they aren't connected. I don't know."

"Think about the train trip, Varney. Remember any of that?"

Varney frowned in thought. "I remember a mad conductor, but that's all." Again he shook his head.

"Did you get any sleep?"

"What day is it?" When Cole told him, he shook his head in wonderment. "I must have."

"But you don't remember where?" Cole prodded.

"Look," Varney said angrily. "I told you, I can't remember! I remember Alec throwing me out of the Primrose bar. That was early. I remember drinking in the Miners Rest. After that, I don't remember. Just people and saloons. Singing, falling, fighting, laughing a lot, people calling us bastards because we told 'em we were."

Watching, Cole felt a quiet despair. It was worse than he had feared. There was nothing to do now but take a chance. "Varney, you used to go to Junction City once in a while. When you did, what did you do there? Where did you go?"

"Why, I always dropped in to say hello to the governor, then I had a couple of drinks at the Grandview or the Prairie. Why?"

"Do you remember drinking in either of those places this time?"

"No," Varney hesitated. "Was I really in

Junction City?"

Cole stood up now. "Yes, you were," he said quietly. "Louise Selby came home on the same car with you three."

"Did I see Dad?"

Cole sighed. "You couldn't have, Varney, or he wouldn't have let you on the train."

Varney finished his coffee now, then lowered the cup to the blanket. He seemed relieved at what Cole had said.

Cole moved again to the chest of drawers and leaned against them. "Varney," he began, "who were those two men you were drinking with?"

"Leave them alone," Varney said swiftly. "They're all right."

"I won't do anything to them. I only want to talk to them to see what they can remember. Who are they?"

Varney looked at him with sharp suspicion but he was silent. Finally, he said, "Well, you'll find out anyway. Albie Wright and Henry Bohannon."

"Why did you pick up with them?" Cole asked curiously.

Varney smiled for the first time this morning. It was an unpleasant smile. "Why, they're both bastards too, Cole. They got to thinking about Macandy's story and felt sorry for me. They'd been through it and they came

158

out to tell me what it was like."

Cole nodded. "Were they with you all the time?"

"All the time I can remember."

"Junction City too?" Cole asked hopefully.

"I tell you I don't remember Junction City! Why? Did something happen there while I was there?"

Cole hesitated a moment. There was no reason why Varney shouldn't know it, and the fact that he did might jar his memory. He watched Varney closely for any reaction to what he was about to say. "Yes, something happened there. Abe Brandell is dead. They suspect murder."

"They're saying I shot him? It's a damn lie," Varney said.

Either Varney was a superb actor or he was telling all the truth he remembered, Cole thought, and he believed that Varney, sick and shaking as he was, could not have reacted quickly enough to the news to dissimulate.

"Abe fell or was pushed down the back stairs of the Grandview on Monday night, Varney. Are you too sick this morning to see what's coming?"

Varney stared at him. There was no anger in his look now, only a beginning fear. He nodded and was silent for a moment. Then he said, "Funny, but I was never mad at him.

He tattled all right, but he tattled the truth."

Cole didn't know just why he believed him, but he did. Reviewing the people Varney admitted to resenting, Abe Brandell's name had never been mentioned. Now Cole pushed away from the dresser. "Can you eat anything?"

"No," Varney said. "I want to sleep."

"All right," Cole said. "I'm heading for town and then Junction City." He waited for Varney's questions or comments but none came. He said, "I'll ask Bert to look in on you around noon. Try and eat, will you?"

Varney nodded slowly, then he said abruptly, "Don't say it, Cole."

"All right, I won't," Cole said. Just what Varney didn't want him to say, Cole didn't know. He had been about to tell Varney to stick close to Mill Iron. Whether Varney thought he would say that or he thought Cole was about to lecture him, Cole didn't know.

Cole got breakfast, looked in on Varney, saw that he was sleeping, then put on his Stetson and sheepskin and tramped down to the corral in the light rain. He and Bert hitched up the livery horse to the buggy and after Cole had given Bert instructions to look in on Varney, he drove off. There was, he thought, a dismal prospect ahead of him. Two riffraff miners stood between Varney and all the hell that would break loose when Varney's visit to Junction City was uncovered.

Before he reached Primrose the drizzle stopped and the gray overcast lifted but did not break. Approaching the town, he saw the new snow reached far down the Rafts. The autumn colors of the aspens and oaks were wiped out by this single storm, a plain warning of coming winter. The day had a touch of foreboding that matched Cole's mood.

In town at the feed stable be traded the livery buggy for his chestnut and headed for River Street. The business section of the town was just coming awake. Clerks were sweeping off the dirt-tracked boardwalks in front of their places of work and the good smell of wood smoke from newly awakened fires was mingled with the rank smell of mud.

Cole headed in the direction of the bridge and turned down River Street whose only traffic was miners with their dinner buckets heading for the shift change at the mines and mills against the mountain. The saloons were emptying now for the beginning of the day shift.

At the Miners Rest Cole reined in at the tie rail. The doors of the saloon were open and the bartender was rolling out beer barrels through the big doors to be stacked in the break of the tie rail where the brewery wagon would presently pick them up. The bar-

161

tender, Cole saw, was the same one who had tried to break up the fight. He was wearing a heavy sweater with raveled sleeves and Cole noted as he stepped out of the saddle that the man was unmarked. The fight, he reckoned, had been just another brawl in a succession of them which the man had learned to handle without harm to himself.

Cole ducked under the tie rail and waited until the bartender hoisted his last barrel atop an earlier one and turned back toward the saloon.

"Rain's over, looks like," Cole observed pleasantly.

"About time," the bartender said and halted. He looked closely at Cole. "Don't I know you?"

"You do, from yesterday. My arm still aches where you laid a pool cue across it."

The bartender smiled but without humor. "The place to fight is in the street, mister. Maybe you'll learn, but the rest of them don't."

"I've learned," Cole said. Then he added, "I'm new in this end of town. You know where Henry Bohannon lives?"

The bartender's small eyes narrowed. "You mad at Henry?"

"Not any," Cole said mildly and waited.

The bartender tilted his head in the direction of the saloon "One street over. Rooming house painted tan. Can't miss it. Cut through the saloon if you want."

"You don't care if my horse tracks mud on the floor?"

The bartender looked puzzled, then glanced at the tie rail and saw Cole's chestnut. He laughed and looked at Cole who was smiling faintly. "Well, he ain't as dirty as some I serve beer, but maybe you better not."

Cole thanked him and rode around the block. He found the rooming house by its scabby coat of peeling paint. Of the slatternly woman who opened the door he inquired after Bohannon and was told to look in the big room upstairs. Cole ascended the stout-railed stairway and found himself in a big corridor with rooms on either side. At the end of the corridor was one big room, a dormitory jammed with canvas cots, row on row. The stink of sweat, unwashed bodies and clothes was appalling and Cole opened his mouth to breathe through it instead of his nose. Blankets were tumbled helter-skelter on most of the cots which were just as the waking miners had left them. Their extra clothes hung from nails at the head of each cot. Of the forty-odd cots, only two held sleepers. Cole went down the narrow aisle and halted by the first sleeper. He had never seen this man. Passing on he came to the corner cot where a shriveled little man, wearing filthy long underwear under his covering blankets, lay watching him. This, Cole was pretty certain, was the man.

"You Henry Bohannon?" Cole asked pleasantly. The old man barely nodded. "Not feeling so good, huh?"

Bohannon tried to speak and was choked by the phlegm in his throat, cleared it and said, "Not so good. Likely Varney feels better than I do, him so much younger."

Cole sank down on the neighboring cot across from Bohannon and regarded the older man with a covert curiosity. Bohannon looked sick and frail and Cole marveled that he had survived the days of drinking just past.

Cole decided to pretend he had talked at length with Varney about their spree. "I'm trying to patch up a few things for Varney in Junction City. How much hell did you raise there, Bohannon? Varney can't remember much."

"One fight," the old man said hoarsely. "We only busted glasses and a couple of chairs that we paid for."

"Varney with you all the time?"

"That I don't rightly remember. He seemed to be around somewhere. He always showed up."

"Did any of you get any sleep while you were there?"

Bohannon looked at him with a sick indifference. "We took a room above the saloon." He frowned and thought. "Yeah, I slept, I guess. Albie did too."

"What about Varney?"

"He slept first."

Cole frowned. "What do you mean first?"

"Well, first in the room." The old man was silent, groping for words that even in sound health he would find difficult to muster. Finally he spoke. "Well, Albie and me slept a little on the train and Varney never. When we got down on the river front Albie got us this room. We'd had some sleep but Varney hadn't and he started to cave in. We took him to the room and come back."

Cole knew it was useless to ask him if he could remember the time. Instead he asked, "Was it dark yet when you took him?"

Bohannon nodded promptly. "So dark we fell on the stairs."

"Then what?"

"We left Varney and come back to the saloon. Kelly's it was. I remember it now. Albie and me met a bunch of fellas and started drinking with them. One of them was mean and Albie and me got in a fight with him. That kind of tuckered us out so we went up to the room."

"Was Varney still there?"

"Yup. We moved him crosswise so the three of us could sleep on the big bed."

"Then what?"

Bohannon frowned. "I ain't sure. I woke up hungry and remembered the lunch at Kelly's bar. I woke up Albie and we went down and ate."

"Why didn't you wake Varney?"

"He wasn't there," Bohannon said.

Cole felt a sudden wrench in the pit of his stomach. "You mean he got up and went out while you were sleeping?"

"I reckon."

"How long were you asleep?"

"I dunno."

"Was Varney in the saloon when you went down to eat?"

"He come back after we eat. We wuz drinking again when he come."

"Where did he go?"

"I dunno," Bohannon said. "He said he went for a walk so he could sober up and drink some more is all I know."

There it was, Cole thought. Varney had been alone for nobody knew how long — an hour, two hours, but long enough to hunt down Brandell. In theory, was Varney sober enough to kill him? Would he even know where Brandell lived? The answer to that last question was that he did know, because everyone else knew. Abe Brandell had been a fixture at the Grandview for a dozen years, moving to a higher floor and a smaller room as his fortunes waned. At first he had been an honored guest, lately only a drunken old man. More often than not he had to be helped to his floor by the porter or desk clerk, sometimes both. Varney would also have known where to find him, even known his room number. The permanent political guests at the Grandview had their names under their permanent key boxes. This saved the desk clerks answering a hundred questions a day. If the key was gone, the politician was in. If the key was there, the man was out.

Cole had the information he had come for and he rose and looked down at Henry. "Where'd you get the money for this bender?"

He thought Bohannon hesitated at answering that question and then the old man said, "Varney had the money. He treated us two bastards on account of he's one. Besides, your dad's rich, ain't he?"

Cole didn't answer. He reached in his pocket, pulled out a couple of silver dollars, tossed them on the blanket and said, "Get yourself a drink and some food."

He left the stinking dormitory as fast as he could and once outside stood beside his horse and breathed deeply trying to flush his lungs. Afterward, he stepped in the saddle and headed for the bridge. There was no need for him to talk to Albie. He had found what he had feared he would find. Sometime during that fateful night that Brandell was killed, Varney had been alone. The hour or hours of his absence were unknown.

He crossed the tracks and the bridge and rode down muddy Grant Street in the busy morning wagon traffic. He put in at the Primrose tie rail and walked through the lobby to the barber shop. Stripping out of his sheepskin, he asked for a haircut and a shave that would rid him of the week's beard stubble. Lying under the steaming towel, his eyes closed; he was for a few minutes utterly alone with himself. Varney was in real trouble, he reflected. It was only a matter of time before the law enforcement agencies in Junction City would learn of Varney's visit there. Even if Sheriff Morehead was a friend of Hal's he would have to check on Varney's visit. Inevitably, he would learn that Varney, a prime suspect now, could give no alibi for the hour or hours he was alone. Cole didn't know what to expect after that. He did know that he himself could not return to roundup or go to

Kansas City with their cattle. This was a time the Halseys must draw together to protect one of their own. The cattle market was good this year and Mill Iron beef was prime, so Fred Enders could easily go with the shippers and handle their sale himself. Meanwhile, Cole knew that he and his father must discover some way to shield Varney, *always supposing he didn't do it,* Cole thought dismally.

Afterward, he ate at a cafe and walked to the depot. Tish was waiting for him on the depot platform when he arrived there. She was wearing a pony coat against the chill morning and its brown, almost formal design, was a small cheerfulness in the gray day. The bare half smile in her greeting and drawn look of her pale face told Cole that she and sleep had been strangers last night. Wordlessly, they moved away from the people who were waiting for the train, now making up in the distant yards. When they halted, Tish said soberly, "I know the news isn't good by the look on your face. What is it, Cole?"

"Varney didn't even know that he was in Junction City," Cole said grimly. "He remembers strange saloons and new faces, and that's about it."

"You talked to the other men?"

"One, and he was enough."

Briefly, Cole gave her the gist of his talk

with Bohannon in the dormitory and when he was finished, Tish was silent, watching his face which he knew was graveside sober.

"Then he had the time alone to do it," Tish said, quiet despair in her voice. "Now what do we do, Cole?"

"Just hope that Varney wasn't seen and identified."

"You think he was?"

Cole's dark and now clean-shaven face grimaced faintly. "My guess is he was."

"Drunken strangers are a common sight in Junction City, Cole. It's the state capital. Everybody visits it and they all seem to make a celebration of it."

"I know three ordinary drunks wouldn't attract attention but I have a hunch these three did," Cole said grimly.

"Why do you say that?" Tish asked.

"I'm guessing they had a chip on their shoulders, Tish. You see, the other two came out to Mill Iron to see Varney because of Red Macandy's piece in the *Times*. Both of them told Varney they heard about him being a bastard. They felt sorry for him because they were too. They wanted to sympathize with him. That's what started this drunk."

Cole ceased talking. Tish waited a moment before she said, "I don't see the connection. How would being bastards identify them in Junction City?"

Cole shook his head. "Varney remembered people calling them bastards, because they told them they were. I think the three of them were proud of being bastards; no, proud's the wrong word. Defiant. My guess is they never spoke without calling each other a bastard. I'll bet they explained it carefully to everybody who'd listen. Here were three genuine, legally certified, died-in-the-wool bastards." Cole smiled faintly. "That sort of humor would get a whole saloon laughing. All the customers would call them bastards. Can't you hear it? 'Come on, you bastards, I'll buy you a drink'."

"Cole, you're guessing," Tish protested.

"Yes, but I think it's a good guess. When Varney first saw me in the Miners Rest yesterday, he said in front of a dozen men, 'Come to get your bastard brother?' If he's said it there, he'd have said it in Junction City."

"But he wouldn't necessarily give his name."

"He'd make a point of giving his name," Cole contradicted. "He wouldn't settle for just being a bastard. He would want it known he was the governor's bastard."

"That's a wicked thing to say, Cole."

"Yes, but I know Varney."

"But why would he do it, Cole? Why?"

171

"To get even with Hal. To get even with the world."

"Damn, damn, damn," Tish said softly, vehemently.

Cole sighed deeply. "Well, I'll know by tonight if my guess is right. I'm going to cruise a few saloons on the river front in Junction City. My guess is they're still talking about those three drunken bastards who really were bastards."

"Do you think Red Macandy will hear the talk?"

"I'd be surprised if he didn't."

"What do you do now, Cole?" Tish asked.

Cole started to speak when the train whistle drowned out his words. They both looked down the track and saw the locomotive begin to pull up to its stop at the platform. "I don't know, Tish," he said wearily. "I'll have to see what's happening in Junction City before I can tell. But one thing I'm sure of." He paused, isolating what was to come. "If they connect Varney with Brandell's death, Varney's got to hide."

"But that'll make him look guilty, won't it?"

"Not as guilty as when he tells them that he can't remember a thing."

The locomotive eased past the platform now and halted its two passengers cars abreast of the platform. The passers-by started to drift toward the train and now Cole said, "Tish, will you help us some more?"

"You don't have to ask. What can I do?"

"If I find they're after Varney, I'll telegraph you. The message will have three words — 'Tell him yes.' If you get that telegram, tell Varney to head for our line shack in Officers' Gulch and do it fast. Tell him to wait for me there."

As he finished, the conductor called, "Aboard."

"I will, Cole, yes." Suddenly, without warning, she moved against Cole, put her arms around his neck and kissed him on the mouth. Then she stepped back and said calmly, "That's what you're supposed to do on a depot platform, Cole. Now good-bye."

12

Red Macandy did not bother to meet the train the governor was returning on. Instead, at train time, he went up to the capitol and took the last remaining chair in the governor's crowded waiting room. The governor's receptionist, Irma Thruelson, nodded coldly to him and made a note on her pad. Red had carefully left the reception-room door open. He knew the governor's trick of sneaking in his office door before calling for the rush of people waiting on him. This day Red wanted to be first, and the way to be first was to know when the governor passed by.

Irma waited perhaps a minute after Red had seated himself, then rose, came to the door and closed it. She did not look at Red either coming or going. Red waited until she was seated, then rose, reopened the door and took his seat again. He and Irma looked down the long room at each other and Red stared her down, ignoring the hatred he read in her glance.

It was only a few minutes before Red heard the sound of heels on the marble-floored corridor outside. When the governor, trailed by Joe Eames and the governor's tall son, passed by the door, Red rose and hurried out after them. The governor had his hand on the doorknob of his private door when Red, skirting Cole and Joe, caught up with him.

"I'm first, Governor. This is important."

"Well, let me get my coat off," Hal said easily. He swung the door open, stepped aside and bowed mockingly and with a gesture signaled Red in first. Red, unimpressed, strode into the big office while the governor, Cole, and Joe Eames followed in that order. Hal shrugged out of his coat and took off his hat which Joe moved up to accept.

"Wouldn't you know it, sir?" Joe said. "We had the office fumigated while you were gone and now we'll have to have it fumigated again." He looked at Red now. "You're costing the taxpayers money, Red."

The governor looked at Joe with mild reproof, tinged with resignation. Red, as if he were occupying the office himself, drew out one of the chairs from the corner conference table and carried it to a place before the governor's big desk behind which Hal already stood.

"Get my list of appointments, will you, please, Joe?" Hal asked courteously.

Joe Eames headed for the connecting door as Cole shrugged out of his worn sheepskin and tossed it and his hat on the table. Halting at the door, Joe said, "Pull up a chair next to Red, Cole. You can't hit him from there."

He stepped out, closing the door behind him. Suppressing a smile, Cole skirted Red's chair and took the leather armchair which faced the side of the desk and was even with his father's chair. From this vantage point, he could watch Red as he lighted up one of his twisted stogies. Cole suppressed his irritation as best he could, for he had had only a chance to shake hands with his father, who along with Joe and a handful of the party men boarded the train at West Haven. Hal had asked why he wasn't at roundup and Cole said he'd explain later. Cole had hoped to have this hour alone with Hal because the train, along with the party men, had allowed no privacy whatsoever.

The reception-room door opened and Joe stepped in, carrying a list. Before he laid it on the desk the governor said courteously, "All right, Red. Let's get going."

"What I've got to say is for your ears only, Governor."

"Then you may leave, Red," Hal said gently. "I wouldn't say good morning to you without a witness."

"You'll regret it," Red said brashly. "But that's your funeral."

"Exactly," Hal said.

Red drew out a folded sheet of paper from his coat pocket and said, "I would like your comment Governor, on the following item, one." He looked up from the notes at the governor, his pale eyes brimming with pleasure. "This morning the sheriff decided to reopen the investigation of Abe Brandell's death. He believes there is grounds for suspicion of murder. Would you like to comment?"

"No. Sam must have grounds for his suspicion. Why should I comment?"

"You'll see," Red said. "Item two. Your illegitimate son, Varney Wynn, was in Junction City Monday night, the night of Abe Brandell's death. He was very drunk and very belligerent. I think you'll have a comment on that."

God help us, Cole thought. *He's put them together.*

Hal looked at Cole now with surprise and hurt in his eyes.

Cole stood up. "Red, step out a minute, will you? Hal will call you first when he's through."

"Well, well," Red said. "Got you that time, didn't I, Governor? All right." He stood up. "I'll give you ten minutes."

Joe Eames said quickly, "You're giving him all the damn time he wants, mister. Will you walk out now or will I throw you out?"

"I'll walk out and if I'm not back in here by ten minutes, I'll just keep on walking. You can read what I think about it in tomorrow's *Times.*"

Joe opened the door, Red stepped out. Joe looked at the governor now and said, "Call me when you're ready, sir."

"No, you stay," the governor said. Now he looked up at Cole and sank back into his chair. "So that's why you aren't at roundup. You

177

could have warned me," Hal said quietly.

"I should have," Cole said miserably. "But the train wasn't the time or place to talk about it, Hal. I figured I would have an hour alone here with you and Joe."

Hal nodded understandingly. "Now tell me."

Joe quietly came over and took Red's chair while Cole told of Varney's spree with his two friends. When Cole said that Varney had no recollection of being in Junction City, Hal grimaced and shook his head. But when Cole told him Bohannon said that Varney was alone for an hour or hours the night of Brandell's death, Hal's face altered into a grimness Cole had never seen in it before.

When Cole was finished, Hal was silent, assessing this news; then he said, "He could have done it, but do you think he did it, Cole?"

"No, I don't," Cole replied. "It's a strange thing, but Varney's mad at the whole world except Abe Brandell. I don't know why it should be that way, but I think it is."

Joe Eames said with a quiet savagery, "Red will print it all, sir. There's no way we can stop him."

"He can't accuse Varney of Brandell's murder," Hal said quietly. "Still, he won't have to, for the simple fact that Varney was here when it happened is damning enough." He shook his head sadly, "That poor miserable boy. Does he know what's shaping up for him?"

"Not all of it," Cole replied. "He doesn't know that he was alone here for long enough to do the job. Tish will give him the news." He went on to tell of his arrangement with Tish to start Varney on his way into hiding.

Hal looked at him for a long moment. "No, I won't have that, Cole. I know you're trying to protect me and Varney, but I won't have it."

"You know what you'll be facing?" Cole asked grimly.

"A little. Tell me what you think I'll be facing."

"Sooner or later Sheriff Morehead is going to want to question Varney. He'll discover that Varney can't even remember being in Junction City."

"Does that make Varney a murderer?" Hal asked quietly.

"No, it only makes a filthy mess for Red Macandy to spoon up every day. You're the one that'll catch it in the face every day too, Hal."

"But if Varney hides out, that'll be worse," Hal said.

"Not worse, Hal. Nothing's worse than

having Varney brought here and questioned every day."

"Sam's a good man, Cole. He won't torment him any more than he has to."

"But he'll have to torment him," Cole said flatly. "Red Macandy will see to that. Red will make a Roman circus out of this, Hal. He'll try Varney every day in the *Times*. He'll dig up everything bad in Varney's past and make it worse."

"He'll still do that if Varney's in hiding, won't he?"

Joe Eames cut in saying, "I think I see what Cole's getting at, sir. Varney won't be arrested and held without good cause, but if Varney is reachable Macandy will be prodding Morehead into never letting him alone. If Varney's hidden, all Macandy can do is scream for his appearance."

"That's a pretty shabby way to treat Sam," Hal said.

"The other is a pretty shabby way to treat yourself and Varney, Hal," Cole countered.

Hal rose and began to pace the floor in front of his desk. He paused and then placed both hands on the back of the chair where Joe was sitting and said to Cole, "All right, what's the end of this, Cole? Varney stays in hiding the rest of his life?"

"He stays in hiding until we find out who

did kill Abe Brandell," Cole said quietly.

"How do we do that?"

"I wouldn't know right now," Cole said wearily. "Still, the only way we can prove that Varney didn't kill Brandell is to find the man who did."

Joe Eames said dryly, "That's a tall order to ask before the election, my friend."

"The election be damned!" Hal said explosively. "I've got a son who's under suspicion of murder. That's more important than my being elected."

"Anyway you look at it, sir, you're going to be crucified every single day from now on," Joe Eames said wryly.

Hal began to pace again. Both hands were jammed and fisted into his suit-coat pockets. Finally he glanced up abruptly at Cole. "I think you're wrong about this, Cole. If I follow your advice and Joe's, I'm saying in effect I will not produce my son until the killer has been found. That's sort of asking for special treatment, isn't it?"

Joe Eames said hotly, "All right, ask for it, sir! Surer than hell if Varney gives himself up, he'll get special treatment. Not the kind you were referring to, either. You think Red Macandy won't dig up a couple of witnesses who saw Varney on the third floor of the Grandview? You think another witness won't pinpoint the time of the fall because he heard the body crashing down the stairs? You think he won't drag out another witness who heard Varney threaten Brandell?"

"He'll do that anyway," Hal said.

"Ah, but the witnesses have to identify the suspect; they can't do it if he isn't here," Cole said.

"But hiding a suspect is not honorable," Hal insisted. "It's against the law."

"You won't be hiding him. You can tell Morehead the whole truth — that the last you knew Varney was at our line camp in Officers' Gulch. Morehead will send a man up there and Varney will be gone."

"You mean you'll hide Varney and not tell me where?"

"Exactly."

The governor shifted his glance to his secretary now. "You like this, Joe?"

"I hate all of it, but I hate this the least."

Hal said slowly and distinctly, "I am defying the laws I took an oath to uphold."

"But I didn't swear to uphold them, Hal. And you're upholding the laws you swore to when your office orders an honest search for Brandell's killer."

Again Hal looked at Joe. "Can you make this sound any better to Macandy?"

"Simple," Joe said. "Tell him that you've

182

asked the U.S. Marshal to bring in your son for questioning."

Hal grunted. "Go get Red."

Joe moved across the room to the reception-room door and opened it and went out. He came back immediately and closed the door behind him and, leaning against it, said, "Red's gone."

Save for the capitol building, the Governor's Mansion was the pride of the whole territory and the young state. It was a two-story brick building with a semicircular portico supporting four Doric columns whose only purpose was to support a balustrade. To the left of the entrance was the huge unused living room which could be turned into a ballroom. On the right was an equally huge and equally unused dining room. The broad staircase in the wide hall led to the second floor which held six bedrooms and a library. The latter was where the governor worked and took his meals and was next to his austere bedroom. Albert, who doubled as coachman and butler, and his wife Portia were his staff. When an official hostess was called for, the governor alternated this much-coveted chore among the wives of the elected officials of the party. Otherwise, he led a lonely and almost solitary life in the evenings, seldom answering invita-

tions so that he could catch up on his paper-
work that his daytime schedule did not per-
mit.

This night he and Cole, who had already
sent his telegram to Tish, finished dining and
were enjoying after-dinner cigars as Albert
left the room on his third and final trip to the
kitchen with the empty coffeepot and cups.
Hal, Cole noticed, had eaten sparingly as if
he had no heart for food. During supper they
had temporarily laid aside all talk of Varney
and discussed the Mill Iron affairs. They had
agreed that Fred Enders would go with the
cattle to Kansas City because Cole's presence
here was necessary.

Inevitably, now, the talk switched back to
Varney, Cole, and his troubles. "Cole, are you
convinced Abe was murdered?" Hal asked.

"We've only got Macandy's word that the
sheriff was reopening the investigation. I
don't think he'd say that if he didn't mean
to print it. And if he prints it, it'll have to be
true."

"I wish I didn't have to read tomorrow's
Times," Hal said glumly.

"Yes, there goes your election," Cole said
quietly. "Unless we come up with a murderer
first, that is."

"If Varney is out, who's left to suspect?"

Cole shook his head. "I don't know, Hal,

184

but I can't get one thing out of my mind. Why was Varney in Junction City the very night Brandell died? Why couldn't it have been any other night? If Varney was drunk for four days, why did he and his friends choose that night?"

"You think his friends chose it for him?" Hal asked.

"Isn't it possible?"

Hal thought a moment before saying, "Speak plainer, son."

"All right. What if it was arranged to have Varney here and very drunk on that night?"

"Who would arrange it?"

"Who wants you defeated?" Cole countered.

"No," Hal said. "Forbes, Burley Hammond, Bowie Sanson, Joe Brinkerhoff, and Seth Lawford are not murderers, Cole. Technically, I suppose they are because of the working conditions they allow in their mines, but intentional murderers, no."

"Maybe some well-meaning friend thought he'd be helping them."

"No, not even that, Cole. There's a lot at stake in this election. It will cost those boys a lot of money if I win, but I don't think they'll murder for money. They're dirty fighters but not killers."

"All right, you've known Brandell for over twenty years. Who'd want to kill him?"

"In his day he sent many a man to the pen. Also he kept many a man from hanging."

Hal was quiet for a moment. "That's a good thought. I'll have to ask Joe to have the warden check the prison records tomorrow to see if anybody's been turned loose who would've held a grudge against Abe — "

"All right. Then find out, if you can, why any of them would choose to kill Abe the night Varney Wynn was in town."

"You can't accept the coincidence?"

Cole stood up. "No. Matter of fact, I'm choking on it." He laid his dead cigar on the ashtray. "I'm going back to Primrose tomorrow, Hal."

"To hide Varney again?"

"That first."

"And what next?"

"Oh, I'll be busy," Cole said.

"I don't know what you're going to do," Hal said slowly. "But look a long time — a helluva long time — before you leap."

"I haven't got much time," Cole said. "I have to leap before Election Day, Hal."

"You don't have to," Hal said sharply.

"Then let's put it that I want to." Cole moved over to the sofa and picked up his coat and hat. "I think I'll get some air, Hal. What room do you want me in?"

"Take your choice. All the beds are made up."

Cole put on his coat and hat and regarded his father with affection. "I'd suggest you get a lot of sleep tonight, Hal. You've got a rough morning coming up."

Hal sighed. "I know, but the sun will set tomorrow night too, just like it did tonight."

They bid each other good night and Cole went down and let himself out the front door. He paused on the edge of the portico and regarded the night. Where once the Governor's Mansion had stood alone on the raw sage flats at the edge of Junction City, its block of grounds was now surrounded by homes of the growing community. Lighted windows were on all four sides of it. Cole took the gravel drive down to the street, heading for the center of town. He knew what he was going to do and where he was going, but there was one thing he wanted to check. His first stop was the covered back stairs of the Grandview. Standing at the bottom, he could see two faint islands of light made by the lamp shining through the landing doors. What did he expect these stairs to tell him, he wondered sourly. Did he think the killer would leave a signed confession on the steps that the sheriff had clumsily overlooked?

Now he headed toward the river front, the oldest and shabbiest part of Junction City, a hangover from the days of the fur trade when the beaver trappers had their choice of going up to the head waters of the Raft or to even higher head waters of the Coronation.

Kelley's Saloon on Water Street faced the wide river with its rotting landings, long since unused. It was a corner saloon and as he crossed the street to it he noted the dark side entrance to the stairway Bohannon had described. Entering the low-ceilinged room he saw there only a handful of drinkers at the bar. Three card games were in progress at the rickety tables. Judging by the appearance of the customers this was a workingman's saloon. Some of them looked like cowhands in from the outlying ranches, while others could have been railroad workers or teamsters.

He went up to the bar and asked for a beer from a young, hard-faced bartender. When the beer was brought him, Cole said, "You have three hell raisers in here a couple of nights ago?"

"The bastards, you mean?" the bartender asked. His hunch had been right then, Cole thought.

"Yeah, I had 'em. All the other saloons down the street did too, I hear."

"Remember the young one, shorter than the other young one?"

"The governor's son? I thought he was making that up because anybody can claim to be a great man's bastard so long as you don't make him prove it. But I guess he was."

"Were they always together?" Cole asked.

The bartender looked at him more closely now. "You trying to prove something?"

"I guess I am. What I want to know is, did you ever see him when he was alone?"

The bartender scowled. "They got in a fight but that was the three of them." A faint belligerence came into his tough face now. "Look, are you fellas hoping I'll change my story? What did this kid do?"

Cole ignored the last question. "What is 'you fellas' supposed to mean?"

"Why the sheriff's office, I reckon. Two of you have been in here twice and so has the young squirt from the newspaper."

"I'm not from Morehead's office and I'm not from the *Times*."

"Then what's it to you where the kid went and what he did?"

Why not tell him, Cole thought. Tomorrow's *Times* would explain to him why Varney's whereabouts that night were important. He said, "I'm Wynn's half brother."

The bartender nodded. "Your name's Wynn?"

"No, Halsey. Cole Halsey."

The bartender's expression of indifference suddenly fled his face. "The governor's boy?"

When Cole nodded the man said swiftly, "The hell." He thrust out his hand. "I'm Homer Kelly. I've voted for your old man since I could vote."

Cole shook hands with him and was surprised at the firmness of the grip. "How are you, Homer?" He straightened up then and finished up his beer, wanting to leave. He had met people like Homer before, people who wanted to brag that they were on a first-name basis with the son of a famous governor. He fished out a coin from his pocket and put it on the bar.

Homer, watching him, ignored it. "I reckon this changes things," Homer said. "Yes, I seen Wynn alone just one time. He come up to the bar to buy a drink he didn't need. He asked me what time it was." Now he gestured to the clock over the back bar. "He was in front of the clock and I told him to take a look. He said he was too drunk to see it, so I told him and he left."

"Told him what?"

"Quarter to eleven. Then, like I said, he left."

"See which way he went, Homer?"

"He turned left. I reckon I know why, but I didn't tell them deputies I ever seen him alone. Not that squirt newspaperman, either."

Cole looked at him curiously. "Why not?

"When I tell you what he asked me, you'll know." He paused and then said with only a trace of censure in his tone, "He asked me which sporting house had the best girls." Homer tilted his head sideways in a pointing gesture. "I told him there is six houses down the street and go look for yourself."

Cole winced inwardly. He should have guessed it, he supposed, since booze and women were associated ever since alcohol was first distilled. Red Macandy would love this, and the thought prompted Cole's question. "Why didn't you tell the deputies and the *Times'* man?"

Homer smiled faintly. "When they talked with me they told me he was the governor's son. I figured your dad had enough trouble without the whores thrown in."

Cole nodded. "He has. Thanks for that, Homer. You don't know which house he was headed for?"

Homer shook his head in negation and Cole asked, "Can you give me the names of the madams?"

"Some, but not all. I'll ask around though."

Cole calculated swiftly. He knew he must return to Primrose tomorrow and talk with Varney and see him safely hidden again. That was the first order of business and by far the most important. When that was done, he could return here to try and piece Varney's alibi together. If the *Times* discovered the sporting house episode — if that was where Varney went — then let them. In exposing it, Red Macandy would at the same time provide Varney with an alibi. Now Cole said, "Suppose I come back in a couple of days for the names of the madams, Homer?"

"I'll have 'em," Homer said with certainty. "Just remember when you hunt 'em up, you want to pick the right time. That's around five. The girls will be sober then and you won't be cuttin' in on their business time."

Cole nodded and now Homer leaned on the bar. "Can you tell me what Varney done that they're asking about him?"

Cole told him of Brandell's death and the reason for Varney's being a prime suspect. "It will be in tomorrow's *Times*, Homer."

"Have they arrested the kid?"

"No, and they won't." Now Cole held out his hand and Homer accepted it. "I wish there was something I could do for you, Homer. You may have saved Varney's hide."

Homer grinned. "You can do something. Bring your father in sometime so I can buy him a drink."

"He'd come in to thank you even if I didn't ask him, but I will."

On the street Cole felt the first real hope

since Tish had come out to Mill Iron with the news of Brandell's death. If some woman in one of the Water Street cribs could cover that blank time nobody could account for, then Varney was safe.

13

Cole boarded the early morning train to Primrose, in his hand a copy of the *Times* which he had bought from the newsboy on the station platform. He found a seat alone and as the train pulled out he opened up the paper. The biggest type in Macandy's print shop proclaimed, SHERIFF SUSPECTS MURDER! The subhead said, BRANDELL CASE REOPENED. GOVERNOR'S SON IN TOWN NIGHT OF DEATH.

It was a cunningly contrived story, Cole thought as he read. First, Macandy announced all the bare details of Sheriff Morehead's change of mind in regard to Brandell's death. Then Red, with Brandell safely dead and unable to sue for libel, told of the current rumor that Brandell was the source of the now famous Wynn deposition which revealed that Governor Halsey had an illegitimate son. The next point Red made was that Varney Wynn, this illegitimate son, was positively identified as being in Junction City the night of Brandell's death. Carefully, Red had refrained from saying that Varney was a suspect, but he managed to imply as much when he said the sheriff's office was checking out Varney's activities while he was in the capital city.

Continuing, Red wrote that the governor was stunned at the news of his illegitimate son's presence in the capital the night of Brandell's death. Governor Halsey, it said, was invited to comment, but had declined to do so. The reasons for his reluctance to comment were unknown.

Then Red went on to say and safely, that this new bombshell had plunged the Halsey camp into deep gloom. Speculation, he wrote, was rife that Governor Halsey in the face of this jarring news might withdraw from the gubernatorial race. Forbes' forces, Red said, were decent enough to refrain from any comment whatsoever.

Everything Red wrote was true, Cole saw, but he had contrived to get his message across with the impact of a mule's kick. Without ever stating it, he said, in effect, that law officers thought a drunken Varney had revenged himself on Abe Brandell for releasing the document which branded him a bastard.

Cole felt a cold rage as he let the paper fall into his lap. Red, of course, did not know of Hal's decision to put the law on Varney when he did not show up for questioning. But when that announcement was made, Macandy would make more political hay out of Hal's order. Cole knew that if the election were held tomorrow, his father would be voted out of office in the deepest and most scandalous disgrace. Even the newspapers friendly to him could not rebut Red's facts. The story, Cole knew, would jar the law into action. He hoped that the code he telegraphed Tish last evening had been acted on immediately, for undoubtedly Morehead was going to telegraph Anse Beckett, the sheriff of Primrose County, to bring in Varney.

Cole looked out the window across the dun prairie that stretched unbroken to the distant snow-covered Rafts. He remembered Tish's kissing him on the depot platform at Primrose. Was that prompted by the same feeling that made a woman kiss a hurt child in pity and comfort, or was it simply Tish's way of declaring a truce in their war of wariness toward each other? Cole knew Tish was genuinely concerned over the fortunes of the Halseys, father and sons. Then how could she be as close to Bowie Sanson who was masterminding the Halseys' hard luck? Finally, just how close was she to Bowie — engagement close or marriage close, or close but drifting away? There was a time when he could have asked her bluntly and got an equally blunt answer, but that time was past.

When the train pulled into Primrose in midmorning, Cole noted with mild curiosity that River Street was alive with men talking in small groups in front of the saloons and eating places. Was it some sort of holiday he had forgotten about?

Cole joined the others and filed off the car onto the station platform. He started to cut across it, heading back for the bridge, when a rangy, middle-aged man came up beside him and said, "You're Cole Halsey, ain't you?"

Cole halted and looked at the man who was wearing a corduroy coat against the chill of the morning. Cole said, "Yes. I know you, but from where?"

"I'm Abel Lynch, Burley's gardener in Junction City."

"Oh sure," Cole said.

"Miss Hammond asked me to get you and bring you back to the house."

"All right." Abel gestured to the buggy at the other end of the platform and now the two of them walked toward it.

"What's everybody doing on the streets?" Cole asked him.

"There was a bad explosion in number seven level of the Star. Four men killed and another five trapped behind the cave-in. They let the shift go except for the rescue men."

The Star was Burley Hammond's biggest and richest mine and it had a deadly reputation for what Hal was fond of calling "preventable accidents."

"When did it happen?"

"Just after the morning shift change. They think one of the shots hung. Anyway, the explosion brought a cave-in."

They stepped into the buggy and Abel lifted the reins. He looked sideways at Cole. "I'm goin' to take it fast down River Street. They recognized the buggy when I come and I caught a bottle on the knee."

"Does Burley know about the cave-in?"

"They telegraphed him right after it happened, I heard. If he comes back on the train tomorrow they better have a double ration of guards. These boys are in a hanging mood."

True to his word, Abel took it fast down crowded River Street. Apparently the miners had been waiting for him, for the buggy was pelted with rocks, pieces of brick, empty bottles and, inevitably, horse manure.

Across the bridge the town was quieter and they moved through the morning traffic toward the big house on the hill, first picking up Cole's horse at the livery stable.

At the gate of the Hammond place two guards armed with rifles and pistols waved them through. A year or so ago, Cole recalled, an accident at the Star Mill had brought a storm of protesting miners to Burley's front door and obviously the Star's management was taking no chances on another front-porch demonstration. Mounting the stone steps, Cole was barely across the porch before Tish opened the door. Her auburn hair, gathered loosely at the nape of her neck, reached far below her shoulders. Cole recalled other days when he would loosen her hair and run his hands through its silky softness. He wondered fleetingly if Tish remembered too and had arranged it on purpose.

"When you telegraphed me, I was sure you'd be back this morning, Cole. I went out to see Varney last night, so he's gone." She turned. "Go on into the library, I'll get us some coffee."

Cole tramped through the big living room that was filled with handsome and uncomfortable pieces that Tish's mother had brought back from Europe. In the library Cole shucked out of his sheepskin and threw it and his hat on one end of the big sofa. Remembering, then, he picked up the sheepskin and took out the folded copy of the *Times* which he was opening when Tish came in with a tray holding the coffeepot and two cups and saucers. Her gray dress with its high neck and long sleeves combined with her loose hair to give the illusion that she should be attending school instead of serving coffee.

"What's happened, Cole?" she asked, as she set the tray on the desk.

Cole came over and spread the paper out on the desk blotter. "Read this first," Cole said.

Tish sat down immediately, coffee forgotten. Cole moved over, poured a cup for Tish and put it beside the paper. He was pouring his own when a soft groan came from Tish.

"That son of a bitch," she said softly, and Cole smiled faintly. He hadn't heard her say that since those long gone days when she used to come to him for the definitions of the cusswords she had picked up from Burley's ranch hands.

Finished, Tish looked up. Anger made her green eyes almost glitter. "Why, he's done everything but try Varney already!" she said hotly.

Cole nodded. "It'll get worse too." He told Tish then of Red's confronting Hal with the news that Cole hadn't had the chance to tell him. Tomorrow or the day after, the *Times* would carry the news that Hal had requested a Federal Marshal to bring Varney in for interrogation, Cole said. He told Tish of Hal's reluctance to allow Varney to be hidden and of Hal's final surrender to Cole's and Joe Eames' persuasion.

"That's like your father," Tish said warmly. "Hiding Varney means fear, and Hal doesn't know the meaning of the word."

Tish glanced with a quiet loathing at the *Times* spread before her and touched it. "You know, Cole, this will defeat Hal."

"What if we found the man who really pushed Abe Brandell?"

"That would do it. But who do you look for?"

Cole had finished his coffee. Now he rose to put the cup back on the tray. Then he roamed his open hand under his belt in back and started to circle the room, talking. He told Tish of his conviction that Varney's presence in the capital the night of Abe Brandell's death was too big a coincidence and that he couldn't swallow it. Varney went to Junction City only three or four times a year, usually as an errand boy to inform Hal of some decision Cole had made or to ask Hal's advice. Left to his own choice of a way to spend his free time, Varney would go to West Haven to see a girl whose reputation left something to be desired. Why then had Varney chosen this one night out of the three hundred and sixty-five in the year to go to Junction City? Cole asked.

Tish didn't answer immediately. Then she said, "Cole, has it occurred to you that maybe Varney did do it? Maybe he took along those other two men so he could claim he wasn't alone. Maybe he was pretending to be terribly drunk. Maybe he really does remember even if he says he doesn't."

Cole halted and looked at her. "It's occurred to me," he said grimly. "But I don't believe it." He hesitated and then added, "I'm not proud to say this, but I don't think Varney has the guts to kill a man. Not even in anger."

"Then go back to the coincidence. Isn't every accident a coincidence? A cow walks across a railroad track just as a train passes. A duck puts down on a lake when there's a hunter there waiting for it. Varney Wynn was in Junction City when the Lord decided Abe Brandell had lived long enough."

"They're not the same things," Cole said shortly.

"Oh, I know they're not, Cole," Tish said, and he was surprised at the sudden sadness her voice held. "What you're thinking is that Varney was taken to Junction City so he would be handy to blame when somebody killed Brandell, isn't it?"

Cole nodded.

"You said it the other night, Cole. Who

stands to gain by putting the blame on Varney?" She shook her head. "I wish you'd never said it." She looked at him closely now. "If I had to choose between two men who would commit a murder, I would point to Varney Wynn. I would not point at my father. I can't help it, but that's the way I feel, Cole."

"I'm not pointing at your father, Tish. I'm pointing at a man without a name but a man who would murder to see Asa Forbes elected governor. Without, mind you, Forbes' knowledge or consent or the knowledge or consent of the men back of Forbes."

"Now we're friends again," Tish said and smiled.

Cole moved over to the sofa, picked up his sheepskin and shrugged into it.

"Stay a little longer, Cole," Tish pled.

"I can't, Tish. There's a good chance that Sheriff Morehead has telegraphed Anse Beckett to pick up Varney. I want to get to Varney right away and move him."

"Oh, let me go with you," Tish said.

Cole was surprised, but before he could answer, Tish came over to him. "Please, Cole." She halted before him.

"We'll have to take Abel and I don't think he should know where we're going or why," Cole said.

"I'll take care of Abel. Can I go?"

"Sure you can." As unexpectedly as the time on the depot platform, Tish reached up, pulled Cole's head down and kissed him.

When he had straightened up, he said dryly, "You know, I like that, but I wonder if Bowie would."

"What about Bowie?" Tish asked.

"That's what I don't know, and you've never told me."

"I can't see him stopping me from giving you an innocent kiss. I can't see him stopping you from giving me one, either."

"Mine wouldn't be innocent," Cole said dryly. "But you're right. He couldn't stop me."

"Wouldn't, I said," Tish said.

"And I said I couldn't."

They looked at each other and in each of their eyes was a challenge. Tish's glance fell away first.

"You go have the horses saddled, Cole. I'll change clothes in a hurry."

She started out of the room, then said over her shoulder, "Tell Lizzie to make up some sandwiches on your way out, will you please?"

Cole put the copy of the *Times* in his pocket, paused in the kitchen long enough to pass on Tish's instructions to the colored cook and then went out, heading for the stables. There he instructed the stable boy to saddle

Tish's horse and then saddled his own chestnut. By the time he had finished, Tish came out. She was wearing a divided shirt and a warm leather jacket. In her hand she was carrying a shell belt and holstered gun. "Abel said you've got to wear this, Cole."

Cole nodded, accepted the gun and as he strapped it on he asked, "Abel happy?"

"Perfectly. I convinced him I was a lot safer riding than I would be in a town full of angry miners."

Moments later he and Tish passed through the gate and took the first street south heading for the Mill Iron line shack in Officers' Gulch.

It was a flawless day, cold but with no wind, and both their horses were full of spirit and were liking the morning too. For some reason the foothill country seemed strangely deserted and empty to Cole and then he realized why. All the cattle and most of the horses normally grazing here were at roundup, the place he should be too.

Tish too seemed to be enjoying this ride over the bleak dun-colored hills. She said to Cole, "I wish Dad would trade our house for something out here, but he won't even think of it."

"Some people are meant to live in towns, Tish. Maybe he's one of them."

"Oh, he is," Tish said sadly. "I think he's

ashamed of the fact that he ever ran cattle."

"Abel said he might be coming tomorrow," Cole said.

Tish glanced at him. "I hope not. He won't like the welcome he's liable to get at the depot."

"He doesn't have to get a welcome."

"How can he avoid one?"

"Well, he owns the biggest chunk of Primrose & Midland stock. If I owned as much as he did, I'd tell the engineer to stop the train outside of town and let me off. I reckon the engineer would do it, too."

"Why, that's it, of course," Tish exclaimed. "I'll telegraph him tonight to do just that." She hesitated as if considering what she was about to say and then rushed into it. "Why do they hate him so, Cole? He's a good man. He's fair and honest too."

Cole glanced across at her. "I know what Hal would say. So do you, Tish."

"I know. Am I quoting right? 'A payroll is people, not just a sum of money owed them'."

"That's about it."

"But he does like people. He likes Hal and he likes you."

Without looking at her, Cole said, "Tish, you're defending him when I haven't even accused him."

Tish was silent for so long that Cole glanced

over at her. She was looking straight ahead, her face strangely troubled.

"Bowie thinks Dad is a great man," she said flatly.

"Yes, Bowie would."

Tish whipped her head around to look at him. "What do you mean by that?"

"Only what I said. Bowie admires money and power. Your dad has both."

"Hal's not exactly poor," Tish said tartly. "And, of course, a governor hasn't any power at all, has he?"

"Are we getting down to what's been eating you these past two years," Cole asked quietly.

"I can't answer that because I don't even know what you mean."

"Well, we're like a couple of school kids saying to each other, 'My old man can lick your old man.' Is it our fathers, Tish? You want to be loyal to Burley and I want to be loyal to Hal. I think they both need our loyalty now. What they don't need is us hacking at each other about whose philosophy of life is the right one."

Tish didn't answer immediately. When she did there was anger in her voice that brought shock to Cole.

"Damn you, Cole, I don't see how you do it. You've not said a word against Dad but I know you dislike him. You haven't said a word against Bowie either but I know you detest him. You haven't said an unkind word to me but I know you despise the way I live and what I am."

Cole's voice carried anger too as he answered. "Correct in all details except you left something out. Remember, I am the man who told you I loved you and asked you to marry me. You said wait. All right, I'm waiting but that doesn't stop me watching and thinking."

A flush came into Tish's face that she couldn't hide. "Do you want me to say yes when in my heart I don't really know?"

"No," Cole said roughly. "I'm just fed up with sitting in the store window while you make up your mind which dolly you'll take home with you."

Afterward both of them were content with the silence between them. Cole felt as if an old wound had been scraped raw. Their quarrel had revealed nothing to Cole of Tish's feelings for Bowie and he was sorry he had pushed Tish as far as he had. He wished savagely that he had never seen her or loved her. Letting her come with him today had been a mistake; letting her kiss him had been another. Why could a man exercise judgment and control himself in all things except his relations with a woman he loved? He was scornful of this trait in others and scornful of it in himself, but he could never change, he knew.

When they turned up Officers' Gulch, there was soon snow underfoot and because it was rather a tight canyon floored with willows and elders nourished by the spring at its head, they dropped into single file, Cole in the lead. As they advanced the snow got deeper and when they came to one of the few sunny spots free of it, Tish said, "Why don't we eat here, Cole?"

They dismounted and Cole started to gather wood for the fire, but Tish told him not to bother. It was warm here in this protected spot and they would be ready to move before the fire had really caught.

It was an awkward lunch. Their high spirits of the earlier morning were gone and they were both relieved to mount their horses again. An hour later they came on the line shack nestled in the timber beside the not yet frozen stream from the spring above. There was smoke coming from the mud and straw chimney of the low, single-windowed log shack. Varney's horse was tethered alongside the cut wood in the unwalled lean-to.

Before they reached the shack Varney, who heard their horses, opened the plank door and stood in it, watching them. His face, clean shaven of a week's beard, was gaunt, Cole noticed, and held the same expression of sullen shame that was on it when Cole last saw him.

Reining in, Cole looked at him. "That family of porcupines still homesteading here, Varney?"

Varney smiled faintly. "Yeah, there was a little argument." He frowned. "Never expected you so quick." Then his glance shifted to Tish who had reined in alongside Cole. "You're taking pretty good care of me, Miss Hammond."

"The mother hen in me," Tish said.

"Well, come in and warm up."

They dismounted. Tish went in while Cole loosened the cinches on the two horses and tied them to the lean-to post.

When he went in, Tish was seated on the stump stool by the small, two-legged deal table nailed to a wall log. The coffeepot was on the stove and a pot and skillet hung on a nail behind it. Two sets of double-tiered bunks made up the rest of the furnishings of this dirt floored, single room.

Varney, who was wearing a heavy flannel shirt over his ordinary work shirt, went over to the crate nailed to the wall which held the supplies, took out a jar of ground coffee and added it to the contents of the pot. Putting the jar back, Varney said, "It won't take long to heat up." Now he looked directly at Cole. "Well, what did you find out in Junction City, Cole?"

For the second time that day, Cole pulled the folded copy of the *Times* from the sheepskin pocket and opened it. He gave it to Varney saying, "Read that first."

Varney went over to the lone window and silently scanned Red Macandy's story. As he read, his face tightened. Finished, he folded the paper and handed it back to Cole, saying, "Looks like his mind's made up."

Cole pocketed the paper, unbuttoned his sheepskin, and sat down on one of the lower bunks. "Well, that's the box you're in, Varney. Today or tomorrow when they tell Hal you're not at Mill Iron, the hunt for you will be on. Hal knows you're hiding here because I told him. He'll tell them too because he thinks he should." He paused. "You'll have to leave here today."

"For where?" Varney asked, and he seemed almost frightened.

"Well, there's the shack down at Goose Creek. Nobody will bother you there and it's where you won't get trapped by the next snow."

Varney said nothing. Now he assembled three of the four granite-ware cups and poured the coffee. Tish, Cole noticed, was watching Varney closely, perhaps wondering if she was observing the actions of a murderer.

When Varney had distributed the cups he sat down on the other lower bunk which held his blankets.

Cole took a sip of his coffee and then set it on the floor between his feet to cool. "Remembered anything about the Junction City trip, Varney?"

Varney shook his head. "No more than I did the first morning. I haven't really had time to try and remember. I've been sleeping, mostly."

"You remember how much money you had on you, Varney, when you left Mill Iron?"

Varney frowned. "Not a lot. Twenty, twenty-five dollars maybe. Why?"

"How much did you have when you got back?"

"A couple of dollars, I guess. What's all this anyway?"

"Who paid for that bat, Varney? Who bought the booze? Who bought the train tickets? Who paid for the room?"

Varney frowned and thought, then shook his head. "If I can't remember anything else, how could I remember that? I just don't know. I guess there was money enough between us." He added wryly, "From the way I'm still feeling that can't have been very expensive whiskey we drank."

"You don't remember going to a sporting house, Varney?"

Varney's glance leaped up at him and then to Tish. Tish looked at Cole now, surprise and protest in her face.

Cole noted both their looks and he said dryly, "We're in too much trouble to be delicate, Varney. Tish, if you don't want to hear this, just leave us alone for a minute."

"I can listen to anything," Tish said. "I'm just wondering why you asked Varney that."

"So am I," Varney said with resentment.

"Here's the way it is," Cole said flatly. "According to Bohannon, you left the room while he and Albie were sleeping. He didn't see you again until an hour after they woke up. He doesn't know how long you were gone while they slept. See what I'm getting at, Varney?"

Varney nodded. "I've some time to account for."

"You do," Cole said. "I talked with Homer Kelly. He's a great admirer of Hal's. When he found out I was Hal's son he told me about you."

"What did he say?"

"He said you came in alone and because you were too drunk to see the clock, you asked him to read it for you. It was quarter to eleven." Cole paused, not for the reason of what he was about to say, but to give Varney time to remember. Varney seemed to be waiting for more, so Cole said, "You asked him which sporting house had the best girls. He told you there were six houses on Water Street and to go look for yourself. You went out then. Remember any of it?"

Varney's face was flushed and he looked furtively at Tish, then back to Cole. "No, I don't. Kelly say I went to one?"

"He didn't know, but that's what we have to find out, Varney. Do I have to tell you why?"

"No," Varney said quickly. "She could account for that time I was away."

Tish said quietly, "You didn't tell me this, Cole."

"No," Cole agreed. "I don't even like to tell it once but it has to be told." Now he looked at Varney. "In all those days, Varney, do you recall a woman, any woman?"

Varney, elbows on knees, raised his hands and put his face in them. He was motionless that way for perhaps a half minute. "One," he said abruptly. "She was on the train. She talked to the conductor before he came over to us. He was mad. Just that one."

Cole sighed. The answer to the two big questions — where did the money for the drunk come from and was Varney in the sporting house — were still unanswered.

213

Cole lifted up his coffee which he didn't really want but which he nevertheless drank. He was aware that Tish was watching him and now he lifted his glance to her.

Tish asked, "Will Red Macandy find out about this and print it?"

Cole shrugged. "Homer Kelly figures both the sheriff and Macandy might check the sporting houses but they will check them for the three men who were together, not for a lone man. He'd love to print it but maybe for once we'll be lucky."

"But you're not going to leave it there, are you, Cole, when it could prove where Varney was?"

"No. I wanted to stay in Junction City to check with the sporting houses but I had to hide Varney first."

"You should have done that, Cole, before they forget. I could have hid Varney again."

"You really think I could have telegraphed you?"

"Why not?"

Cole sighed. "Tish, do I have to tell you that every interesting bit of information that goes over that telegraph wire is copied down for your father to read. I think my instructions to you might have proved interesting to him."

"You can't really believe that," Tish said angrily.

"I believe it so strongly that the telegram I *did* send you was a code, remember? If it had been clear and carried the message, your father's men would have beat you to Mill Iron and they would have Varney now."

"You simply can't prove this!" Tish declared vehemently.

Cole could but it didn't seem important now. He said, "I can. You see, it's just part of the power that Bowie admires — that I was talking about." He stood up, moved over to the water bucket, scooped some water into the cup, rinsed it and threw the rinse water on the dirt floor. "Time to light out, Varney. Just take your blankets. There's grub and cut wood at Goose Creek." Now he ventured to look at Tish. If he had expected to read anger and denial in her expression, he saw only the same sadness as when she had spoken earlier of her father.

The three of them rode down Officers' Gulch together; at the mouth of it they said good-bye to Varney whose course was straight east into the flats where Goose Creek, a tributary of the Raft, meandered through gently rolling country before joining the big river.

Before they parted, Cole said, "Varney, if they find you, don't open your mouth. But especially don't pull a gun on anyone. That's all Red Macandy needs to make it even worse for Hal."

On the ride home they were both silent. Tish was in a mood to match Cole's taciturn one. They were both regretting things that had been said today — things that had subtly altered their relationship. Neither one of them knew in just what way.

It was dark when they turned the horses into the corral at the Hammond place.

"Have supper with me and stay the night, Cole. There's no sense riding out to Mill Iron just for a bed."

"Thanks, Tish, but you've had enough of me today. Besides, I have things to do tonight."

"It's bound to be an ugly night, Cole. Please be careful." Then in an entirely different voice she said, "I think I'm lonelier than I've ever been in my life, Cole."

"That makes two of us, Tish. Good night."

14

When Cole Halsey had left his chestnut at the feed stable, he went into the Primrose House and stopped in the wide doorway of the dining room. He saw there were only a couple of people still eating at a far table. Louise Selby was setting the tables for breakfast and Cole guessed he had missed supper. He was turning to go when Louise Selby saw him and motioned him in.

Cole threw his coat and hat on one of the lobby chairs and came over to her. She was a nice-looking girl of his own age with a sturdy matronly figure which was testimony to the heavy excellence of the food served up by the kitchen she bossed. Her father owned the Primrose House, but it was really Louise who ran its every department.

"I'm not too late, Louise? I can go downstreet if I am."

"Sit down, Cole. I've sent the girls home, but we'll rustle up something."

Cole seated himself at a table whose red-checked tablecloth matched the others. Louise poured him a glassful of water and then asked quietly, "Seen today's *Times?*"

Cole looked up at her, noting the soberness in her face. Her chestnut hair was a little awry at the end of her work day, making her look a little like a harried mother.

"He didn't leave much out, did he?" Cole said.

"There goes the election," Louise said bitterly. "I could just cry. Matter of fact, I have."

"Don't give up on Hal. He's tough."

Louise nodded mutely but her expression

showed she hadn't much hope. "Ham and eggs suit you?"

When Cole said they did, she left for the kitchen. It was strange, he mused, how his father had the total and absolute loyalty of those who knew him. Asa Forbes was known and liked in Primrose, but the only votes he would get from this county in the coming election would be those of his family and close friends. The rest of the state was something else, Cole knew. They might sympathize with Hal, but the revelation of a bastard son who was clearly under suspicion of murder would be too much. These facts couldn't help but color the judgment of a people who wanted to be proud of the man they elected.

Cole ate his supper that, he suspected, was cooked by Louise herself, asked her to save him a room for the night, then sought the street and turned toward the river.

As soon as he crossed the bridge he felt the presence of tension. Men were still talking in small groups that seemingly were traveling aimlessly except that there was a clear pattern of progress between the many saloons. Against the mountain, dozens of flares were burning around the shafthouse of the Star, sending up flickering shadows into the night.

Cole headed first for Bohannon's rooming house. He let himself in and climbed up the stairs and tramped back to the ever-stinking dormitory. Every cot was deserted which meant that Bohannon was up and about. He supposed that Bohannon shared the anger and anxiety every miner felt for his trapped brothers in number seven tunnel.

It wasn't until Cole was down on the street again that he remembered he was still wearing Abel's gun and shell belt. He must remember to leave them at the Primrose House for Abel to pick up before he took the train tomorrow.

Since Bohannon had patronized the Miners Rest before, that saloon seemed a logical place to start looking for him and Cole headed up the dirt cross-street for River Street. The miners were still milling around the plank walks and in the street, still waiting for some news from the trapped shift.

When he opened the big door into the Miners Rest, the babble of talk became a roar. Billows of tobacco smoke drifted up to cloud the overhead lamps. Many of the men had been drinking since the accident this morning and some of them, Cole saw, were drunk and quarrelsome. The long bar was so crowded that the customers had spilled over to the card tables. No games were in progress. Four bartenders were trying to serve the crowd. The bartender who had broken up Cole's fight was now roaming the crowd, his sawed-off pool cue dangling from the right wrist by a thong like a policeman's club. He was refereeing the quarrels that broke out, ever ready to hurl a drunk out onto the street. Cole waited at the end of the bar until the man reached him and then put a hand out to stop him. "Remember me?"

The man looked at him and then smiled faintly. "Sure."

"I'm looking for Bohannon again," Cole said.

The bartender seemed surprised. "You haven't heard?"

"Something happen to Bohannon?" Cole asked.

"It's more than something," the bartender grunted. "He's one of the five trapped in that cave-in."

Cole grimaced. "Sorry to hear that. When I saw him last, he wasn't in any shape to work."

"Well, he made it in this morning, but I don't think he'll make it out," the bartender said dryly.

"Any news?"

"None of it's good," the man growled. "They've tried to drive a pipe through, but the rockfall was big stuff. They're afraid to use powder for fear of starting another and timbering takes time — and money."

"Well, let's hope Bohannon makes it. Can you tell me where I can find his partner?

Name's Albie Wright, I think."

The bartender's face altered imperceptibly from an expression of gloom to one of caution. He frowned. "The name of Bohannon's parter is Gus Swanson."

"No, this lad's name is Albie Wright. He's the one that went on the drunk with Bohannon and Varney Wynn."

"Yeah, I read about that one in the paper. Don't look so good for Wynn." He frowned, as if pretending thought. "Albie Wright," he murmured. "That don't ring a bell."

"You don't remember him then?"

The bartender shook his head. "Try the other saloon, mister. He ain't one of our regulars."

Cole felt instinctively that the man was lying but there was no way to prove it here and now. Cole said, "I'll do that. Thanks." He headed for the door and as he opened it, he looked back and saw the bartender watching him.

Cole stepped out onto the boardwalk, then moved quickly to the big window which was painted opaque up to the shoulder height of a tall man. Now Cole rose on tiptoe. He could see the bartender, his legs straddled, his head bowed in thought, tapping his left palm with the pool cue and it seemed to Cole a gesture of indecision. Abruptly then, the man turned and headed for the end of the bar. Rounding the free-lunch table, he started back down the back bar, knocked on the door, apparently was bid entry, and went inside, closing the door behind him. Had his own question about Albie Wright prompted this sudden move?

Cole moved farther down the big window to keep the door behind the bar in sight. He waited so long that his patience wore thin and he was about to turn away when the bartender reappeared. Now he walked down between the bar and back bar, walking slowly and looking over the customers. Abruptly then, he stopped and while Cole could not see to whom he signaled, he could see his beckoning gesture. Neither could Cole see who, in the press of the crowd, came forward to the bartender who leaned over and held a brief conversation. Afterward, the bartender traveled the length of the bar, apparently to begin his cruising through the crowd again.

In a matter of seconds a man shouldered through the crowd and headed for the street door. Cole had to assume that this was the man the bartender talked to, a burly and bearded miner who seemed in something of a hurry.

Turning away from the window, Cole crossed to the sidewalk's edge and his back was to the door when the man came out and turned right toward the light of the flares at the shafthouse. Cole let a couple of passers-by get ahead of him before he swung in to follow the man who must be a messenger. The man turned right at the end of the block and Cole fell in behind him, just far enough to keep his dim form in sight through the darkness. From the man's quick gait, Cole guessed that it never occurred to him he was being followed.

The farther from River Street they got, the meaner the shacks and the worse the rutted road became. When the shacks began to thin out, the man crossed a scattering of vacant lots, angling toward a kerosene flare. As Cole came closer, he suddenly stopped in the darkness and saw that the flare was meant to light the entrance to a big wall tent which, Cole knew, was backed by yet another couple of tents in line. The tents, common in mining camps, would be floored and hold as many cots as could be jammed into them. This was a miners' dormitory, the cheapest place a man could get out of the weather and off the ground. The tent flap was pinned back and in the flare's light Cole saw the messenger enter, say something to an invisible man behind the table whom Cole knew would be the well-armed cashier with instructions to collect a quarter from everyone who entered.

Now Cole saw the messenger pay up and

vanish in the darkness. If there were a message to Albie Wright, it could only be that the governor's son wanted to talk with him, which was more of a warning than a message. *Why would Albie need to be warned*, he wondered. On the other hand, maybe the messenger was carrying a summons.

Cole felt a vast impatience now. He could follow the messenger into the tent and perhaps in that smelly darkness find him talking to Albie Wright, but once he found Albie warned, he would get nothing from him. He decided to wait then and moved off the worn path into the darkness. While he was waiting, he tried to puzzle out this strange sequence of events. Undoubtedly, the room that the bartender had entered and come out of was the saloon's office and now he tried to recall who ran the Miners Rest. Since Cole had never frequented River Street and its saloons, he didn't know all the men who ran them. He thought, though, that the man's first name was Dave, his last name unremembered. That would be simple to check later. Presumably then, this Dave somebody had a message for Albie Wright which was prompted by Cole's inquiry for him. Well, Red Macandy's story today had probably started many things in motion and maybe this was one of those things.

It was only a matter of minutes before the

messenger emerged from the tent, a tall young man following him. Even at this distance, Cole knew this was Albie Wright, for he was still wearing Varney's well-worn Stetson which he had traded Varney for his miner's wool hat.

Cole had only a moment to make his decision. Should he let Albie vanish in the night, perhaps for good, or should he follow him to a probable rendezvous with someone in the Miners Rest? Or should he intercept Albie here before he had a chance to be instructed as to what to say if Cole questioned him?

Suddenly, he knew what his decision had to be. The important thing was to learn who sent for Albie and that might lead to the reason why he'd been sent for. He waited silently in the dark, letting them pass, afterward falling in behind them.

The messenger with Albie beside him retraced his steps to the Miners Rest. When they reached the boardwalk Cole was only a dozen paces behind them. They entered without looking around and Cole moved on, taking his old place at the window. The messenger, he saw, headed straight for the crowded bar, but Albie skirted the bar and knocked on the door behind it. He was bid enter, because he palmed open the door and stepped inside.

Swiftly now Cole moved through the saloon

doors, rounded the end of the bar and opened the door without knocking. Albie Wright was standing beside a roll-top desk at which was seated a grossly fat man in shirtsleeves. Both of them turned their heads as he entered and closed the door behind him. Leaning against the door, Cole looked around the room at the whiskey posters, then regarded the two men.

"Looking for someone?" the fat man asked politely.

"Who would you be?" Cole was equally polite.

The big man's face showed no impatience; he spoke as if he were addressing a curious child. "Dave Hardy. I own this place. You're Cole Halsey."

Cole nodded. "I interrupted your conversation. Go ahead — or do you want me to finish it for you?"

Hardy looked amused. "If you can."

Now Cole looked at Albie, studying him briefly. He had a weak face and intelligent eyes. "All right. Albie, you're not to talk with me. Tell me nothing. There's no way I can find out, because Bohannon's dead." He did not look at Hardy, but kept his glance on Albie. "Close?"

There was a blaze of surprise and puzzlement in Albie's eyes. Now Cole shifted his glance to Hardy, whose beefy face held even more amusement.

"No I was telling Albie to step out and bring Jess and Frank to me. Get along, Albie," Hardy said.

"No, you stay, Albie," Cole said.

Hardy brought his left hand up and there was a gun in it, taken from a clip in the knee slot of his desk and kept there for just such occasions as this. He pointed it at Cole.

"Get along, Albie."

Cole said mildly, "Go ahead, Albie. I found out what I came here to learn."

He stepped aside and Hardy said quickly, "Don't cross between us, Albie. Circle and get his gun. Then get Frank and Jess."

Albie made a half circle to Cole and lifted his gun, then backed away, skirted Cole widely and went out.

The two men looked carefully at each other, and then Cole asked mildly, "What'll beating me up get you?"

"Another story for Red Macandy, I reckon."

"Better make it a good one because I'll be back."

"You're always welcome in the Miners Rest," Hardy said blandly.

Cole looked around the room. "This building would make a nice fire."

"Oh, the governor's son doesn't burn buildings. He gets in saloon brawls. He tries to beat up on the man who got Varney drunk."

It was neat, Cole thought bitterly. What lunatic notion had made him come here?

Before he could answer that, the door opened and two of the housemen, one of them his old friend, came in. Albie, trailing them, shut the door. Hardy said to the two, "Rough him up good, boys."

It couldn't be called a long fight, but it was a good one while it lasted. They jumped on Cole in professional style, each going for and capturing an arm. Then one man held his arms while the other started in on him, first going for his solar plexus. Cole sagged purposely just in time to take the blow on his breastbone; it hurt, but didn't drive the breath from him.

Cole now jammed the heel of his cowman's boot down on the instep of the man pinioning his arms. Almost at the same time he caught a roundhouse blow in the head. The blow, plus the instinctive reaction of a man flinching from a stamped instep, allowed Cole to break free. He drove for the corner of the room and put his back against the wall. They came at him, but for a few precious moments he managed to fight them both off. As one man backed away for a fresh charge, Cole glanced past him to see Hardy still seated at his desk, watching this. In his pleasure at the sight of the beating, he had placed the gun, which had served its purpose, on the desk top. Then both men charged together, trying to pin him against the wall. Bracing a foot against the baseboard for purchase, Cole drove between them; once clear, he headed straight for Dave Hardy two steps away. The fat saloon owner too late grabbed for the gun. Cole came at him with a savage kick in the belly. Hardy gave a great bray of agonized pain as Cole's boot drove home, driving Hardy's chair back and taking the huge man with it in a thunderous crash to the floor.

Then they were on his back and Cole felt his knees buckle under their combined weight. He was driven to the floor, face down, and now the rain of blows and kicks came. Covering his face with his hands as best he could, he drew his legs up but the battering on his head and back continued. The last thing he remembered was seeing Hardy stretched on the floor on his side, vomiting.

Cole came back to consciousness to find himself sitting on the plank walk, propped up against the building next to the Miners Rest. His body felt broken and he tried to breathe as gently as he could against the pain racking his chest. His face felt cool and wet and he knew the wetness was his own blood. Turning his head slowly, he saw that his hat lay primly beside him. He didn't doubt that a couple of miners, tired of tripping over him where he lay after being pitched out of the saloon, had dragged him out of the boardwalk traffic and propped him up. Looking down at his hands, he saw his knuckles were raw and bleeding, probably from being tramped on, since he had not landed enough blows in the fight to break his skin. He could not guess the hour but there were fewer men on the street and they were mostly drunks. Turning his head slowly, he saw the flares still burning at the shaft-house.

The big problem now was to get to his feet. First, he put on his hat and then, holding his breath, he managed to get his throbbing leg bent to the side of him and heaved himself to his knees. Then, a hand braced against the store front, he came achingly erect, his legs spraddled to keep him from falling to the walk. Every bone and every muscle had somehow been reached and hurt by the two men. His first tentative steps toward the bridge were uncertain and he wondered how he would ever make it alone. If he hailed one of the drunken miners, the man would undoubtedly pull him down again in trying to help him. He remembered then the watering trough in front of a saloon up the street where he had first stopped in the search for Varney.

Ever so slowly, using the building fronts as support, he traveled up the street and found the trough, filled with scummy water. Beside the trough he took off his hat and because there was no place to put it except the road, he turned the crown down and floated the hat. Then he leaned down and plunged his head into the water of the trough. It beat into every cut on his face and head but its chill shock revived him. He scrubbed his face and head as best he could with his sore hands, then picked up his hat, shook the water from it, and straightened up.

The Primrose House was across the bridge and three blocks beyond. It was, he thought grimly, the longest journey he would ever have to make except for the last one. An hour later he reached the Primrose veranda. From the bridge his course had taken him close to every store front in the three blocks. Holding onto one of the hotel veranda posts, he managed the three steps up and moved with infinite care through the lobby doors and into the lobby. The night bell of the Primrose House desk which would summon Louise or her father, he ignored. He went behind the desk to the keyboard and saw the key to room 3, a ground-floor room, was hanging from its hook. Taking it, he made his slow way past the Selbys' three-room apartment and found room 3 more by feel than sight. It was unlocked and he went in, closed the door behind him, moved over to the bed and fell upon it face down. Once he had rested, he would get out of his clothes, he thought wearily, but morning found him just as he had fallen still dressed in his blood-smeared and torn sheepskin.

15

Cole made the morning train to Junction City only beacuse the chambermaid's scream at the sight of him sprawled across the bed wakened him. On the train he managed to sleep all the way to Junction City, not even waking while the train waited at the Y for two cattle trains from roundup. There he took a hack up to the Governor's Mansion, directing the driver to the kitchen door. Here Portia paid off the driver because Cole was unable to get his hand in his pocket for the hack fare. He managed the back stairs alone and took the room next to Hal's. Portia heated water for his bath and while he was bathing, she took his clothes to clean. When she returned she gave him the unnecessary information that the governor was up north electioneering and that while he was gone, she was boss and that as boss, she thought he should go to bed. Only when Cole told her that he was going out, that he was bigger than she was and that he didn't mind hitting a woman, she laughingly agreed to round up some sort of a wardrobe.

After his healing bath came the bandaging. Portia, who thought that a man's hurt should be reflected in the number of bandages he wore, lost her argument. Cole submitted to one bandage on the raw knuckles of his left hand. His hat would cover the cut on his head and his clothes would hide his other bruises. The mark on his cheekbone was no worse than a razor cut.

When finally Portia brought in a warm sheepskin of Hal's that was the twin of his own, Cole was left to himself in this unlived-in bedroom. He lay back on the bed's counterpane and studied the ceiling, trying to piece together, and assess the importance of his successes and mistakes of last night. On the debit side, apart from the beating he had taken, was the fact that undoubtedly the *Times* would carry the story of his brawl in a Primrose saloon. Red Macandy would make it clearly evident that Governor Halsey had not only one scapegrace son now hiding under suspicion of murder, but another son who was given to barroom brawling and revenge on an innocent man. That, in itself, was debit enough but added to it was the almost certain fact that Albie Wright would disappear. On the credit side was Cole's certain knowledge that Dave Hardy knew what was behind Varney's appearance in the capital the night of Brandell's death. Also on the credit side, although it was minor, was the kick in the belly Cole had given Hardy. That, Cole reckoned, was a lot more hurtful than the beating he himself had received. There was just a chance that he might have ruptured Hardy's liver, but if that were so, Hardy would be dead by now and he would be in jail. Altogether, the debit was considerably larger than the credit, a truly dismal sum of misfortune.

Cole now rose, moved down the hall to the library and noted the time on his father's big wall clock. It was time for the next move. Putting on his sheepskin and hat, he walked down the back stairs where he found that Albert had joined Portia. Albert was dressed in a long, blue, silver-frogged overcoat. When he saw Cole, he rose, his black top hat in hand. Albert regarded him closely and then looked at Portia. "To hear her talk, Mr. Cole, you were one of the walkin' dead. You look pretty good to me."

"What are you doing home, Albert?" Cole asked.

"When the governor's away, we quit early. I took Miss Thruelson and Mr. Eames home. I was ready to put up the horses when Portia told me you might be going out."

Cole smiled. "I've never been gladder to see you, Albert. You and your horses, that is." Albert laughed and opened the door.

"Supper's at six-thirty, Mr. Cole," Portia said.

"Keep it on the back of the stove, Portia. I may be in later," Cole said and stepped out into the crisp late afternoon. The governor's carriage pulled up at the kitchen steps and Cole swung into the seat next to the driver's seat. Albert brought out a blanket from the back seat and shook it out preparatory to throwing it over Cole's legs. Cole looked at him and said dryly, "You're worse than Portia."

Albert smiled. "I figured you'd say that," he said, and carefully refolded the blanket and returned it to the back seat.

Cole told him to deposit him a block from Kelly's Saloon on Water Street. On the drive they discussed Hal and how he was bearing up under the strain of trying to wage a political campaign while at the same time trying to defend his son from a probable charge of murder. Cole had forgotten that Albert, naturally, would not know Varney who, as a rare visitor to the governor, his boss, would have visited him at the State House. Hal always made a habit of giving a double eagle to any of the Mill Iron hands who dropped by, telling them to spend it on the town. He had sense enough to know that a visit to the Governor's Mansion or a dinner there would only embarrass them and interfere with the pleasure they were looking forward to, and he had doubtless done this with Varney. Albert was curious about Varney, Cole knew, but he would have to wait upon events before meeting or learning anything about him, Cole decided.

At Cole's direction, Albert took a roundabout way to the stop he designated.

"Do you want me to wait for you here, Mr. Cole?" Albert said, after Cole had climbed down to the rutted cross-street.

"Why don't you wait for me at Ballard's Livery, Albert. It's warmer than sitting out here."

"Can you make it that far, Mr. Cole?"

"Yes, dammit, Albert, I can," Cole said in exasperation, and then he smiled. Albert nodded, understanding that Cole was not mad at him but at his own physical condition. After he drove away, Cole started slowly down the boardwalk; his soothing bath had limbered up his muscles and he set off at an almost normal pace for Kelly's Saloon. As he pushed through the saloon doors, he saw that Kelly had only a scattering of customers at the bar in the back. Going up to the bar, Cole noted that the wall clock Varney had asked Kelly to read for him said a quarter to five. Homer saw him, came over with a smile on his tough face as he shook hands across the bar.

"Been expecting you," Kelly said. He regarded Cole carefully, noting his bandaged left hand on the bar top. "You look a little different."

"I feel a little different," Cole said. He let it rest there and Homer, sensing Cole didn't want to explain the bandage or the bruises, asked no more questions.

Now Homer reached into his upper vest pocket and drew out a piece of paper which he unfolded and spread out on the bar.

"I made a map where these sporting houses are. I marked them with an X and wrote the name of the madam alongside the mark. See if it makes sense to you." Cole studied the paper and then nodded.

"Most of them have got a colored maid that answers the door, takes your hat and coat and gets your drink order. They'll likely tell you they aren't open yet and if they do that, ask for the madam by name. If they still won't let you in, ask them how they'd like to spend the night in jail."

Cole folded up the list, tucked it in his shirt pocket and said, "I'm obliged to you, Homer. If I find anything, you'll be the first to know."

"Good luck, Cole."

On the street again, Cole turned left and slowly moved down to the next block. By then, he was out of what had originally been the warehouse district. Here were cheap eating houses, saloons, and secondhand stores. The first sporting house on his list turned out not to be a residential house after all, but the second floor of a saloon. He climbed a set of stairs that ended at a door where he yanked the bell pull. He heard the clang inside and waited. Presently the door opened a crack and Cole saw part of the colored maid's face. She said, "We're not open, mister, but be sure to come back later."

"I want to talk with Mrs. Scholtz," Cole said firmly.

"You a policeman?"

"I'll tell Mrs. Scholtz who I am." Cole's voice was cold. "Now open up."

Obediently the maid opened the door and Cole was in a big room that held many comfortable chairs, a rug, two big sofas, and a marble-topped corner table holding liquor and glasses. The lamps had not been lighted yet and it was a dim room smelling of booze, cheap perfume and cigars.

"Take a chair," the colored girl said. As she passed Cole heading for the door at the far end of the room, he saw that she was already in uniform — a very proper black dress with lace collar and cuffs.

She disappeared through the door and Cole gratefully sat down. He didn't know how he was going to go about this preposterous search for the girl who could remember Varney.

When the door opened, a slight woman wearing a dark wrapper came into the room, circled the pair of sofas centered back to back and halted before Cole, who had risen. She was a woman of fifty and her ravaged, once-pretty face now held all the warmth of a prairie blizzard. In a scornful voice, she said, "You're no policeman. Now please get out. The girls aren't ready; they haven't eaten yet."

"Can you get them together here?" Cole asked.

"No. Why should I? What for? Who are you?"

Cole reached in his pocket and drew out a handful of double eagles. Opening his palm, he said, "I've got fifty dollars here for the girl who can remember a man I describe. Maybe it's you. Can you get them in here?"

"That's pretty easy money," Mrs. Scholtz said slowly. "Will it get the girls in trouble?"

"It'll get one girl fifty dollars," Cole said flatly. "No. No trouble."

"Come on back. They're all in the kitchen, waiting for supper." She turned and led Cole through the room, down a long corridor from which six doors opened, three to a side. Already Cole could hear the chatter of female voices in the lighted kitchen at the end of the corridor. Mrs. Scholtz led the way into the kitchen and Cole, hat in hand, followed her.

There was a big round table in the far corner, at which five women were seated. The sixth was at the big stove. At his entrance, the chatter ceased so abruptly that Cole could hear meat frying in the skillet on the stove. The girls were not dressed for the night. Four of them wore stained and powder-spattered kimonos; the one at the stove wore an apron over a plain house dress. All of them had their hair curled tightly to their heads and held by strips of greasy ribbon or cloth. One looked to be in her twenties, the others in their thirties. They were, Cole thought, as unattractive a collection of women as he had ever seen without powder or paint or bright clothes to relieve their dowdiness. Three of them, he noted, were drinking raw whiskey from water tumblers. One was smoking a cigar.

The young one said, "Well, honey, I was expecting you later. Let me get fixed up."

"Be quiet, Bonnie, let him talk. There may be fifty dollars in it for you or the others."

The mention of money brought a sudden interest into the faces of the girls. Cole again pulled out the coins, all double eagles, and showed them in the palm of his hand. Cole said, "I want to know if you remember being with one certain man. This man called himself a bastard."

"Himself?" one of the girls asked.

"Yes. Not you, himself."

"I remember one," Bonnie said. "When would this be?"

"Last Monday night. Eleven, let's say."

"That's right," Bonnie said.

"All right. Describe him."

Bonnie pretended to think. "About thirty. As tall as you, dark hair like yours, but curly."

"Any of the rest of you remember?" Cole asked.

One girl laughed raucously. "He'd only have one girl a night and it sounds like it was Bonnie's night."

Cole shifted his glance to Bonnie. "Nice try, Bonnie, but your mistake."

"Hell, I'd be dumb if I didn't try," Bonnie said cheerfully. "What's this all about?"

241

"It's all about fifty dollars," Cole said. "Thank you, ladies." Cole nodded to Mrs. Scholtz, turned and left the kitchen.

Bonnie called after him, "You come back, honey."

The colored maid was in the parlor when he returned and let him out. It was a chore to descend the stairs and when he reached the street level he sat on the lower step and rested a moment. Taking out Homer's map, he consulted it in the fading light. The next house, he noted, was almost across the street from this one. Glancing up he looked across and up the street and located it. This sporting house was really a house wedged in between two saloons. Its three steps abutting the plank walk led to a narrow porch decorated with cut-out gingerbread fretwork. It had once been painted white but now it was a dingy gray.

Cole angled across the street and slowly mounted the steps and knocked at the door. It was opened promptly by a handsome middle-aged woman wearing an apron. She wore steel-rimmed spectacles and for a moment Cole thought he had made a mistake. "I'm looking for Lettie Gustafson. I must have the wrong place."

"I'm Mrs. Gustafson," the woman said. "You're too early. We're open when the lamp is in the window."

This woman, Cole thought, had the appearance of a kindly, overworked schoolteacher. He supposed, however, that if she took off her spectacles and apron and changed into a bright dress, she could look like the madam she was. "I'm not a customer," Cole said. "But I want to talk to all your girls."

"Now that *is* something," the woman said. "You a preacher? You going to save 'em?"

Again Cole reached in his pocket, got a fistful of coins and showed them to her. "If any of your girls or even you can remember a man who could have been in here Monday night, she'll get fifty dollars."

The schoolteacher look was replaced by a pleased rapacity in the woman's expression. She stepped aside, saying, "Come in."

Cole stepped into the parlor which, like the other parlor, held a couple of sofas and several chairs plus an ornate sideboard which was stocked with bottles of liquor and glasses. Inevitably in the back corner was an upright piano.

Mrs. Gustafson skirted him, then went over to an end table holding a lamp, struck a match and lighted it. "Sit down," she said. "I don't think the girls have started supper yet."

Beside the entrance to the stairway at the far end of the room there was a heavy red-velvet curtain and the woman disappeared behind it. As Cole sat down in the nearest chair, he reflected that there was still some of the schoolteacher in Mrs. Gustafson, for the room had been aired of tobacco smoke and liquor fumes. The curtains in the front window, which were discreetly parted for the lamp to be lighted later, were frilly and clean. The brass cuspidors shone brightly.

Now he heard women's voices, growing more distinct each second; then the curtain billowed, letting four girls into the room followed by Mrs. Gustafson.

Cole rose as the girls in a group regarded him with curiosity. Like the girls in the other house they were not dressed yet for the evening. They wore wrappers of outing flannel and like the other girls, the hair of three of them was curled up and tied with strips of rag or ribbons. One girl, the best looking, wore her hair loose and down her back. Now the group broke up; two girls went over to the sofa and the others took individual chairs. Like the girls across the street, these girls weren't yet ready to receive customers. They were neither powdered nor painted and were completely indifferent as to their appearances at the moment. They all seemed to be in their late twenties, two blondes and two brunettes.

Mrs. Gustafson came over to Cole. She

turned then and said, "Girls, I told you what this man said in the kitchen and you didn't believe me." She turned to Cole. "Tell them."

Once again Cole pulled out the money and jingled it. "There's fifty dollars for one of you if you can remember a certain man. If he was in here, he came in last Monday night."

"What did he look like?" one of the girls asked.

"That's what you're going to tell me," Cole said. The girls exchanged puzzled glances. "You'll remember him because he was very drunk and kept calling himself a bastard."

The girl on the sofa with the long hair straightened up. "Why, I had him," she said quickly.

As in the other house, Cole said, "Describe him."

"He was maybe five inches shorter than you and he had pretty blond hair. He didn't weigh much but he wasn't exactly skinny. He had a thin face and a beaky kind of nose."

Cole felt a sudden excitement, for she had described Varney as accurately as he could have himself.

"I think it's your fifty dollars, Miss — "

The squeals and groans of the girls drowned him out. They didn't go over to the lucky girl but sat where they were, alternately looking at Cole in wonder and at the winner with envy.

Cole crossed over to the girl and gave her the fifty dollars in gold pieces.

"Thanks, mister. Is this all I have to do?" the girl asked.

"I'd like to talk to you alone. What's your name?"

"Marty."

"May I talk with her alone, Mrs. Gustafson?" Cole asked.

"Come on, girls," Mrs. Gustafson said. "Marty, remember supper's ready."

The girls trooped out. Now Cole sat down next to Marty who immediately rose and went over to the sideboard. "That calls for a drink. Want one?"

"I'd like one," Cole said. He watched her pour two stiff drinks into two tall glasses.

"Water in yours?" she asked.

"Plain, please."

She returned to the sofa now, gave Cole his drink and, standing, saluted him with the glass. "Here's to more lucky days like this." She put down half her drink while Cole took a sip of his and then she sat down beside him. She was a frail thing, Cole saw, with a rather thin face that wasn't quite pretty. Her hair, long and golden and shining, would be her vanity, Cole knew. Her pale eyes were bold and bright, probably made so by the drinks she had had before he came.

"What do you want to know, mister?"

"Everything, Marty. You do the talking. Tell me what you remember."

Marty didn't even frown in her endeavor to remember. "He came in alone and he was awfully drunk. Two of us were free and he picked me. I'd had a helluva time with the man before him and I hoped he'd pick Dolly. I tried to get him to take her but he wouldn't, so I took him upstairs.

"He gave me twenty and I started out of the room to get change from Mrs. Gustafson. He said, 'No, it's yours.' He lay back on the bed. While I was getting ready, he said, 'Do you know, I'm a bastard, a real bastard?' I said, 'That's nothing new to me. I just got rid of one.' Then I climbed into bed and I'm damned if he wasn't asleep — passed out."

"Did you leave him then?" Cole asked.

"No. Like I said, I was tired. He paid me good and I didn't want him to feel cheated when he woke up, so I covered him and me up and I slept."

"Beside him?" Cole asked.

"Right alongside him, same bed."

"How long were you with him?"

"I can't remember. Must have been a couple of hours, though."

"He couldn't have got up while you were

sleeping and come back before you woke, could he?"

"No," Marty said flatly. "I slept in snatches because he kept waking and talking."

"Could you understand what he said?"

Marty shook her head. "None of it made sense but it kept coming back to bastard. He'd say, 'Bastard, bastard, bastard,' like he was telling someone. Then he'd say it again and sound mad."

"Didn't Mrs. Gustafson wonder why you were so long?"

"She sure as hell did," Marty said. "She came in once and told me to get rid of my drunk. I waved that twenty-dollar gold piece in front of her nose and told her to get the hell out of the room, that I'd earned my sleep."

She finished her drink. Cole waited for her to gag on the raw whiskey, but she didn't. Her throat tautened and that was all. Cole said, "Go on."

"That's about all. He woke me up crying once. Then one of the girls wondering what was going on knocked on the door. That waked him and me too. He sat up and looked around him like he didn't know where he was. I told him he paid me and hadn't got what he come for. He just laughed and said, 'To hell with it. Keep it.' I put on my dress and helped him downstairs. He was still pretty drunk. He went over to the sideboard, took a swig of whiskey, waved to me and went out. That's about it."

"Do you know what time that was?" Cole asked.

"Late. Or early, I mean. Maybe two-thirty, three. All the girls but Dolly were sleeping."

She got up now, possibly prompted by her recollection of Varney's trip to the sideboard. She went over, poured herself another drink and sat down. "You believe I earned my fifty, mister?"

"I believe you, Marty."

"I liked the kid. I felt sorry for him," Marty said.

"Sorry enough to help him?" Cole asked.

Marty thought a moment before she said, "Well, maybe. Tell me how."

"Day after tomorrow I'll bring him in. I'll come right from the depot with him. That'll be around three. Can you be dressed to go out with me when we get here?"

Marty looked at him warily. "Go where?"

"To tell a couple of men just what you told me tonight."

"Will I get the kid in trouble?"

"You'll get him *out* of trouble, Marty."

"Sure, I'll go," Marty said. "I owe him something, don't I?"

Cole stood up. "Not as much as he owes

you, Marty." He looked down at her and said soberly, "Do you forget things when you're drinking, Marty?"

She smiled. "You mean will I remember promising you? Yes, I will."

"Thanks, Marty. I'm obliged to you."

"No, it's the other way around. It ain't every night I make the price of three or four new dresses."

"See you in two days, Marty," Cole said and moved toward the door.

"Say, who are you, mister?" Marty asked then. Cole halted and looked at her. "Mrs. Gustafson would kick my head off if she heard me ask a customer's name, but you're not a customer."

"You'll find out when I come back for you, Marty. Fair enough?"

Marty nodded. "Fair enough, Handsome. Good night."

When Cole stepped out onto the board-walk, it was night. He was a half block toward Ballard's Livery where he would be meeting Albert before he remembered his promise to Homer. Retracing his steps he went in Kelly's now crowded saloon. Kelly was busy and Cole waited patiently at the bar until Kelly came up to take his order and recognized him. "I got what I wanted, Homer. Mrs. Gustafson's. A girl was with him for about two hours."

A broad grin split Homer's tough face. Somebody rapped a coin for service down the bar and Cole said, "I'll be back in a couple of days and tell you about it."

"Do that," Homer said. "I'm glad it worked."

Cole again sought the street and headed for the livery. *People can surprise you,* he thought. A tough Irish bartender had helped him because he was Hal's son. An alcoholic little whore had remembered enough of her Sunday school lessons to be honest with Varney and to pity him. Now Cole could admit to himself that before finding Marty he had feared a lot of things that hadn't happened. If Marty had been less generous and more suspicious, she could have spooked at his questions and lied, or even left town. Cole knew they would talk at Mrs. Gustafson's about the mysterious stranger who paid a girl fifty dollars to recall a man who had called himself a bastard. Maybe the story was already spreading and would come to Red Macandy's attention, but the big, big thing was that now Varney had an alibi for those blank hours which could be backed up by Marty, Mrs. Gustafson, and Dolly. Cole knew he was no closer to Brandell's killer than when he had started, but he was sure now that Varney was safe.

Cole was weary when he reached the livery

and found Albert waiting patiently on a chair behind the stove in the office. Outside Cole accepted his help climbing into the carriage and did not protest when he covered his legs with the lap robe. Once the team was in motion Cole directed him to go home by way of the depot. Once there Cole went into the big building, across the empty, unlighted waiting-room and approached the station agent's window. He asked to send a telegram and was given paper and pencil. He addressed the telegram to Tish in Primrose and sent this message: VARNEY IN CLEAR. ASK JOE PERRY TO SEND A MAN TO GOOSE CREEK AND BRING VARNEY TO PRIMROSE. RETURN TOMORROW.

He was about to sign his name when he added the words, HOW ARE YOU, BURLEY? to the message. He knew this would either anger Tish or make her laugh and that it was hardly kind of him to ask a favor of Tish while taunting her father. Still, he let it stand, signed his name and paid. The agent looked at the clock and said, "I can make it tonight if Benny ain't left early. It'll go out first thing in the morning though for sure."

Back in the carriage, Cole directed Albert to the Governor's Mansion. He found himself looking forward to Portia's supper and even more to a long night of healing sleep, but before that he must write a note to Hal.

16

Next morning the conductor held the train long enough for Cole to buy a paper from the newsboy and then signaled the train in motion. Once seated in the crowded car next to a man he didn't know, Cole unfolded the paper. Again Red Macandy was using his boldest type to headline the front-page column one and two story. Column one's headlines said: GOVERNOR ORDERS ONE SON BROUGHT IN. The adjoining column was headed OTHER SON IN SALOON BRAWL. The first story began,

Pressure brought to bear on Governor Halsey forced him to announce yesterday that he had ordered law enforcement officers to find and seize his illegitimate son, Varney Wynn, and bring him in for questioning as to the part, if any, he played in the murder of Abe Brandell.

The rest was just a rehash for emphasis of the whole Varney Wynn story. Cole put his attention then to the second column story, which began,

Cole Halsey, oldest son of Governor Halsey, was involved night before last in a nasty brawl in Primrose. Young Halsey, apparently bent on getting revenge upon the man he thought had seduced Varney Wynn into joining him in four days of dissipation, encountered his victim in the saloon. Reports from eye witnesses indicate that young Halsey assaulted Albie Wright, Wynn's companion, and that a vicious fight ensued. Trying to halt the combatants, David Hardy, owner of the Miners Rest, was severely injured by young Halsey. According to witnesses, Halsey received a sound thrashing at the hands of Wright's friends.

There was more, of course. Cole was identified as "foreman of the governor's big Mill Iron ranch, formerly known as a man of even temper, not given to public brawling. It was thought that young Halsey, under great stress due to the revelations of his half brother's conduct during the past few days, became temporarily deranged."

It was a typical Red Macandy story, factual but written with an unconcealed bias by inference. It said in effect that poor misguided

Governor Halsey was being punished by whatever gods there were, those instruments of punishment being his two worthless sons. Hal, Cole knew, would be appalled when he read this issue of the *Times*. Together with what the *Times* had printed before regarding Varney's bastardry and his dissipations, it made the whole Halsey tribe appear to be a collection of immoral paranoiacs. Cole wondered then if the account of his brawl wouldn't break Hal's already overburdened heart. All that was needed to destroy Hal utterly would be the revelation that Varney had spent a night in a sporting house that fateful Wednesday.

Cole looked at the rest of the front page. One column was given over to a speech by Asa Forbes who was touring the southern part of the state. It was the familiar plaint that his opponent was trying to hobble capital investments by restrictions that would strangle the state's growth.

In the lower corner there was an inch of type not headlined. It said that an explosion in the Star mine day before yesterday caused the death of nine miners. The cause of the explosion was unknown, but the management was investigating. Red Macandy, true lackey that he was, did not bother with a casualty list or the name of the Star's owner.

When the train pulled into Primrose, Cole stepped out into a windy gray day. He thought that Tish, anxious to hear how Varney's alibi was established, would meet him or at least send Abel, but neither of them were visible on the wind-swept platform. He was sure now that his taunt at Burley had angered Tish and had probably angered her enough so that she hadn't asked Joe Perry to send a man summoning Varney in.

Cole buttoned the collar of his sheepskin and headed for the bridge and livery. Some of the stiffness in his legs was fading; as he walked down River Street he saw that it was still thronged with miners. Today though there was a difference in their appearance. Many of them were clean shaven and were wearing their best clothes as if to celebrate something. When Cole stopped one miner to ask what was going on the man looked at him contemptuously. "Just a big funeral this afternoon is all — a funeral for nine men."

Cole regretted more than ever his flip remark to Burley in the telegram. Burley would be saddened by the death of these men, he knew, but not saddened enough to spend some of his money to make his mines safe to work in.

At the livery Cole learned that a man had left early this morning to get Varney and Cole calculated that Varney would be here sometime in midafternoon.

Cole asked for his horse which he rode as far as the Primrose House. He entered the Primrose House by way of the lobby hoping to see Louise Selby and thank her for getting him on the train yesterday with the aid of the hotel's hack. She was not around, and Cole walked into the bar which was deserted save for a solitary drinker at the back end. Its emptiness told him that roundup had not yet finished. Alec greeted him quietly and Cole took his bottle and glass over to one of the empty gambling tables and sat down. Alec, observing the unwritten rule that if a man sat down he wanted to be alone, went back to his other customer.

Cole did want to be alone, for he knew this day he had to find Albie Wright and pick up the search where he had dropped it. But would Albie Wright be here? Wouldn't Dave Hardy have told him to get out of town, to disappear? That depended on whether Hardy had time to tell Albie much before Cole broke in on him. The *Times* had said Dave Hardy was seriously injured in the brawl. So seriously, Cole wondered, that he was unable to talk with Albie after the fight? But suppose Albie was here still? Would Albie talk if he was offered money? If he were to offer Albie more money than he had been paid to drink with Varney, maybe Albie would feel no obligation to keep quiet. But why was he so sure Albie wouldn't talk for nothing, he wondered. Well, for one reason he had hit Albie at the finish of Varney's spree. Another reason was that Albie had come at Dave Hardy's summons. The third reason was that Dave Hardy might have threatened him there in the office before Cole broke in.

Cole had his drink, paid Alec and went out to his horse. He supposed the place to look for Albie Wright was either the Miners Rest or the tent dormitory. He decided to head for the tent first and accordingly put his horse down Grant Street and across the bridge. Passing the Miners Rest he saw that it was crowded with miners drinking up for the mass burial. Although smoke was coming from the mill chimneys and the hoist shack, it was doubtful, judging from the number of men on the streets, that the Star was operating with anything like a full shift.

The tent dormitory in daylight was even less inviting to behold than it had been at night. It lay at the edge of a pile of tailings surrounded by scarred and weed-grown land that looked as if it was used as a dump. The dirty gray canvas of the behemoth was billowing in the wind as he dismounted and tied his horse to the flare post.

Cole stepped through the flap and halted. To his right was a table on which reposed a cigar box half-filled with quarters. Seated with his back to the potbellied stove was a bearded man with eyes that were cold and mean. In front of him, resting beside the cigar box, was a pistol.

"Know a man here named Albie Wright?"

"I don't know no names," the man said sourly. "You go in there, you pay your two bits. Don't care if you stay a minute or a week, it's two bits."

That made sense, Cole reflected. With day shifts giving up their cots for the men coming off night shift, with drifters, drunks, transients, one-night stayers, men who were sick and men who were about to be sick coming and going, it would be impossible to keep track of any one man. Cole paid up and walked in.

There was just enough light coming through the canvas to see by, and Cole made his way down the right center aisle. Perhaps a third of the cots were occupied and as Cole walked slowly past them, looking for Albie's weak face above the blankets, he felt a sudden pity for these men. These were the men without any possessions except what they had in their pockets, homeless and womanless and rootless, many of them strangers in a foreign land. They came in to find a few hours of blessed oblivion in stinking, lice-ridden blankets. Somewhere ahead of him a tearing, rumbling cough came from one of the blanketed figures. How many men had died in here, unnoticed by indifferent strangers on either side of them, Cole wondered.

Then he found Albie, who was lying on his back, blankets pulled up to his chin, eyes open and staring at the gray ceiling.

Cole halted and looked at him a long moment, making sure. Then Albie became aware of being watched and his glance shifted to Cole. There was no expression in his face, not even curiosity.

Cole moved into the narrow space between an empty cot and Albie's and halted, looking down at Albie. "Remember me?"

"What if I do?"

"You've got a gun of mine."

"I ain't got it. It's at the saloon." Albie's voice was hoarse, but it did not hide the surliness.

"Want to get it?" Cole asked.

"Hell with you. It ain't mine."

Cole sat down on the adjoining empty cot and regarded Albie, wondering how to get to him. "Bohannon's dead, I hear."

"Boo hoo," Albie said mockingly.

"Want to earn some money?" Cole said.

"None of yours."

"All money's the same. Mine's just like anybody else's," Cole said mildly.

"What do I do for it? Beat up Varney for you?" Albie said jeeringly.

"No. I can do that myself. All you do is talk."

"About what?"

Cole leaned forward. "Who paid you and Bohannon to go on that drunk with Varney?"

Albie said promptly, "Save your money. Nobody."

"Then why were you hauled out of here to see Dave Hardy the other night?"

Now Albie raised up on his elbows, revealing the filthy long underwear he wore. "How the hell would I know? I barely said hello before you rammed in."

"Then what did Dave say to you after they threw me out?"

"After they threw you out, they carried Dave out. Puking blood too."

"He didn't talk with you?"

"You think he could?" Albie asked sarcastically.

Cole regarded him in silence for a moment, then decided to take the chance. "I think he wanted to tell you not to talk with me, not to tell me who paid for that drunk. But I'm willing to pay you."

Albie lay down and looked at the ceiling. "Why? I got all the money I want. Look around you. Nice place, ain't it?"

"That's what I mean."

Albie looked at him fiercely. "Nobody paid me, damn you! Now go away and let me sleep."

"Fifty dollars?"

Albie came up on his elbows again, fury in his face. "You can offer me your whole damn ranch and I wouldn't tell you, because there's nothin' to tell. Nobody paid me."

"You're lying," Cole said quietly. "What does it get you? Are you planning on going to the man and asking for more money than I offer?"

"That's a damn good idea 'cept for one thing. There ain't no 'him'."

"I'll pay you more than he will."

Albie shook his head in wonderment. "By God, Varney was right. You'll try and bend a man till you break him. But not me. You think I'd tell you if anybody paid me? You'd have to kill me first."

From across the room, somebody called wrathfully, "Shut up over there."

"What is it about me that gravels you so?" Cole asked quietly.

"Everything!" Albie said bitterly. "He's

your little brother and you cuff him around like he was a saloon dog! Don't tell me you don't because I seen you! I had a big brother like you. That's why I'm here!" He was so mad he was close to choking. "You ask me I'd say you was the bastard in that family, not Varney!"

"All right, but what if I said you'd save Varney from being arrested if you told me who paid you."

"I'd have to hear him say that, not you!"

Cole heard footsteps approaching and turned his head. The bearded clerk-collector came to a halt at the foot of the bed, his pistol dangling from his hand. He pointed to the tent flap with his other hand. "You," he said to Cole. "Outside, and quick about it."

Cole rose and without looking at either man moved out to the aisle and walked up it and went outside to his horse. More than ever he was certain that Albie Wright was paid, but he was equally certain he could never make him admit it. *Never?* he wondered then.

Cole rode back to River Street, crossed the bridge, went up Grant and turned right at the cross street that ended at Burley Hammond's gate. There were two men with rifles guarding it, one of them Abel, and it was only then that Cole remembered he hadn't picked up Abel's pistol at the Miners Rest.

He reined in and said, "I owe you a gun, Abel. You making out without it?"

"We could fight a war with what we've got inside."

"Any trouble?"

"Oh, when they get drunk enough some of 'em come. But not close, though. We let 'em shout a bit then run 'em back."

Cole nodded. "Tish home?"

"Been inside since that ride with you."

Cole moved up the drive but took the left fork which led to the back of the house and the stables. He tied his horse to a corral post and headed for the back porch and the kitchen door. There he had his hand raised to knock when the door swung open and Tish was facing him. She was wearing an apron; her sleeves were rolled up and her hands and forearms were dusted with flour. There was a smudge of it across her cheek, Cole noted, but what surprised Cole was the look of smoldering resentment in her face, an expression akin to the look he had seen on Varney's face countless times.

"I saw you pass the window," Tish said tonelessly. "Come in."

"Maybe I'd better come some other time."

"Well, I can think of times you've been more welcome, but come in. I want to hear how Varney's in the clear."

She stepped back and lifted the apron straps over her head as Cole moved in and closed the door. He nodded to Lizzie and saw that he had interrupted their joint bread making.

"Lizzie, I'm quitting on you," Tish said. "If I stayed any longer, I'd ruin the whole batch anyway."

She turned so quickly she missed Lizzie's smile and went through the dining room and living room and into the library, Cole trailing her. Once there, she headed straight for the chair behind the desk, saying, "Funny, the only two rooms in this house I can stand is this one and my bedroom." She sat down. "I'm in a foul mood, Cole, I warn you."

"I'd never have guessed it," Cole said dryly.

"Why did you put that greeting to Burley in your telegram?"

"Common politeness. Is he here?"

"No. Our men at the mill told him to stay away."

"A pity. If he was here you could ask him if he got my greeting. He wouldn't lie to you."

Tish glared at him as he stripped out of his sheepskin and threw it and his hat on the sofa, then sank into the easy chair facing the desk. "About Varney, now," she said.

"It's a little rough, but I think you've paid

for your ticket."

"Damn right I have," Tish said angrily.

Cole told her then of his search of the sporting houses and of turning up Marty. He explained in detail how Marty was sure Varney couldn't have even left the room during the time they were both fitfully sleeping. Tish got the picture and her face reflected her distaste, but at the same time it held a certain sadness.

"Tomorrow I'm taking Varney in so Marty can identify him for sure; then we're going to the sheriff."

Tish was silent now. She turned her head and looked out the window and Cole, regarding her profile, thought she had never looked more beautiful or desirable.

"Poor lonesome Varney," Tish said softly. She turned her head to look at Cole. "How he'll hate you when you tell him this."

Cole only nodded, aware that Tish was studying him.

"You're not doing so badly in the black-sheep department yourself," she said then, gesturing to the copy of the *Times* on the desk top. "Is Red Macandy lying about you this morning?"

Cole told her of the brawl in Hardy's office and the search for Albie Wright that started it. He told her of his absolute conviction that Varney had been framed and that

Albie Wright could confirm this if he would. He also told of his fruitless effort to get Albie to talk earlier this morning, and Tish listened so carefully that she was leaning toward Cole as he finished.

"I know where this is pointing, Cole. Maybe it's true Albie was paid. Maybe some lunatic planned to put the blame for Brandell's murder on Varney. But if you find him are you going to say that Dad and Bowie and Fred Brinkerhoff and the Stevens brothers and Asa Forbes knew of it and supplied the money? Does Hal believe they did?"

"Hal doesn't. I don't. But the man has to be found, Tish."

Tish shrugged. "Find him then. But it's too late, Cole. Hal's licked already."

"You think he should quit?"

Tish sighed. "I would in his place. Today's paper makes his election impossible. If Macandy hears Varney was in a sporting house it'll be even worse. Hal's too good a man to be crucified by Red Macandy."

"He'll stick. Do you know why?"

When Tish said she didn't, Cole rose, asking, "Did you read all the paper this morning, Tish?"

"Just about you and Varney."

Cole came over beside her and spread out the paper and pointed to the inch of type at the bottom of the page. Tish read it and then looked up at him.

"It's not much, is it?" she said.

"No names of the dead. No account of the cave-in. No reasons given for it. Just nine nameless miners had hard luck doing dangerous work."

Tish rose. "We're back to Dad again."

"No. I'm only telling you why Hal will run for re-election."

Tish walked slowly over to the door. "Go away, Cole. I'm not mad. I'm just more confused than when we talked about it before. I'm tired of talking and I'm tired of thinking. My loyalties keep getting in the way of everything. Please go away."

Cole moved over to the sofa and put on his sheepskin. He passed her as she stood by the door, touched her arm gently and went on through the house and out the back door.

17

That same morning Bowie Sanson was up and shaving in the bathroom when he heard the knock on the door of the suite's living room. He called, "Come in," knowing it was the waitress with his breakfast. As he finished, he heard the girl moving about and then she called, "Get it while it's hot, Mr. Sanson."

"Right now. Thanks, Eileen."

He shrugged into his bathrobe and went through the bedroom into the living room. Eileen had moved the lamp from the table between the two front windows and pulled it across a window where he could look at the town as he breakfasted. His usual breakfast was neatly laid out, the *Times* folded beside his coffee cup.

Bowie sat down, deciding to eat his cold stewed apples last and tackle the eggs and ham first while they were still hot. He took a couple of bites, poured some coffee, drank it, then unfolded the *Times*. Red's biggest type alerted him. Announcement of the governor's ordering of a search for Varney Wynn was expected. It was the story in the second column that drew his attention. Reading the headline he exploded in a laugh of delight. Cole in a saloon brawl? Unbelievable. But there it was and there was Forbes' election in the bag.

He read the story with relish until he came to the mention of Albie Wright and then a sudden chill came to him. It passed immediately, but it left a residue of uneasiness as he finished the story. While he ate, he recalled his dealings with Henry Bohannon and Albie

Wright. Dave Hardy had never mentioned Bowie by name in their introduction. Even if Cole had made Albie talk — and it certainly read as if he hadn't — what could Albie tell him? Only that a man had paid them to get Varney drunk and take him to Junction City. Still, Dave Hardy wouldn't let it get that far. He'd have warned Bohannon and Albie not to answer any questions and pay them besides. He'd probably already done it, since he was an honest man in his way, a careful one, too, a man who once bought stayed bought.

But as he dressed, Bowie came to a decision. He'd better go to Primrose tomorrow — today's train had already left — for several reasons, the first, of course, being to confer with Dave Hardy about the steps taken to silence Henry and Albie. He had to see Asa Forbes on Monday. Then there was the threat of the strike which was apt to follow the cave-in at the Star. Burley had been talked into remaining in Junction City while keeping in touch by telegraph with the Star's superintendent in Primrose. It had not been a satisfactory means of communication yesterday and that condition wouldn't improve. Burley had to have a capable man on the spot, and that man was himself. Then there was the matter of Tish. He'd let that ride long enough. Now, with her father in a spot of trouble and with

Bowie helping him out of it, it might be a good time to press Tish to announce their engagement. If Cole Halsey was any factor in her decision and he wasn't, this story in the *Times* would finish him. All three Halseys were in the deepest kind of trouble; they were discredited thoroughly and this brawl of Cole's would clinch Hal Halsey's defeat.

Yes, he'd have to go to Primrose and he silently cursed the early departure of the Primrose train. He'd missed it today and tomorrow would have to do.

Finished dressing, Bowie put on his overcoat and hat and went out to the street into a chill overcast day. He had a ten o'clock appointment with Burley which was a half hour away, so why didn't he drop in on Red Macandy and congratulate him on today's *Times*, he thought.

Red was alone at his big square desk when Bowie entered. The look of apprehension with which he greeted all callers vanished at the sight of Bowie and the closest thing to a smile he could muster came into his face.

"Red, what a story!" Bowie said immediately. "Congratulations. We didn't need the saloon brawl, but it really nails it down for Asa."

"I was lucky," Red said modestly.

"How'd you get the news so quick?" Bowie

asked, as he came over and half-sat on the edge of Red's desk.

Red pushed his chair back a little. "I got me a smart kid in Primrose. I give him a couple of bucks for the ordinary Primrose stuff, but he gets five bucks for the big ones. I think I'll add another five for this one."

"Anything more about it that you couldn't print?"

"Yeah. It didn't happen in the saloon proper. It happened in Dave Hardy's office. Cole had been asking around for this Albie Wright and when Dave heard about it he sent for Albie. He must have wanted to warn him to watch out for Cole. Cole must have seen Albie because he followed him right into Dave's office. Dave sent Albie out for a couple of Dave's muscle boys. They came and worked Cole over in the office. Anyway, he broke away from them long enough to give Dave one hell of a kick in that fat belly of his. Then the boys finished the job on Cole and pitched him out in the street. After that, they carried Dave home. My kid says he looked hurt real bad according to the men who saw him."

There was nothing alarming here, Bowie thought. Cole probably wasn't in any shape to go after Albie again.

Red went on. "My kid usually mails his

stuff in, but this time he knew he was on to something. He wrote it up and gave it to one of the train crew to bring to me."

"Can you get anything more out of the story?"

"A follow up? Don't need one." Red pointed to the paper on which he'd been writing when Bowie came in. "Front page editorial for tomorrow. I'll head it 'Our State Is Shamed.' I'll say we're a disgrace in the eyes of all the other states and in the country. I'll call on Halsey to resign immediately if he has any honor in him. I'll say there's a movement under way to impeach him if he doesn't."

"Is there?"

"Hell no, but there will be. I'll call for a special session of the legislature." Red frowned and looked sadly at Bowie. "I'm surprised you and Asa haven't thought of that. Hal's wide open for a morals charge."

Bowie said dryly, "I've thought of it. I'd be a hell of a campaign manager if I didn't, but Asa wouldn't hear of it. We're high class."

Red laughed derisively. "That's a luxury no politician can afford." He leaned forward. "Why, hell, Bowie, you aren't electing your man. Halsey's defeating himself, you're not defeating him."

"I happen to agree with you, Red, but that's the way Asa wanted it. Anyway, Halsey's done for, whoever did it."

"Whoever did it?" Red echoed. "Why, you're looking at the man who did it. Me. I printed the things you didn't have the guts to say, and you know it."

"For money," Bowie said dryly.

Red grinned. "Yes, that helped."

Before Joe Perry's messenger and Varney were in sight of Primrose, Varney was talked out. The young man who had fetched Varney from the Goose Creek line camp was wondering if his companion wasn't a little crazy. During the ride through the gray day into a steady wind which blew the words back in a man's throat, Varney had talked unceasingly. Gregarious by nature, Varney had been too many days alone and he had tried to make up for it by talking of horses, women, speculating on the roundup and the weather. The hostler told him of the mine accident and Varney questioned him, shouting into a wind that made half his questions unhearable. In despair the hostler gave up trying to answer but still Varney talked.

Within sight of Primrose, however, Varney fell silent too. He wondered what was ahead for him and why he had been sent for. Two days ago he had been told to hide and now he had been yanked out of hiding with no explanation. It had been at the order of Miss Hammond, the hostler said. Well, Cole had trusted her so he had to trust her, but it was confusing.

As they rode into Primrose, Varney expected to be flagged down by someone he knew and to be told that the sheriff wanted him, but his presence went unremarked. In the street in front of the livery he said goodbye to the hostler and afterward reined in. What was he supposed to do now, he wondered — hunt up Miss Hammond and ask why he had been summoned or should he report to Anse Beckett, the Primrose County sheriff?

As he was considering the choice, Joe Perry appeared in the livery driveway and called, "Cole's at the hotel, Varney."

Varney waved his acknowledgment and put his horse in motion. If Cole was here why had Miss Hammond and not Cole sent for him, he wondered. He left his horse at the Primrose House tie rail, looked in the bar and saw Cole was not there, then he went through to the lobby heading for the desk. Louise Selby was behind it and Varney approached her reluctantly, remembering that she had come home from Junction City in the same car with him. Louise saw him before he reached the desk and she said, "Cole's in room 3, down the hall, Varney." Varney veered off into the corridor and knocked on the door of room 3. A sleepy voice called, "Come in," and Varney entered.

As he did, Cole came to a sitting position on the farthest of the two beds and gave Varney a sleepy wave of greeting with his bandaged hand. At sight of him Varney felt the old resentment and simultaneously the shame for feeling it. Then his attention narrowed and he remarked the bandaged hand, the cut on Cole's cheekbone, which was a twin to his own, and the dark bruise on the shelf of Cole's jaw.

"You've been in a fight," Varney said.

Cole gestured to the desk. "It's all in the paper, Varney. Read it." As Varney crossed the room he shrugged out of his duck jacket and took off his hat, throwing both on the chair before the desk.

As he began to read the *Times* Cole crossed behind him to the washstand and poured some water in the bowl and with his unbandaged hand splashed his face and the back of his neck with water. Afterward, he toweled his face dry and moved over to the dresser. He chose one of the three cigars on its top and lighted it. By that time, Varney was finished reading. He felt a fleeting pleasure that at last Cole was in the kind of trouble usually reserved by the fates for him. He looked at Cole and said, "What would Red Macandy do without us?"

Cole smiled crookedly. "He'd find somebody else because that's the way he is."

Varney moved over to the bed and sat down. "Where are we now, Cole? Am I going to jail, or what?"

Cole seemed to forget the lighted cigar in his hand as he slowly began to circle his room.

"No, you're not going to jail, but I'd better start from where I left you." He told then of his hunt that came for Albie Wright, how he found him and of the brawl and beating in Dave Hardy's office. Varney listened carefully, feeling an obscure pleasure but some puzzlement too.

"This mean anything to you, Varney?" Cole asked abruptly.

"Not much," Varney said. "Why were you after Albie?"

"To find out who paid him to get you drunk."

Varney came alert now. "Did somebody?"

"I'll talk about this later, Varney, but listen now, will you."

Cole told him then of going back to Junction City and of his search of the sporting houses for a girl who could remember Varney. He told of finding Marty at Mrs. Gustafson's who remembered him and had been with him those missing hours that had been unaccounted for. As Varney listened he felt a wild relief that was tinged with shame and anger. His time away from Albie and Henry was accounted for, so he did not kill Abe Brandell. He felt a shame because in his drunken loneliness he had hunted out a whore to comfort him and angry that Cole should have discovered it.

"Remember any of it?" Cole asked.

Varney shook his head no. "Could this Marty be lying for her fifty dollars?"

"She wasn't lying," Cole said quietly and he told Varney how he had questioned the girls in both houses by asking all of them if they had a drunken customer who kept calling himself a bastard. As Varney listened he cringed inwardly and deeper shame flooded through him. At that moment he hated Cole for revealing his weakness and his self-pity.

When Cole finished, Varney was silent. He watched Cole who had suddenly discovered that his cigar had gone out. Cole walked over to the dresser and put the cigar down on the saucer ashtray.

"I reckon she isn't lying," Varney said.

"That twenty dollars you gave her, Varney. Does that mean anything to you?"

Varney shook his head. "What should it mean?"

"You told me out at the line shack you had between twenty and twenty-five dollars with you when you started out on that spree. You gave Marty twenty, leaving you less than five. Know who bought all the booze the first day? Who bought the train tickets? Who bought all the booze the second day and night? Who paid for the room and the food you must have eaten? Not you, because you wound up with two dollars, you said."

"Why, it had to be Henry and Albie."

"Where'd they get the money?" Cole asked slowly. "Henry lived in a stinking boarding-house dormitory. Albie sleeps in a lousy tent where a bed costs twenty-five cents a night. Where'd they get money for your spree?"

"Why, they're miners and miners get wages."

"Then why weren't they mining instead of drinking? If they had to drink, why did they have to go to Junction City to do it?" Cole shook his head. "No, Varney, a miner has to scratch to live on what Burley Hammond and the others pay. He has to scratch every day. He doesn't take four days off and blow his savings on a pick-up friend like you. Can't you see that?"

Varney hadn't thought about it much but now that Cole pointed it out, he could see that it was unlikely that Albie and Henry would have their own money for this dissipation. "You think somebody gave them money to get me drunk, don't you?"

"I'm sure of it," Cole said flatly. "I'm sure they were told to take you to Junction City so you'd be there when Abe Brandell was killed. I think you were framed, Varney. Do you think you were?"

Yes, Varney thought, and with conviction that everything fitted too neatly in place to leave any doubt. "I think you're right, Cole. I think this is aimed at" — he hesitated — "Dad. I've always been a black sheep so it was easy, wasn't it?" There was oddly no bitterness or self-pity in his tone of voice. Varney saw Cole frown, puzzled at their absence.

Cole then said, "Yes, I think it's aimed at Hal, but I can't think that Asa Forbes and the men behind him would ever murder Abe Brandell or have it done."

"Then who did?"

"That," Cole said, "is what I'm trying to find out through Albie. I hunted him down this morning." Cole went on to tell then of his visit to the tent dormitory and now Varney listened as closely as he could, watching Cole's marked face filling with new excitement and new hope.

When Cole was finished he added his own observations of his fruitless meeting with

Albie. "You see, Varney, he wouldn't help me because he likes you. You told him enough about my treatment of you to make him hate me. He hates me more than he loves money."

"Then try Bohannon."

"Albie's all we've got, Varney. Bohannon was killed in the mine accident day before yesterday."

Varney felt a deep regret because he liked the old man who, Varney thought, hadn't liked him much.

"Let me try Albie," Varney said.

Cole smiled. "I was hoping you'd say that, because it just might work, Varney." He gestured toward the paper. "Put that paper in your pocket and after supper hunt Albie up. Read it to him. Tell him you're on the dodge. He doesn't have to know anything about Marty saving your neck. Tell him you're in real deep trouble. Tell him whoever paid him to get you drunk would know who killed Abe Brandell. Tell him they'll hang you, Varney, unless he talks."

"Yes," Varney said softly. "Sure." He looked at Cole then and thought, *Why has he done all this for me?* and then he thought with the old bitterness, *It isn't for me, it's for Dad.*

18

A copy of the *Times* in his coat pocket, Varney went into the Miners Rest around eight that evening. It was jammed with miners, most of them still in their funeral clothes, who, whatever their country of origin, were drinking to erase the memory of death. Varney nodded to a couple of miners who remembered him from the days he had spent here. It surprised him that none of them asked him why he hadn't been arrested until it occurred to him that few of these men could read and all were wholly uninterested in the scrapes Governor Halsey's sons had got into.

Slowly Varney eased his way along the bar through the crowd looking for Albie. He could not help but overhear their talk of the strike at the Star Mine and Mill. He heard Burley Hammond cursed a dozen times along with Evans, his mine superintendent. This talk had been heard often before after a mine accident but it would come to nothing, Varney knew. The miners were ignorant and unorganized and too concerned for their jobs to risk action.

Down toward the end of the bar he saw Albie's back and pushed through the miners' line, four deep at the bar. Reaching over a miner's shoulder, he touched Albie. Albie turned and when he saw Varney, he smiled. Because of the uproar in the place, it was useless to try to talk, so Varney beckoned to him and then elbowed his way out of the crowd. It was a minute before Albie appeared and then he came with a mug of beer in each hand. Varney noted the haggard look in Albie's face and saw too that he had a dirty piece of flannel wrapped around his throat. He was still wearing that hat Varney had traded him, he noticed.

Varney led the way past a poker game to the far corner table where it was quieter, and they sat down.

"You look like hell," Varney said, when they were seated. "You sick, Albie?"

"Yeah. I feel like it, too," Albie said hoarsely. "I ain't really over that drunk yet."

They both took a swallow of beer, then Albie said, "Saw that damn brother of yours this morning and we damn near had a fight. He tell you about the beating he got?"

Varney nodded. "I wish I'd seen it."

Albie laughed, but his laugh turned into a paroxysm of coughing. Afterward he took another swallow of beer and said, "What've you been up to, Varney?"

"You haven't heard?"

"Nothing about you."

Varney pulled the copy of the *Times* from his jacket pocket, unfolded it and laid it before Albie, who said, "Hell, I can't read. What does it say?"

Varney turned the paper toward him and read the headline aloud, afterward looking at Albie.

"My God!" Albie exploded. "Your old man's as bad as your brother!"

Slowly, Varney read the entire story in which Red Macandy reviewed the reasons for the governor issuing his order to bring Varney in.

Albie listened with growing amazement and when Varney finished, Albie said, "That's really in the paper? About us getting drunk?"

Varney nodded. "And maybe me killing Abe Brandell."

"You never! Did you?"

"I don't think I did," Varney said. "But I can't be sure, Albie. I was so drunk I don't even remember being in Junction City."

"I can't remember much either, but I bet you never." A look of puzzlement came into Albie's face. "If they're looking for you, why ain't you in jail now?"

"I will be," Varney said glumly. "But I had

to see you first."

"To tell me to say you was with me all the time? Hell, I'll say that."

"Thanks, but they'd never believe you," Varney said. "No, that's not why I had to see you, Albie. I know I didn't kill Abe Brandell, but to prove it I got to find who did."

"I'll help you," Albie said hoarsely. "But where do we start looking?"

"You can help me without looking if you will."

Albie looked baffled. "How's that?"

"Tell me who paid you to get me drunk, Albie." Varney leaned forward now. "I *got* to know, Albie. I *got* to or I'll hang."

Albie leaned back in his chair and his glance slid away from Varney to his beer. He was frowning and Varney couldn't tell whether it was from the effort to remember or if he were framing a refusal.

"Why was I in Junction City on that certain night, Albie? I can't remember whose idea it was to go there, but I don't think it was mine. I think it was Henry's or yours."

Albie stared into his beer as if hypnotized.

"Dammit, Albie," Varney begged. "You've got to tell me. If you were paid to take me to Junction City that day, it ties up with Brandell's killer. Can't you see that?"

"Yeah. I can see it," Albie said, very slowly.

285

Varney continued. "All that time I didn't spend any money, Albie. You and Henry paid for everything. You don't have that kind of money, neither of you. Do you?"

Albie sighed deeply and then raised his glance to Varney. "We was paid, all right, but we never knew why. We was given money and all we could drink if we'd get you drunk and keep you drunk and take you to Junction City the day we did, Monday."

"Who paid you, Albie? Please tell me," Varney begged.

Albie shook his head. "I don't know and that's the truth, Varney. I don't know his name. Dave Hardy called Henry and me to his office two days before. There was this man there, too. He made us the proposition and we took it. We was to go out and see you claiming we was both bastards and felt sorry for you. We was to bring you in town, get you liquored up and keep you here a day so's people would know you was drunk. Then we was to take you into Junction City the next day. We was to bring you home the day after and stay drunk as long as we wanted."

"What did he look like?"

"Thirty maybe. Kind of heavy-set. Blue eyes. Wearing clothes like yours. Maybe a rancher, I don't know. I never seen him before."

"Was Dave Hardy there?"

At Albie's nod, Varney said, "Then he heard him. He'll know, won't he?"

"He will if he lives," Albie said. "Your brother kicked him in the belly and from what I hear, he's damn near dead. That woman of his opens the door with a gun, they tell me, and she's mean enough to shoot you."

Albie, facing the door, had been looking at Varney but now his glance lifted beyond Varney. "Here it is, Varney," he said softly.

Varney was momentarily puzzled, but he turned his head in the direction of Albie's glance. A tall man wearing a jumper jacket, cowman's boots, and shell belt was coming toward them. He was also wearing a star. He came up to the table, halted and said pleasantly enough, "Hi, Varney."

"Hello, Anse. I wondered if I'd have to walk into your jailhouse before you saw me."

The middle-aged sheriff, a lean man who looked weather-beaten in spite of his sedentary job, smiled. "Cole told me you were around town." Anse Beckett looked at Varney. "I don't like it much your being here, Varney. I'd like to send you off to Hal stone cold sober."

"You going to lock me up, Anse?"

"Nothing like that," the sheriff said. "I'm going to take you up to the hotel where Cole

287

can keep an eye on you."

Varney laughed and rose. He looked at Albie, winked and said, "Thanks, friend."

The ride to the hotel with the sheriff was embarrassing to them both. Anse Beckett was Hal's old friend and Varney knew the sheriff would prefer to kick him all the way to the hotel instead of ride with him. But Varney didn't care. He was turning over in his mind the information Albie had given him. What it came down to was that Dave Hardy had the key information. How could he get it from a sick man whose woman was more than glad to shoot at you?

At the livery stable the sheriff waited for Varney to turn in his horse and then Varney walked back to Primrose House, the sheriff on his horse paralleling his course. Beckett was taking no chances of losing him until he was in safe harbor, Varney thought wryly.

Varney climbed the steps of the Primrose House veranda and then he turned and waved to Beckett who waved back and rode on. Varney saw by the light of the lamps on either side of the lobby entrance burning dimly that the long row of barrel chairs stretching down the veranda were empty. Almost as if he had planned this, which he hadn't, Varney turned and walked way down the veranda and slacked into one of the chairs. The day's wind had died down and the night held a crispness that Varney didn't even notice.

He was not ready to face Cole yet, he knew, because there were many things he had to sort out and put in order. To begin with he felt inordinately proud of what he had done tonight. He had got the information from Albie that was so necessary, so he had succeeded where Cole had failed. If now he gave Cole Albie's information Cole would take over, just as he took over everything else in Varney's life. Cole had bailed him out of his drunk, found Marty and tracked down Albie, hidden him and had put together all the clues which added up to a frame up, only had tried and failed to get Albie to talk. Cole had allowed him to do nothing to save his own hide except this tonight.

It was strange but true, Varney thought sourly, that when he was just plain Varney Wynn, before he was the governor's bastard son, he had made out all right on his own. He had done the work assigned him, had his own girl, drank when he had the chance and stayed out of any bad trouble. It was only when he became the governor's son that Cole really put the ring in his nose. Since then he had been led, ordered, threatened, and forced, but now he had information upon which he and he alone could act. After all, he was the one who'd been framed. What kind of man would he be if he let his big brother fight this, his most important battle, for him?

The decision made, Varney began to speculate on how to reach Dave Hardy. Should he try him tonight? Caution said no. To find out where Hardy lived he would have to go back to the Miners Rest. If Anse Beckett found him, he'd jail him for sure, but even if he succeeded in finding Hardy's house on the other side of the tracks, this was the wrong hour to try and persuade Hardy's woman to let him talk to Dave. Tomorrow he and Cole would be going to Junction City. Cole, of course, would dog him every minute until he had been cleared by Sheriff Morehead. After that, he was free to work alone. Of course, Dave Hardy might die while he was in Junction City but if he was that close to death, he probably wouldn't even be able to talk tonight. Well, Hardy's death was a chance he had to gamble on.

His decisions made, Varney rose, walked through the empty lobby, heading for their room. The sound of men's voices in the bar sounded pleasant, tempting him, but then he remembered that Alec might refuse to serve him and would tell Cole he'd been in.

He went on down the corridor and opened the door of their room. The table between the beds held a lamp turned low and by its soft light Varney could see Cole sleeping in the bed closest the window. He closed the door gently but not gently enough. Cole stirred, sat up, saw him and turned up the light. With a kind of shock, Varney regarded Cole's upper body. It was a mass of multicolored bruises, each blending into the other across his chest and down his shoulders and his arms.

"Find him?" Cole asked.

Varney remembered then to look discouraged. "I found him. Nothing."

"Not even a hint?"

Varney took off his hat, shook his head and climbed out of his coat, talking. "He's got some damn notion in his head that makes him mule stubborn." Now he looked at Cole. "You know what I think? I think Albie's going back to whoever paid him and ask for more money to keep his mouth shut."

"I was afraid that would be it," Cole said in a discouraged voice. "Was he afraid?"

"Sure, but I'm not through with him yet, Cole. You stay clear and let me talk to him some more."

"All right." Cole lay down and stared at the ceiling while Varney undressed and climbed into the other bed. He was reaching up to put his palm above the lamp chimney, preparing to blow into it to douse the lamp when Cole said sleepily, "Another day, and not even a dollar."

"You wait," Varney said, and thought, *You'll do the waiting, I'll do the moving now.*

19

Bowie Sanson came off the Sunday train at Primrose and headed directly for the Miners Rest across the street. As usual at this hour it was almost empty and Bowie took it to be a sign that the miners had returned to work.

In the near-empty saloon he inquired after Dave Hardy's condition and was told that Dave was still a mighty sick man. Bowie asked where he lived and was given directions.

Leaving the Miners Rest he walked down River Street in the gray chill day. He was wearing a Stetson, cowman's boots, and a leather jacket he'd always affected on his visits to Primrose.

At the corner of Grant and River Streets he turned left on Grant and within a block he was among the small houses and seedy rooming houses that he had seldom noticed before. Why, he wondered, did Dave Hardy choose to live in this shabby section of town when he was the sole owner of a prosperous saloon. Then he remembered Dave's woman. Rumor had it that Dave was living with her without benefit of marriage, a condition that was easily accepted this side of the river but roundly denounced on the other side.

Two blocks down petering-out Grant Street he turned right and saw the newly painted white house with its yard that the bartender told him to look for.

Bowie mounted the steps, crossed the porch and knocked on the glass-paneled door.

He waited several moments and knocked again, this time more loudly. He heard movement inside now and the door opened a crack. A woman's rough voice with seemingly no source said, "Go away. There's a sick man in here."

"Mrs. Hardy, I'm Bowie Sanson, an old friend of Dave's. Is he conscious?"

There was hesitation before the voice said, "Barely."

"Then he'll want to see me, Mrs. Hardy. It's very important or I wouldn't be here."

"I'll see," the voice said, and the door closed. Bowie turned his back to the door and wondered what he would tell the woman if she refused him entry. He hoped his name meant something to her but he supposed it didn't.

He heard the door open and turned and saw

framed in the doorway a full-figured woman whom he guessed would be in her late thirties. Her hair was a brassy red, unmistakably dyed. Her face had once been pretty but was now too full and it was marred by gray eyes set too close together. She was wearing an outing-flannel wrapper to whose collar and cuffs she had sewn masses of lace. Her uncorseted figure was fulsome and Bowie would have bet that this wrapper was her uniform save when she was on the street.

"He'll see you but you mustn't be long."

Bowie took off his hat. "Thank you."

She turned, said, "Follow me," and Bowie tramped through the small living room whose principal feature was a large horsehair sofa containing a scattering of garishly covered pillows. A coal fire was burning in the big-bellied stove in the corner, making the room oppressively hot. The woman led the way down a narrow corridor opening off the far wall of the room, then turned into the first room on her right and was momentarily lost to sight.

When Bowie entered the room he saw that it held two beds and in the far one lay the massive bulk of Dave Hardy.

Bowie walked slowly past the first bed and into the space between them where he halted and held out his hand. "Dave, I'm sorry to hear you're stove up. How are you, really?"

Dave raised his flabby hand and weakly shook Bowie's. "Not too good, Bowie. I hurt awful."

The woman was watching Bowie with a curiosity she did not bother to hide. "Sit on the bed," she said then. Bowie sank down on the bed and glanced at the woman. "Could we be alone?" he asked.

"No," she said promptly. "What he knows, I know, and what I know, he knows. Ask him."

Bowie glanced at Dave. "Everything?"

"Everything," Dave said.

Bowie looked at her with a closer appraisal. A lot of men, of which he would never be a member, consulted their women on investments, land values and such, but Dave Hardy's business was one of which a woman could have little or no knowledge. True, he was a political force and maybe he had sought her advice there but much of his work was secret, sometimes rough and usually dirty. But Dave had said everything and Bowie had to believe he meant it.

Now he turned to Dave and said, "I read about the brawl in today's paper. Macandy said Cole was after Albie Wright. Was he?" Dave nodded. "Did you talk with Albie?"

"Cole came in too quick. I didn't have a chance, Bowie."

"But did you talk with him afterward? Did you get word to him to get out of town?"

"I was too sick. My God, I was sick!"

"This Albie Wright then, where do I find him and where do I find Henry Bohannon?"

"Bohannon's dead. Killed in that Star cave-in. Albie just drifts around. He's in my place a lot of the time. He sleeps around in them bed tents. Lately it's been that one out by the main tailings."

Bowie rose. "I'll find him then. I think it's time to sweeten him up."

"Move him out of here, Bowie."

"Maybe I'll do both. I don't want to tire you any more, Dave, so I'll leave. Anything I can do? Anything you want?"

"Rose's taking care of me fine, Bowie. Thanks."

"I'll be back when you feel better, Dave."

Rose led the way out of the bedroom and into the living room and put her hand on the doorknob.

"He's had a doctor, hasn't he?"

"Twice a day."

"What do they think's the matter with him?"

"They don't know for sure. A ruptured spleen maybe."

"Nonsense! He'd be dead, by now, wouldn't he, if that were true."

"I only know what they tell me," Rose said, in a voice that sounded as if she held small hope.

Bowie patted her heavy arm and said, "Take good care of him. I know you will. He's too good a man to lose."

She nodded grimly and let him out, as he tipped his hat and said good-bye.

As he walked back toward the business district, he assessed what Dave Hardy had told him about Albie. It was not good, not any of it. Dave had tried and failed to warn Albie and had not followed it up. True, he could have been in too much pain to think of it but, nevertheless, Albie Wright was wandering around with information that had to be concealed, the importance of which he was ignorant. Now Bowie thought back to that first meeting with Albie and Henry. He had asked Dave not to mention his name and Dave hadn't, but Albie would recognize him, surely. He had to get to Albie as soon as possible with money to buy his silence. Bowie wondered then if Cole had been in touch with Albie. Varney was in hiding and could not have been in touch with Albie and Bowie doubted that Cole was in any shape to hunt Albie down. Nevertheless, he couldn't take a chance.

On his way back to the depot to see if there was a hack still hanging around, he decided that this evening, under cover of darkness, he must find Albie Wright. At the depot he was in luck for he found a hack unloading early arrivals for the train that would depart for Junction City in another half hour. He got his bag from the waiting room, stepped into the hack and directed the driver to Burley Hammond's place, where he was passed by the guards and was deposited on the front steps.

Lizzie answered his ring and stood aside for him, saying, "We got your telegram, Mr. Bowie. Miss Tish's in church, but she said to make yourself at home. I'll take your bag up to your room."

Bowie handed her his bag and said, "I'm surprised Mr. Hammond let her go to church."

"Nothing bad can happen to you when you're in church, Mr. Bowie."

Bowie was about to ask her if she had ever heard of Saint Thomas à Becket but knew that would be lost on her. He strolled into the living room, looked at the fragile chairs, then, like all the Hammonds, went on into the library.

He had barely time to light up a cigar before he heard the Hammond carriage deposit Tish at the front door. She came immediately into the library and Bowie rose to meet her. He put a hand on each of her upper arms and kissed her on the cheek before she had time to take off her coat or remove her hat.

"Heavens! I haven't been to Europe, Bowie," she said. "Why this sudden affection?"

"Because you look like you need it, Tish." He helped her off with her coat and silently admired her long sweep of dress, whose color closely approximated that of her auburn hair.

"Well, I guess I did," Tish said. "This has been an awful week, Bowie. Everything about it's been awful." She smiled crookedly at him. "Dad's not here. Why don't we have a glass of sherry?"

Bowie nodded and went over to the tall glass-end bookshelf, whose lower desk level shelf served as a liquor cabinet. Bowie took out the decanter and two glasses, poured the sherry into them and carried them to the easy chair where Tish had seated herself. He gave her one, then rounded the desk. Before he sat down he lifted his glass. "To us, Tish."

Tish smiled and lifted her glass, then sipped her sherry. Bowie took a drink and then sat down.

"Have you ever thought, Tish that you don't have to go through this alone?"

Tish said tiredly, "Everybody goes through everything alone."

Bowie shook his head emphatically. "If we

were married, Tish, all your troubles would be on my shoulders. Even if we were only engaged, they would be."

"No, Bowie. That's one of the troubles too."

"Easily lifted. Just say we're engaged now to be married in two months."

Tish shook her head gently. "But I don't know all of you, Bowie — how you always think, how you like children and how many you'd like us to have." She paused. "Come to think of it I've never seen you speak to a child."

"I can't very well carry one around with me to speak to," Bowie said defensively.

"But we're always talking about unimportant things like your law cases or politics or how Judge so-and-so favors this approach and how the Star would make more money with some kind of new concentration method. We never talk about people except how they can be influenced our way. The little things about you I've got to learn, and I can't. I really can't separate you from my father because you think and talk and act alike."

"That's the nicest compliment you could pay me, Tish. The little things, as you call them, are what all of us learn in marriage. If you waited to learn everything about me we'd be married when I'm eighty." He paused, wondering if this was the time to push, and decided it was. "I won't wait that long, Tish. In fact, I won't wait very much longer."

Tish considered this and Bowie watched her. A fleeting pain seemed to cross her face and vanish. "I'm afraid you'll have to, Bowie."

This was the time to really push, Bowie thought, and he said carefully, "Then I'll consider myself free, Tish."

"You always have been."

"No, not in my own mind. I want to marry you, Tish. You are the one I love and I always will. But a lot of men have had to settle for less, and maybe I'm one of them."

"Are you trying to tell me that if I won't marry you you'll start looking around?" Tish asked, incredulity in her tone of voice.

Bowie hesitated, then said quietly, "I'll have to, won't I?"

"Bowie!" Tish cried. She rose and rounded the desk and flung her arms about him and kissed his cheek. "Look around, Bowie! Find the nicest girl in the world — nicer than me! Oh, Bowie, you're free now! So am I! Don't you see?"

Bowie sat appalled. Her words and their meaning registered, but he could not believe them. She had taken him at his word, when he only meant to mildly threaten her.

Now she broke away and did a pirouette of joy as he watched her balefully. Halting, she came back to him, her smile holding a heart-breaking happiness.

"Bowie, I could never have loved you the way a wife must love her husband! It's not that I couldn't love you for all the fine things you are. It's that I couldn't love you for the things you're not! Oh, Bowie, find a girl who really loves you. If she does, you'll love her and marry her."

"What are the things I'm not?" Bowie asked angrily.

"It doesn't matter, Bowie," Tish said gently. "You won't change, and I wouldn't have wanted to change you. You're fine as you are."

"But not fine enough for you?"

"No. Different is the word. I've said it, Bowie, and I won't take any of it back. Go find your nice girl and forget me."

There was a knock on the door and Lizzie stuck her head in. "If you folks are ready, Miss Tish, dinner is too."

Bowie sat stunned, the taste of ashes instead of sherry in his mouth. He rose, as if in a dream, and followed Tish into the dining room and seated her.

Tish talked endlessly during the meal while Bowie only half-listened, speaking only when he had to. He was cudgeling his brain for some way to retrieve his error, but in his heart he knew there was no way. Her very gaiety and sudden high spirits told him she was wildly happy to be honorably rid of him. Hadn't she said, "I won't take back any of it"? He could propose daily and she would always reply that it was settled, that they were both free.

Tish said something to him which he hadn't heard and Bowie said, "I beg your pardon?"

"I asked if Dad reads all the telegrams that go out over the wire? Does he have a copy sent to him?"

Bowie's flush was uncontrolled. "Oh, come now, Tish. He's got more to do than that."

"Maybe he doesn't read them. Does he have copies sent to him?"

Bowie answered reluctantly. "Why, it's his line. I suppose he gets a copy of very important messages, some bit of news that might affect his financial interests and various things." He frowned. "Why d'you ask?"

"Cole says he does read the messages, especially the Halseys'."

"When did he say that?"

"Why, just yesterday."

"Is Cole here now?" Bowie asked, trying to keep the apprehension he felt from his voice.

"No. He and Varney took the train into Junction City today."

"Varney's surrendered?"

"Yes. Cole called him out of hiding and they're going in to see the sheriff."

"You mean Cole's able to get around?"

"Oh yes," Tish said. "He even went to Junction City the day after the fight."

If Cole was able to travel, he would have been able to search for Albie Wright, Bowie thought, and on the heels of that thought came another that was comforting — if Albie had told Cole who paid him, Cole's first act would have been to hunt Bowie down. Still, Cole and Varney were on their way to Junction City, weren't they, maybe to search for him? Bowie suddenly lost all appetite.

He said with an air of casualness that was hard for him to muster, "The paper said Cole was hunting for Albie something or other to beat him up. Is that true?"

"Yes," Tish said carelessly. "Cole's got some notion that somebody paid Albie Wright to get Varney drunk and take him to Junction City. He found Albie, but Albie denied he was paid."

I'm in time, then, Bowie thought exultantly.

"That's a silly business," Bowie said. "Varney's got drunk on his own before and he will again."

He saw Tish open her mouth to speak and then close it.

"You were going to say something. Don't you agree?"

"I was going to say I don't know Varney well enough to have an opinion."

That wasn't what she was going to say, Bowie felt, and he wondered briefly what she was hiding. He said resentfully, "Cole seems to have confided in you, Tish. I'd think after that disgusting brawl he got in, you wouldn't want anything to do with him."

Tish looked up quickly. "What's disgusting about trying to find the name of the man who paid Albie? That man would know who killed Abe Brandell."

Bowie put down his fork. "Does Cole believe that?"

"Of course. So do I."

Bowie asked curiously, "But why should he confide that to you?" He saw the flush come into Tish's face and he persisted, "Are you special friends?"

"We always have been. You know that."

"Is he the reason you stayed on here this week instead of coming back to your family?"

Tish said angrily, "You have no right to ask that, Bowie."

"I know I haven't, but I did. Is he?"

"Yes," Tish said defiantly.

"You love him." It was not a question, but a statement.

"All right, I do!"

They were silent a moment, Bowie staring at her angrily and Tish's eyes reflecting an anger equal to his. "How long has this been going on?" Bowie asked then.

"Ever since I can remember, only I didn't know it."

"Are you going to marry him, Tish?"

"If he asks me again, but I don't think he will."

No wonder she had called his bluff so quickly back there in the library, Bowie thought. This put the final, irrevocable seal on their break. What had happened this week between Cole and Tish to change her mind? He didn't know and he shouldn't care. Then his native shrewdness told him that he must go carefully. His whole career was riding on his close friendship with the Hammonds and it would be insanely dangerous to quarrel with Tish. What he should do was acknowledge his defeat with grace.

He nodded now and smiled sadly. "He will, and you'll marry him. May I be godfather to your first child, Tish?"

"If this fairy tale comes true, you may, Bowie."

Again it was Lizzie who interrupted their conversation as she brought in the dessert.

After dinner Bowie told Tish that he had to

spend the afternoon with Pete Evans, the Star's superintendent. He would very likely have supper with Pete, so Tish should not count on him joining her for the evening meal. Afterward, he went up to his usual room and found that Lizzie had unpacked his bag. The small-caliber pistol which he had brought along for protection in case trouble-seeking miners identified him as a company man lay on the dresser top. Bowie slipped it in his jacket pocket, went downstairs and left the house.

He spent the next four hours at Pete Evans' place discussing the probability of the miners striking, the advisability of doing more timbering in the unsafe areas and a raise in the miners' wages. This would be compensated for by increasing the length of the shifts. It was dark when he rose to go and Mrs. Evans, a buxom and kindly looking woman, came into the parlor and asked him to stay for supper.

"I promised Tish I'd be back for supper, Mrs. Evans. Thanks," Bowie said, then on the spur of the moment, "You know, when I come to Primrose you people are always wining and dining me. I have an idea. Why don't you and Pete meet me at the Primrose House tomorrow noon. I'll have Asa Forbes and Tish with me. I'll tell Louise to get up something special for us."

They agreed with pleasure and Bowie went out.

When he reached Grant Street he turned down it toward the bridge, wondering how he was going to find Albie Wright. He thought it unlikely that anyone would be sleeping at this hour, but he nevertheless decided to try the bed tent first. In the darkness he had a hard time finding it but the flare finally attracted him and identified it. Halting outside the circle of light cast by the flare, he examined the long canvas length of the tent or as much of it as he could see, and was appalled at the shabbiness of it and the seedy neglect of the ground around it. While he was wondering how this business was operated, a drunken miner moved past him and went through the tent flap, first reaching in his pocket for a coin which he tossed on a table, only the corner of which Bowie could see. A hand picked up the coin and the miner vanished into the dark interior. Should he go up and ask for Albie Wright? Bowie wondered. He decided against it for whoever was taking the cash at the table might remember that a man too well and differently dressed to be a miner had inquired after Albie Wright.

Well, what should he do? He could not stand here the whole evening, waiting for Albie Wright to appear. That left the Miners Rest, into which he dare not go for fear of being seen searching for Albie or, if he found him talking with him.

He hadn't decided what to do as he approached the Miners Rest on the boardwalk. Ahead of him he saw a man standing on tiptoe and peeking over the painted part of the window to see inside the saloon. Bowie halted and waited till the man found who he was looking for and went inside. Bowie moved up to the window and looked over the milling men inside. In deference to the mine owners, the Primrose Council had long since passed an ordinance that ordered the saloons to close at eight o'clock on Sundays. This was to ensure that the miners would be reasonably sober on the Monday morning shift. The result was that the miners simply began drinking earlier, which was what they were doing now.

Bowie could not hope to pick out Albie from that jam of men. He did note, however, that there was a back entrance to the saloon and that fact gave Bowie an idea. He retraced his steps to the corner and walked down to the alley that ran behind the Miners Rest. It was pitch black here and the only light that showed was an occasional glint when the back door of the saloon was opened.

Bowie moved down the alley and halted by the door and set himself to wait. A couple of men came out, turned his way and passed within a foot of him without seeing him. Bowie settled himself against the wall, waiting, and was soon rewarded by a man who turned in the alley from the street and headed up it. He passed Bowie and was reaching to open the door when Bowie spoke.

"Do you know Albie Wright, my friend?"

He was answered in German and the man went inside. Two men came down the alley soon after, but Bowie was looking for a loner. They passed him, not seeing him, and went in. At last, a lone man entered the alley, passed Bowie and was reaching for the door when Bowie asked the same question.

"I know him," the man said.

"Send him out here, will you? I'm supposed to take him to Dave Hardy's place."

"Why don't you go in and find him?"

"Hell, I don't know him," Bowie said.

"All right."

The man went in and Bowie settled himself for a long wait. However, he was pleasantly surprised for within a minute the lanky frame of Albie Wright stepped out into the night.

"I'm right here, Albie," Bowie said pleasantly. "Let's go."

"What's he want with me?" Albie asked suspiciously.

"He wants to give you money," Bowie said.

"Who are you? I can't see a damn thing."

"You wouldn't know me," Bowie said easily. "Let's get going."

He stepped up to Albie and together they tramped up the alley toward Grant Street. Bowie knew that when they reached it there would be enough light for Albie to identify him. He put out an arm now and halted Albie.

"I've got the money here. Might as well give it to you now and save myself the walk. Hold out your hand."

Albie did and Bowie felt around for it, found it and put in Albie's palm two double eagles.

"What's it for?" Albie asked.

"For keeping your mouth shut."

"About what?"

"About getting Varney Wynn drunk."

There was a long silence and then Albie said, "I know your voice. Who are you?"

"It doesn't matter."

"I reckon it don't at that," Albie said. Bowie, perhaps his sense of hearing heightened by the darkness, thought he detected a faint anger in the timbre of Albie's voice and his hand dropped into his jacket pocket. A second later he felt Albie's arms thrown about him. Suddenly, almost in his ear, Albie shouted, "Help! Help!"

For the briefest of moments Bowie was sorry this had to happen and then he lifted his massive arms quickly and easily broke Albie's grip. Swiftly, he jammed with the gun into Albie's belly, tilted it up toward his heart in the same movement and pulled the trigger. The breath blasted from Albie's lungs in a gagging groan and Albie fell away from him and Bowie heard the thud as his body hit the ground. The sound of the shot, Bowie knew, had been muffled by the closeness of the gun to Albie and by his clothes. Now Bowie looked up and down the alley, saw no one, then knelt and reached in Albie's right pocket. Then he stayed his hand and straightened up. If the money were not stolen by the first man who found him, it would serve to bury him, Bowie thought.

20

When Cole and Varney reached Junction City that same Sunday Bowie left it, they went immediately to the hack stand at the end of the platform and climbed in.

"You know Mrs. Gustafson's house on Water Street?" Cole asked.

The driver nodded. "You're too early."

"Drive there anyway, will you?"

They angled away from Main Street toward the poorer section of town. The day was gray with the promise of snow just as it had been in Primrose and Cole wondered if they would wind up the roundup in an early blizzard. Somehow the roundup seemed a year in time and a continent in space away. He had spent more time on trains this last week than he had normally spent in six months.

Cole glanced at Varney now and wondered why he seemed so subdued today. He supposed he was trying to hide the disappointment he felt at his inability to get information from Albie Wright last night. Well, he was one of that vast brotherhood of men who did not take defeat lightly, Cole thought grimly. He had not told Varney all of what was coming this afternoon, and Cole knew he wouldn't like any of it.

The driver pulled up at the plank walk in front of Mrs. Gustafson's unpainted house. Cole said to him, "You wait for us, we won't be long." Then he looked at Varney. "Better come along, Varney."

The two of them ascended the steps. Cole knocked on the door. It was answered by Mrs. Gustafson who with her spectacles, her sober dark-blue dress, looked more like a schoolteacher than ever.

"Afternoon, Mrs. Gustafson," Cole said,

touching his hat. "I think Marty is expecting us."

"She is," Mrs. Gustafson said pleasantly. "Come in."

Cole led the way into the prim clean room. There was a fire in the pot-bellied stove at the side of the big front window and the crackling of its burning wood almost drowned out Mrs. Gustafson's words as she said. "Sit down, I'll get her."

She disappeared up the stairs and Cole moved over to the sofa. Varney stood looking about him, examining the room.

"Remember any of it?"

Varney sighed and shook his head and then they both looked at the stairwell as they heard footsteps descending. They saw first the high shoes, then the skirt of a green dress and then Marty stepped into the room. She looked, Cole thought, as demure as any girl at an ice-cream social.

"Hello," Marty said. She looked from Cole to Varney and then she smiled, "Hello, Baby." She took a few steps forward past Cole and halted before Varney who was blushing furiously. Then she turned to Cole. "That's my seventy-dollar boy and no mistake. What's his name and what's yours? Remember, you promised."

"Later, Marty," Cole said. "That's a pretty dress."

"I'm glad you like it. It's your money."

"We've got a hack waiting outside, Marty. You'll need a coat."

"We got time for a drink?" Marty asked.

"You take one," Cole said mildly. "Varney, have one with her. I think it'll help."

Varney nodded and joined Marty at the sideboard. She poured out a stiff three fingers of whiskey into each of the two glasses, handed Varney his, saluted him and tossed off her drink. Her pale and shining hair was done on top of her head, somehow adding a kind of beauty to her almost plain face.

She put down her glass, gave Varney a friendly pat on the arm, and disappeared behind the big red curtain.

"Remember her?" Cole asked.

Again Varney shook his head. "God, I wish you wouldn't ask me that any more," he said, almost angrily.

"That'll be the last time," Cole said.

Varney tossed off his drink and had barely set his glass down when Marty came into the room. She was wearing a black coat with a fur collar and a black hat with white feathers on it. "Well, out into the winter day. Where are we going?"

Cole smiled faintly. "Like I told you, Marty. To see two men." He crossed to the door and held it open while Varney followed

her out. She climbed into the carriage un-
assisted and Varney took the seat beside the
driver.

Cole climbed in beside Marty. "The State
House, driver," Cole said.

Instantly, Varney turned to look at him just
as swiftly as Marty looked at him. "What the
hell is this?" Varney said.

"I thought we'd sightsee a little," Cole said.
"It's Sunday."

"Honey, you picked a real day for it,"
Marty said tartly. "If you've got time to kill,
we could kill it back in the house."

The driver put the team in motion and they
headed toward the business district and the
big capitol building on the hill beyond.

"You going to throw in a boat ride too,
honey?" Marty teased. "It's a great day for it."

"Easy, Marty," Cole said. "I've got reasons
for all this."

"Name one," Marty said.

"You'll see."

When they rounded half the big graveled
drive and were alongside the steps, Cole said,
"Stop, driver."

Marty looked quickly at him. "Here?"

Cole stepped out and held out his hand.
Puzzled and mute, Marty let him hand her
out of the hack. Varney climbed down.

Cole said to the driver, "Wait here for us,

will you? Better tie your team and come inside where it's warm."

"My time's worth something, mister."

"You'll be paid for it." Cole turned now, put his hand under Marty's elbow and the three of them, with Varney on the other side, climbed the steps, entered the seemingly empty building and turned left.

"Where we going?" Marty demanded anxiously.

"We're almost there."

As they passed the door to the reception room, Marty halted. On its frosted glass was painted in gold leaf, *OFFICE OF THE GOVERNOR.*

"Oh, no," Marty breathed.

"No, it's the next door, Marty, not that one."

This little deceit seemed to satisfy Marty and Cole moved her on, then palmed open the next door, holding Marty's arm. As they walked into the big room Sheriff Sam Morehead, sitting in the easy chair, came to his feet and so did Governor Halsey who had been seated behind the desk.

Cole felt Marty's arm go rigid as she gave him an imploring look. Cole smiled and gently pushed her forward. By now she knew she had been tricked and she was scared. Cole halted her before the desk and said, "Marty, may I present Sheriff Morehead and Governor Halsey."

"Oh God," Marty moaned.

The sheriff nodded courteously while Hal, his close-cropped hair seeming grayer than it had been, came around his desk, and put out a hand. "Pleasure to meet you, my dear."

Marty put out her thin hand. She smiled timidly at first and then openly as most people did when they discovered that their governor was a warm, friendly man who meant it when he said it was a pleasure to meet them.

"Introductions aren't over, Marty. I'm Cole Halsey and this is Varney Wynn. We're half brothers."

Sheriff Morehead gestured to the chair he had risen from. "Sit down, Marty."

While Hal shook hands with Cole and Varney, the sheriff moved back to the conference table to move some chairs up. Joe Eames stepped into the office then, was introduced to Marty, then also helped with the chairs.

After Hal had gone back to his desk and sat down, all the others except Cole sat down too.

"Marty, everybody here knows where you work. Don't be afraid that something will happen to you. Nothing will. Are you afraid?"

Marty smiled timidly. "A little."

"Well, relax then, while I tell them how I found you."

Cole began with his visit to Kelly's Saloon and his discovery through Homer Kelly that Varney, at a quarter to eleven that Monday night and alone, had asked for the best sporting house. A good bit of the time during his visit back to Primrose, Cole said, he kept wondering how any of the girls in the six sporting houses could possibly remember a lone man, and the solution had finally come to him. Upon his return he had taken Kelly's list of the madams and started his rounds of the sporting houses, asking the assembled girls if any of their customers on that fateful Monday night had identified himself as a bastard. There was fifty dollars for the girl who could come up with Varney's description.

In the second house Marty did. She had, Cole said, described him exactly.

"Hold on a minute, Cole," the governor said. "Isn't that the equivalent of bribing a witness?"

"I don't think so, Hal," Cole said. "If I'd offered one of the girls fifty dollars to say she'd spent a couple of hours with Varney, then I'd surely be guilty of bribery. But I offered fifty dollars to the girl who could remember and describe Varney and I don't think that's a bribe."

Cole's glance shifted to Sheriff Morehead. "Sam, the county has already spent more than fifty dollars in wages trying to check out what Varney did in Junction City, hasn't it?"

"Considerably more."

"Charged to investigation," Cole went on. "Well, that's what my money went for, isn't it?"

Morehead looked at the governor. "I think he's right, Hal."

The governor nodded and Cole thought he looked definitely tired. There was a strange sadness in his face but in his eyes there was the same old indomitability. "All right, Cole, go on."

Cole looked over at Marty. "It's your story now, Marty. Tell it the way you told it to me. Don't cover up anything just because you're in the governor's office."

Marty nodded and began a little timidly, first talking to Hal. Then she shifted her glance to Morehead and kept her attention on him. Cole could understand that she was awed by Hal's position but not a bit awed by Morehead's. The sheriff had dealt with whores and talked their language. Her account was factual, detailed, and salty. Through it all, Varney listened carefully, watching her, his face wooden. Listening to it again Cole remembered what must have been a timeless simile — harder than a whore's heart. Marty's heart was hard all right, but there was some charity there too. Marty finished her story saying, "When Cole asked me if I would tell my story to help the kid, I said I would." She looked at Hal. "I didn't know it would be you I'd tell it to."

"Thank you, my dear," Hal said courteously and he looked at the sheriff. "Satisfied, Sam?"

Morehead nodded. "The way my men pieced it together, that accounts for the only time Varney was alone. Yes, I'm satisfied."

"Does Macandy have to know this, Sam?" Cole asked.

"No," the sheriff said flatly. "I'll tell him that Varney surrendered, accounted for all his time, and was released."

"He'll want to know how Varney accounted for it?"

"Simple. Our investigation shows that Varney and his two friends were never separated," the sheriff said. "From what you tell us about Homer Kelly, he'll keep his mouth shut." The sheriff's glance shifted to Marty. "That leaves you, Marty. If I even hear a rumor that Varney was at Lettie Gustafson's, I'll know where it came from. You'll be on the next train if I hear it."

Marty smiled impudently. "Why, Sheriff, I like it here."

Cole rose and, seeing him, the rest of them

did, including the governor. Hal walked around the desk and again shook hands with Marty. While he was doing so, Cole moved over to Joe Eames and said, "Joe, I've got a hack waiting outside. Can you take Marty back to her house while Varney and I talk to Hal?"

"I will indeed. I will even let her walk over me to get in the house." He shook his head almost in disbelief. "All I can say is that when Varney picked out a soiled dove, he picked out the right one."

Sheriff Morehead shook hands with Hal and left immediately. After telling Cole he would meet him in the corridor, Joe ducked into the reception room to get his coat and hat. Cole and Marty walked to the door and stepped out into the corridor. There Marty halted and looked up at him. "Golly, he's class," Marty said. Then she added slowly, "I ain't never seen a man like him before."

"None of us have," Cole said.

At that moment, Joe stepped through the reception-room door into the corridor.

"Joe will see you home, Marty. Again, I'm obliged."

Marty's not-quite-pretty face broke into a smile. "Don't thank me, just come in and see me." Then the smile faded. "No, I guess you wouldn't, would you?"

"I would and I will. I'll stop and have a drink with you, Marty."

"That's not what I meant, but good-bye, Cole."

He watched her join Joe and the two of them headed for the entrance.

Back in the office Varney was putting the chairs back around the conference table. Cole sat in the remaining straight chair, leaving the two chairs for Varney. "How did it go up north, Hal?"

The governor said, "I had my head above water until you got in that scrape, Cole." He hesitated. "Was that necessary?"

Cole reiterated his conviction that Varney had been framed and that he was out to get the man who framed him, but Hal was already shaking his head.

"We've gone over that, Cole, and I don't believe it. Is that what you were trying to beat out of that lad in the Miners Rest?"

Cole told him then of his beating and of his and Varney's vain attempts to get an admission from Albie Wright that he had been paid.

The governor listened without comment and when Cole was finished, he said, "You intend to go on trying to get this Albie Wright to talk?"

"Varney does," Cole said and they both looked at Varney. He had been slacked in the easy chair, his sullen face watchful. Under their scrutiny he straightened up.

"I'm going to try, Dad."

"Please be a little less violent about it than Cole, will you?" Now he looked searchingly at Varney. "This afternoon was pretty rough on you, Varney. It was pretty rough on me too. Still, I can see why Cole thought it was necessary."

Varney only nodded.

Hal straightened up and said firmly, "Well, that's all behind us. What's ahead of us I couldn't guess." Now he stood up. "Boys, I've got a deskful of letters to write. Why don't you go up to the house and I'll see you when I get rid of them." He went to the reception-room door, then halted by it and turned to regard them. "Those," he said, "are two of the longest faces I've seen in many a day."

21

During the night the previous day's promise of snow had become a reality. Across the flats the storm driven by a west wind buffeted the train, plastering the windows of the car's right side with big wet flakes that were riding parallel to the ground. They scummed the car windows and finally caked them so heavily it was impossible to see out.

At Primrose, protected by the sheltering Raft Range, the snow was angling down from the west and when Cole and Varney stepped out onto the platform they found it carpeted with three inches of the heavy stuff that was building by the minute. Varney, who had told Cole that his first move when he got to Primrose would be to hunt up Albie Wright for further questioning, now said, "Where'll you be?"

"I'll wait for you at the hotel, Varney. If Albie will come with you, bring him along and we'll take him out to Mill Iron. There must be some way we can soften him up."

"That just might do it," Varney said. He buttoned up the collar of his mackinaw, waved good-bye and cut across the tracked platform heading for River Street and the Miners Rest. It would be easy enough to tell Cole later that Albie had refused to come out to Mill Iron, but since he had all the information Albie could give him, he wasn't even going to try and see him.

The Miners Rest, now that most of the men had gone back to their normal shifts at the mines and the mill, was almost deserted and Varney got immediate attention from Jess, the morning bartender.

Jess halted before Varney, nodding, waiting for his order. Varney ordered a whiskey and Jess lifted a glass and bottle on top of the bar. He waited until Varney paid up, then started to go when Varney said, "Wait a minute."

Jess came back and regarded Varney stonily.

"Can you tell me where Dave Hardy lives?" Varney asked.

Jess' glance dropped to the bottle and the the already filled glass in front of Varney. "You figuring on drinking more than one of those?" Jess asked.

Varney looked down at his glass. "I hadn't figured on it. Not that it's any of your damn business."

"What do you want to see Dave for?"

"That's none of your business either," Varney said.

Jess said, "He don't see nobody."

"I know he's sick, but he'll see me."

The bartender's eyes narrowed a little. "You aimin' to make trouble for Dave? If you try it, that woman of his will shoot you in the belly before you can even start it." The bartender paused. "Come to think of it, I bet she does anyway."

"Why would she?"

"Hard luck always goes in threes, don't it?"

Jess said enigmatically.

"What's that supposed to mean?"

"You're the last, ain't you?"

Varney frowned. "The last of what?"

"The last of the three bastard drunks," Jess said. "Bohannon got it in the mine and Albie got it last night in the alley. You'll likely get it on Dave Hardy's front porch."

"What did Albie get last night?"

"Shot dead," Jess said. "Didn't you hear? We found him out in back this morning when we was sweeping out."

The shock Varney felt was followed almost immediately by a feeling of quiet exulation. He had all the information Albie would ever have been able to give him even if he had lived. "A fight?" he asked.

"No marks on him. Somebody just jammed a gun in his belly and that was it."

Now Varney had his drink. He put down the glass and said, "Albie was all right, but I reckon he's better off dead."

"Nobody's better off dead," Jess said coldly. "You couldn't have done it, could you?"

"Not from Junction City," Varney said. "I just came in on the train. If the sheriff won't believe that, tell him to ask Cole. He was with me."

Jess turned his head then and looked at the near-empty back bar. He walked down the room a few steps, picked up a six-gun from the back bar and returned with it to Varney. He laid the gun on the bar, saying, "Your brother lost that in the ruckus the other night."

Varney nodded and unbuttoned his mackinaw and ran the gun under the belt. Then he asked patiently, "Do you tell me where Dave Hardy lives or do I ask somebody else?"

Jess gave him directions and Varney stepped out into the swirling snow and turned downstreet. Albie Wright had been killed. But why? he wondered. Was his death connected in any way with the big drunk?

As he trudged along in the wet snow Varney turned over this possibility in his mind. Surely Albie wasn't worth killing for the money he carried and Varney couldn't remember Albie ever speaking of an enemy. Then was he jumping to a wrongful conclusion if he guessed that whoever killed Albie did it to keep him from talking? So, whoever did it was the man who originally planned and paid Albie and Henry for the big drunk.

By the time he had reached Grant Street and turned left he knew he was right. It explained Albie's death and nothing else did. The killer could have read in the *Times* that Cole's fight in the Miners Rest was the result of his attempt to talk with Albie Wright. To prevent Albie from talking to Cole he killed him. It was that simple.

Varney found Dave's house, mounted the steps and knocked on the door. He waited an interminable while, knocking again and again before the door was suddenly opened. A big woman in a gray wrapper confronted him holding a gun that was pointed at his belly.

"Get away quick from here, kid, and stay away."

Instinctively Varney raised his hands waist-high in protest. "No. No. My name's Varney Wynn. I've got to see Dave Hardy."

"No, you don't. Now git."

"If I don't see him, he's headed for jail for sure. Tell him that will you?"

Rose regarded him for a moment and abruptly turned and closed the door. In moments she was back. The gun now dangled from her hand and she said, "Follow me."

She led Varney into the bedroom where Dave Hardy was lying in the farthest of the two beds. Varney halted at the foot of the first bed and nodded.

"Now you see him," Rose said. "Why was he headed for jail if you didn't?"

Varney looked at the massive bulk of Dave Hardy and Dave regarded him with equal curiosity. Varney had seen him before but had never spoken to him, while Dave couldn't remember ever having noticed Varney.

Varney said then, "You know who I am?"

"Halsey's bastard," Dave said weakly.

"That's right. Who paid Henry Bohannon and Ablie Wright to get Halsey's bastard drunk?"

"Ask them," Dave whispered.

"They're both dead."

Varney watched Dave's weary glance shift to the woman. Varney turned his head to look at her but she was looking at Dave, her face expressionless.

Then Dave spoke. "Since when is Albie Wright dead?" he asked Varney.

"Since last night. Killed in the alley behind your place."

There was a long silence after Varney spoke and he let it run on.

"About my being in jail," Dave Hardy said weakly. "Why would I be put there?"

"Because you know who paid Henry and him. Albie told me you did. You called him and Henry into your office. This fellow was there. He was about thirty and big. He asked if they wanted a free drunk and when they said yes, he told them to go pick me up at Mill Iron. You guaranteed them free booze at your saloon while they kept me drunk."

"A lie," Dave whispered. "You can't prove any of it."

The woman spoke suddenly. "You're a fool, Dave."

Dave's glance shifted to her. "Why am I?"

"Because you're next."

Varney looked from the woman to Dave. Again they were looking at each other as if they were communicating without using words.

"He got to Albie. He can get to you and to me. He's got to."

Dave sighed but he continued to look at the woman. She said, still looking at Dave, "Tell him before we're dead."

The room was so quiet then that Varney could hear Dave's labored exhalation of breath. Finally Dave dragged his gaze from the woman and looked at Varney. "It was Bowie Sanson."

Varney frowned. "Should I know him?"

The woman spoke now. "A Junction City lawyer. Asa Forbes' campaign manager. He's going to marry Burley Hammond's girl, they say. He was here yesterday. He wanted to find out where Albie lived. He wanted to pay him to keep quiet."

"Did Bowie Sanson kill Abe Brandell?"

"Rose," Dave whispered.

"We don't know," the woman said. "Why don't you figure out why you were taken to Junction City the day Brandell was killed?"

"Rose," Dave Hardy whispered angrily.

"The hell with it, Dave," Rose said roughly. "You thought so and I thought so. Now that Albie Wright's murdered, we know. A murder to hide a murder." She looked at Varney now. "Out you go, young man. You got what you came for."

Varney nodded, and said politely, "Thank you both."

The woman let him out and neither of them said good-bye.

Once on the street Varney walked aimlessly in the pelting snow, trying his poor best to think what he should do now. The enormity of what Dave Hardy and his woman had told him could not be wholly absorbed at once. Bowie Sanson, the woman said, was Asa Forbes' campaign manager. Varney, up to last week a ranch hand with no interest in politics, had never heard of him. But his effort to place the blame for Brandell's murder on Varney was a political move aimed squarely at his father, Governor Halsey. But Asa Forbes was a good man, Varney knew, which meant that Forbes knew nothing of what Bowie Sanson had planned. Burley Hammond was a Forbes backer and certainly he would never countenance murder on behalf of his political candidate. Neither would the other mining men, all solid and respected men. They were not asso-

332

ciated with his framing and the two murders, but they all stood to win by his father's defeat.

He had to assume then that all of this was Bowie Sanson's doing — his own framing and the deaths of Abe Brandell and Albie Wright. Suddenly, it came to Varney that Bowie Sanson must still be in town, unless he had fled on a horse. But why should he run? Varney thought. Only Dave Hardy and his woman could tie Sanson to Albie's murder and surely nobody could ever tie Bowie Sanson to Abe Brandell's murder. The way it was done argued that Bowie had to be alone in order to make it look accidental. So, if nobody saw Bowie Sanson commit either of the murders, he could never be convicted.

There was a chance, though, that Sanson might flee town on the train, which would be leaving in minutes now. Varney vaguely located himself in the swirl of the snowstorm and began to trot toward the depot. Cole's gun in his waistband jabbed him in the groin at each step and now he lifted it out and placed it in the big right-hand pocket of his mackinaw.

When he arrived at the depot platform he saw dimly through the swirling snow the made-up train approaching from the distant yards. The platform was empty but Varney knew its passengers would all be in the warm waiting room. He pushed inside and found the room almost full of people. Slowly he cruised the crowd, nodding to a few people he knew, but he saw nobody answering the description of Bowie Sanson.

Now, as the train approached the platform, Varney moved out into the storm. When the mixed train coasted to a halt, he placed himself just to the side of the entrance to the lone passenger car. The passengers filed out of the depot and were joined by others who had been waiting in their buggies, but none of them was a man of Bowie Sanson's description.

Varney waited out in the storm until the train pulled out and then he sought the warmth of the depot stove in the waiting room. He was alone there and he put his back to the stove, his mind searching for answers to even more questions. Unless Bowie Sanson had sneaked into the car when it was in the yards, he had not taken the train, so he might still be in town. *If I find him, what am I going to do with him?* Varney wondered. For a fleeting moment, he wanted Cole at his side and then he rejected this with all his will, even denying to himself that he had ever thought it. No, this was his own problem and Cole must never know it existed. All right, what was he going to do with Bowie Sanson?

The heat from the stove came through his

trousers and he moved off a little. The only thing that could be proven against Bowie Sanson was that he paid two strangers money to get him drunk and take him to Junction City on a certain day. Sanson could admit that without any harm to himself, arguing that it was acceptable politics to disgrace the son of an opponent if he was already disgraced. *And, God knows, I'm open for it,* Varney thought. It came to this then, that there weren't grounds even for Bowie Sanson's arrest. A fury of frustration came to Varney then. He could make charges that were unprovable and find himself jailed for uttering them. Worse, if it had not been for a sporting girl with a good memory, he could be right now charged with the murder of Abe Brandell. Varney's wild temper, never far beneath the surface, surged up in him, and he had never felt lonelier in his life. There were people to turn to like Cole and his father, but he could not. For once, just for once, he was on his own and would stay on his own.

Where to look for Bowie Sanson was the next question he asked himself. The woman had said Bowie Sanson was rumored to be engaged to Tish Hammond, but he could not very well go to the Hammonds' and ask for Bowie. And what would he say to him if he did find him there?

Now Varney, warmed through, moved over to the door of the waiting room and went out into the storm, heading for the bridge. Should he act now while Bowie was in town? What good would waiting do? He could never uncover proof against Bowie in an eternity. Suddenly, irrevocably, in that blinding drive of snow, Varney made up his mind.

As he moved up Grant Street in the slush of the boardwalk, he cast about for a way to begin his search for Bowie. The most obvious place to inquire was the Primrose House, the best hotel. Of course, he would run the risk of running into Cole, who was waiting for him there, but that was a risk that had to be taken.

He climbed the steps of the Primrose House veranda and paused long enough to shake the snow from his coat and hat and then he moved inside, heading directly for the desk at the far side of the lobby. The dining room, he noted, held a few people and would hold more when the bar began to empty. The slight, graying owner of the Primrose House, Mr. Selby, was behind the desk and he looked up as Varney halted in front of it.

"Good day, Mr. Selby," Varney said. "Is there a Bowie Sanson staying with you?"

"No, he usually stays with the Hammonds, Varney. But I think he's in the bar if you want to see him."

Varney thanked him, turned and headed toward the barroom. Through the door he could see the men lined along the bar.

He was halfway across the big lobby when he saw Tish Hammond seated with a woman he didn't know on one of the big leather sofas. Her face was half-turned away from him and he passed without her looking up. Then he halted in the doorway of the barroom. Even when he saw Cole, his back to him, seated at one of the tables with three of the Mill Iron hands, he felt no alarm. It never entered his mind that the presence of the hands meant roundup was over. Slowly, carefully, he looked at the men at the tables and then at each man at the bar. Then he saw Asa Forbes talking with a blond-haired, heavy-set man of about thirty, dressed in unworn range clothes cowman's boots, and leather jacket.

Now, right now, Varney thought, and moved into the room. When he halted by Forbes who was chatting with Bowie, Forbes looked at him and then smiled.

"Why, hello, Varney," Forbes said, and extended a hand which Varney ignored. He was looking at the other man.

"Are you Bowie Sanson?" Varney asked quietly.

"I am," Bowie said. "You're Varney Wynn, aren't you?"

Varney tried to make his face expression-less, but his lower lip was trembling.

"You killed Abe Brandell and Albie Wright, didn't you?" Varney said. "Would you like to tell Asa or shall I?"

The look of consternation that came into Bowie's face was something he could not hide. His heavy face went slack with shock.

Still looking at Bowie, Varney said, "Asa, listen to this. Bowie paid two men to get me drunk and take me to Junction City so I could be seen the night Abe Brandell was murdered. Dave Hardy saw Bowie give the men the money and their orders. Bowie killed one of the men last night, but I got — "

Bowie's hand plunged into his pocket and came up with his pistol. Too late, Varney drove his hand into his mackinaw pocket for Cole's pistol. He had it and was dragging it out when the hammer caught in the lining of his pocket. It was then that Bowie shot him in the chest.

Varney staggered back against an occupied chair, caromed off the man sitting in it and fell, and then the barroom was in pandemo-nium. Many of the seated men rolled off their chairs to the floor and the men at the bar on either side of Bowie and Asa Forbes backed away, stumbling over each other to get out of the line of fire.

Only one man was moving toward Bowie and it was Cole Halsey. His hands were empty and he was weaponless. He halted by Varney and knelt and saw the blood staining Varney's shirt and running from the corner of his now slack mouth. Now Cole slowly raised his head and his glance settled on Bowie.

"So it was you," Cole said.

Bowie's face was ashen. He glanced beyond Cole to see the people crowded in the doorway. Among them was Tish. A lost look of despair came into his face then and Cole watched the courage ebb and empty from his handsome face and once-bold eyes. Slowly, then, Bowie turned the gun to his own chest. Asa Forbes struck out at his hand but not in time to halt the trigger pull. The sound of the shot was muffled, almost apologetic. Bowie's upper body slid down the bar and he fell, turning, onto the brass rail, then rolled over onto his back.

EPILOGUE

From the *Capital Times:*

BOWIE SANSON KILLER SUICIDE

FORBES WITHDRAWS FROM RACE

At Primrose yesterday Bowie Sanson, eminent capital lawyer and campaign manager for gubernatorial candidate Asa Forbes, shot himself to death after shooting and killing Varney Wynn, son of Governor Halsey. This shocking scene was witnessed by more than fifty people who were in the Primrose House bar, noon scene of the murder and suicide.

It was held by Asa Forbes that Bowie Sanson's murder of Wynn and his own public suicide was tantamount to a confession that he was the killer of Attorney Abe Brandell, whose broken body was found last week on the back stairs of the Grandview Hotel. In view of this shocking revelation that his campaign manager probably killed Brandell, Forbes issued the following statement:

"I am withdrawing my name from the ballot and myself from politics. Neither I nor my friends could know that a man of Bowie Sanson's public character would have committed such a crime. We were wrong. We were totally without knowledge of Sanson's plot to place Varney Wynn under the suspicion of murdering Abe Brandell. However, we share a measure of his guilt by trusting him. My deepest sympathy goes out to Governor Halsey, who lost a brave son at the hands of a cowardly murderer. . . ."

THORNDIKE-MAGNA hopes you have enjoyed this Large Print book. All our Large Print titles are designed for easy reading, and all our books are made to last. Other Thorndike Press or Magna Print books are available at your library, through selected bookstores, or directly from the publishers. For more information about current and upcoming titles, please call or mail your name and address to:

THORNDIKE PRESS
P.O. Box 159
Thorndike, Maine 04986
(800) 223-6121
(207) 948-2962 (in Maine and Canada call collect)

or in the United Kingdom:

MAGNA PRINT BOOKS
Long Preston, Near Skipton
North Yorkshire,
England BD23 4ND
(07294) 225

There is no obligation, of course.